A Secret to the Grave

Jane Blythe

First published in 2012 by Dorrance Publishing

Bear Spots Publications
Melbourne Australia

bearspotspublications@gmail.com

ISBN: 0992418011
ISBN-13: 978-0-9924180-1-4

Cover designed by QDesigns

PROLOGUE
TEN YEARS AGO
NOVEMBER 20TH

8:13 P.M.

"Are you sure we're doing the right thing?" Chelsea asked with a sidelong glance at her boyfriend.

"I don't see that we have a choice," Jasper replied, his gaze remained fixed on the road.

Rain was pouring down outside and inside the car was almost as cold as it was outside. Chelsea reached over and turned up the heat, holding her hands above the vent and rubbing them vigorously, trying to warm them up. Watching mesmerized as water cascaded down the windows, the whir of the windscreen wipers as they flicked backwards and forwards barely keeping up with the pounding rain.

Shivering as guilt and fear threatened to engulf her. Chelsea wished she were out in the rain, letting it wash away her troubles. When she was little she had loved nothing more than to run and play in the rain. She loved the feel of raindrops bouncing off her skin, of her wet hair dripping down her back, her soaked clothes clinging to her skin. She loved the freedom of being part of nature, of the wildness of the rain, and always felt better, calmer, more at peace after a storm. As a child, she used to sneak out of her bed at night after everyone was asleep to play in a storm.

"I don't know, Jasper, maybe there's another option, another way."

Turning his gaze briefly from the road, he shot her a reassuring smile before repeating the words she had already heard him say a hundred times. "We've been through this, Chels, there is no other option. Tess was right, this is the only way out."

"I know," Chelsea sighed. "I just wish there was a way out of this that didn't involve something so dramatic. Something so unchangeable. So final. Once we do this we can't take it back."

"Everything's going to be okay," Jasper soothed. "You'll see."

They both lapsed into silence. Neither of them could quite believe what they were about to do. Weeks of planning had all led up to tonight. Despite their trepidation, they both knew they were doing the right thing, the only thing they could do under the circumstances.

Jasper glanced in the rear vision mirror, even though they had not seen another car in miles. They were alone on the deserted country road. There had not been a car behind them since they left the city, and only two pairs of headlights had come towards them in the last hour.

Several minutes passed in silence. Both of them lost in their own thoughts. Chelsea once again watched the rain cascade down the window, the steady drumming and the patterns the dripping water made soothed her, comforted her.

"It's nearly time," Jasper announced, jolting her back to reality.

She turned to look at him. "We're really gonna do this." She was not sure whether it was a question or a statement.

"We're really gonna do this," Jasper echoed.

He turned to look at her and she saw in his eyes that he was as scared as she was. The realization comforted her, knowing that they were in this together. She reached over and laid her hand on top of his. "I love you," she whispered.

Moving his hand from under hers, he lifted her hand and pressed it to his lips, kissing it softly. "I love you too. Forever."

Feeling tears start to slide down her cheeks she ran her hand through his hair. "Together forever," she whispered.

Locking his eyes onto hers Jasper nodded, it was time.

Taking each other's hands, Jasper pressed his foot down on the accelerator, sending the car racing towards a cliff. As the rain continued to pour down, thunder crashed and a flash of lightening lit up the sky. Chelsea thought it was an appropriate send off.

Moments later the car sailed off the cliff. It seemed to hang in the air before falling slowly, crashing into the raging water below.

NOVEMBER 20TH

8:24 P.M.

Janice Peters hummed softly to herself as she turned off the car engine and reached across to grab her shoes from the floor in front of the passenger seat, where she had tossed them when she had got in the car earlier. Janice hated to drive with shoes on, especially high heels like the stylish pink pair that dangled from her hand.

The bottom of her shoes were covered in mud so she decided not to put them back on, she had just had the carpets in her apartment cleaned and she didn't want to track dirt all over them. It had been raining for days. The skies were grey, sheets of rain soaking everything and everyone. The gloomy weather perfectly matched her mood.

Climbing out of the car she pushed the door closed then opened the back one and reached in, grabbing two bags of groceries from the backseat. Balancing them and her handbag in her arms, she bumped the door closed with her hip.

Starting towards the elevator one of her shoes slipped from her grasp and clattered as it landed on the ground, the sound echoing loudly in the underground parking garage. Muttering wearily under her breath, she maneuvered the bags into one arm and awkwardly bent to retrieve the shoe.

Walking as quickly as she could under her load, Janice paused when she heard a noise behind her, turning quickly to see a shadow flit silently across the garage. Turning, she continued at almost a run, cursing softly to herself when one of her stockinged feet stepped on something sharp. Not bothering to stop and see what it was, she kept moving towards the lift, praying that for once she wouldn't have to wait several minutes for the ancient machine to reach the parking lot.

Pushing the up button on the wall beside the elevator doors she looked over her shoulder scanning the garage, looking for any sign of movement. Tapping her foot impatiently as she watched the light move slowly indicating that the lift was finally nearing her.

Letting out a strangled scream as a hand gripped her shoulder.

Heart thumping so loudly she could hardly hear the voice of the man behind her. "Janice, dear, you dropped your keys."

Struggling to calm herself, she turned slowly, looking up into the smiling face of Mr. Pickering, the old man who lived directly below her. Giving him a shaky smile she took her keys from his outstretched hand. "Thank you."

"I scared you," he said, his smile turning into a frown. "I'm sorry, I didn't mean to, I thought you heard me."

Smiling reassuringly at her elderly friend. "No, I'm sorry. I guess I'm just a little on edge at the moment."

Gesturing at the bags in her arm, "Do you need some help?"

"I'm fine. You should have called me, I could have got you something while I was at the store," she said, gesturing at his own grocery bag.

The ping behind them announced the arrival of the elevator. Mr. Pickering held his arm across one of the open doors that had a habit of closing on you before you were inside. "What's got you so jumpy?" he asked, as the lift slowly shuddered back to life.

"Just tired, I haven't been sleeping so well the last few nights," she answered, rubbing a hand over her tired eyes.

"Something bothering you, sweetheart?" he asked, peering at her closely.

Shaking her head wearily. "It's nothing," offering another half-hearted smile.

Creaking to a stop at Mr. Pickering's floor, he cast her another worried glance. "You want to come over for dinner? Katherine would be thrilled to see you." His wife had Alzheimer's and most days she couldn't even tell you her own name.

Although Janice usually loved visiting the sweet old lady tonight she was too wired. "Some other time, Mr. Pickering."

"Are you sure?" he questioned unconvinced. "A home cooked meal, great company. Come on, dear, you can't lock yourself away alone forever."

She shook her head uncertainly, all of a sudden overwhelmed by the need not to be alone on this night. She *was* tired of being alone, but it was the price she had to pay. "Some other time," she repeated softly.

"I'll hold you to that. Take care of yourself, dear," he called through the closing lift doors.

Leaning back against the wall Janice let out a deep sigh as she looked at herself in one of the mirrors that covered each of the lift's three walls. She looked terrible, she was pale and there were dark circles under her eyes. All she wanted was to take a long, hot shower, cuddle up in her pajamas and slide under her covers.

The elevator door slid open as it reached her floor, shaking herself Janice started down the hall, clutching her shoes and bags in one hand as she unlocked her door with the other. Once inside she dropped her things on the floor and pulled the door closed behind her.

Janice loved her apartment. It was her favorite place to be. She had lived here for three years and over that time she had worked hard to make her home her cocoon. Other than a few of the women from work she had no friends. She didn't go out. She had never had a serious boyfriend. The majority of her time and energy went into her work. In her spare time she had begun to collect antique furniture. The Pickering's had got her started and she had visited a few antique stores with them, her collection was coming along nicely, although it was nothing compared to theirs.

Setting the grocery bags on the counter, she'd deal with them later, then moving tiredly down the hallway she turned on the shower, and slipped out of her clothes, leaving them where they fell. She hated the suits that she wore for work, the tight fitting sweaters and short skirts, the high heels that always made her feel uncomfortable. She had always been a jeans and sweatshirts sort of girl, she never felt at ease when she was all made up.

As she waited for the water to heat, she went to the kitchen, grabbed one of the frozen meals from the stack in the freezer and stuck it in the microwave. Janice was definitely not a cook, sandwiches were about the extent of her culinary talents. Since she lived alone she mostly just ate frozen meals for dinner, her freezer was always filled to overflowing with an eclectic array of choices.

Returning to the bathroom, Janice climbed into the shower, standing under the steaming water she tried to let the heat wash her anxiety away. Usually a shower could calm her down after even the worst of days. The pounding water was like a wonderful, relaxing massage.

Today, however, it refused to work it's magic, and after several minutes she felt no better than when she had got in and reluctantly turned off the tap. Not bothering to dry off she grabbed a soft pink robe from the back of the bathroom door and pulled it tightly around herself.

Opening the bathroom door she froze in her tracks.

A man stood in the middle of her bedroom. He was dressed from head to toe in black, with black gloves, and a black ski mask covering his face, his eyes staring calmly at her through slits in the mask.

For a moment neither of them moved, then with her heart racing and pulse pounding, her survival instincts took over. Casting a glance at the phone on the bedside table, it was only a few feet away and yet it seemed like miles, fighting back her fear Janice made a desperate run for it.

The man also sprung into action. Leaping across the room in

what seemed like one giant jump and tackling her to the ground, knocking over her bureau in the process, sending her make-up scattering and clattering across the floor. She struggled against him, but he was bigger and stronger than she was, and within moments he had overpowered her. His hands were clamped like irons around her wrists, and he straddled her stomach.

Thrashing wildly beneath him, she choked back a sob as she struggled to draw a breath beneath the crushing pressure of his weight against her chest. 'He's going to rape me then kill me' Janice thought, more horrified by the thought of being defiled than by the thought of being killed.

She opened her mouth to scream but the sound stuck in her throat when she heard him laughing. "What do you want from me?" she whimpered.

He said nothing, just climbed off her but kept a firm hold of her wrists, his grip so tight that Janice thought the bones would simply snap. He began to drag her across the smooth wooden floorboards of her room.

Her mind for some reason transported itself back to the day she had the carpet pulled up and the floorboards restored. She remembered the pride she had felt as she'd looked at the beautiful room, the shining wooden floorboards perfectly setting off the antique furniture she had chosen so carefully. It had been the first room that she had finished decorating, her first room in her first home, it had been part of her plan to take control of her life. Then she had moved on to the living room, she was halfway through it and if this monster killed her she would never get the chance to complete it.

Janice kicked her feet out wildly as he pulled her across the floor, trying desperately to get away from him. Her feet catching and tangling in the bedding along the way, he barely slowed, just yanked her free and continued to drag her, almost dislocating her shoulder in the process.

Reaching the full-length nineteenth century mirror, he yanked her to her feet, wrapping an arm around her neck, so tightly that she had to stand on her tiptoes in order to draw a shuddering breath.

"Please, just tell me what you want," she whispered as she stared at the masked man, hoping against hope he would just take what he wanted and leave her alive.

He said nothing, just reached up and pulled the mask off.

Janice gasped, her heart stopping as she stared in shock at the face in the mirror beside her. Any hope she had of getting out of this alive vanished and she had to remind herself to breathe. She shook her head as she stared at the mirror, at the man's empty, soulless eyes staring back at her, as if that could somehow erase what she was looking at.

"No," she murmured despairingly as she started to sob, tears falling down her cheeks, her own grey eyes staring back at her, completely devoid of hope.

NOVEMBER 21ST

Rain was pounding down like millions of unseen drummers beating the rhythm of their tiny hearts, as he left the café, two cups of coffee in his hand. Starting down the sidewalk he watched, mesmerized, as raindrops dripped into a puddle, dimpling like hundreds of tiny bullets in a body.

Shaking his head to force himself not to think that way, but it was too late, his mind was already back in the past. The body flashed before his eyes. The bullets flying through flesh, leaving what seemed like hundreds of red dots in their wake. Shock and disbelief flashed through eyes that then went eerily blank as the body fell to the ground.

A horn honked and Detective Parker Bell found himself back in the present, his partner waving at him from the car across the street. Once again, he shook his head to try and focus it on the task at hand, and quickly crossed the road.

"So what have we got?" Parker asked as he shook the rain from his clothes and slipped into the passenger seat of his partner's car.

"Female, name is Janice Peters, age twenty-five, abducted from her apartment sometime during the night," Detective Skylar Wyatt replied, taking the coffee cup that Parker offered him and opening the lid. "This is black, I like my coffee white," he complained, narrowing his emerald green eyes at his friend.

Parker had known Wyatt for twenty years, ever since he and his twin sister had moved in with the family who lived next-door to the Wyatt's. Parker had been ten and Wyatt fifteen, Parker had been angry and withdrawn, Wyatt had been a sophomore football star. Wyatt had taken him under his wing, the two becoming firm friends despite the age difference. They had been partners for three years now.

It was a long-standing tradition between the two of them, Parker only drank his coffee black, Wyatt only drank his white, and both were always trying to turn the other. "Suck it up, buddy," Parker laughed and then sobered as his partner pulled out into the traffic and he thought of where they were headed.

"We got a picture?"

Wyatt kept one hand on the steering wheel while the other dug into his pocket and pulled out a photo, passing it over. Parker studied the serious face of the young woman staring back at him. She had shoulder-length, light brown hair and solemn grey eyes, framed by long, dark lashes. Hoping that this pretty young woman with her whole life ahead of her was still alive, he stuck the photo in his shirt pocket.

"Who called it in?"

"An elderly neighbor," Wyatt answered, they were headed in the same direction as most of the rest of the traffic, making their journey impossibly slow. The rain, which had been pouring down relentlessly for days on end, meant that everyone was driving, no one braving the wet to walk or ride a bike. "Apparently he went to check up on her this morning, knocked on the door, and when he got no answer he let himself in with his key."

"What did he find?" Parker asked, winding down his window, he hated the feeling of being cooped up inside a small space. Cold air whipped through the car sending Wyatt's strawberry blonde hair and Parker's own wavy black hair flying. Raindrops were dripping inside and onto the arm of his royal blue sweater, leaving dark little dots everywhere they fell. He thought again of the small dots of red blood, but forced the picture from his mind.

Wyatt glared over at him. Parker shrugged, "It's stuffy in here."

Wyatt was always cold. Today he was dressed in a black suit, white shirt, burgundy sweater, and his huge, black woolen overcoat. He had begun wearing the overcoat back in September when the weather was still mild.

Sighing, Wyatt said nothing and returned his gaze to the road where the cars were crawling along at a snail's pace. Their drivers huddled inside, readying themselves for the snow that would not be far away and the long winter that was to come.

"He found the microwave still beeping and grocery bags on the counter. There were signs of a struggle in the bedroom, so he left immediately and called the police. He sounded so shaken up on the phone that the 911 operator was worried he might have a heart attack."

Sensing there was more to the story than Wyatt was telling him. "And . . ." he prodded.

"It's pretty bad," his partner began warily.

Parker felt his stomach drop. Wyatt never exaggerated, usually tending to understate things. If he said it was bad, then it was going to be horrible. "How bad?"

Shooting him a concerned glance Wyatt hesitated. It was Parker's first day back at work after an incident a couple of months ago, and he knew his best friend wanted to make sure he was okay.

"There was a note," Wyatt finally announced.

"A note?"

"Yeah."

Parker waited impatiently for him to continue, but Wyatt said nothing. "So what did it say?" he pressed.

"That whoever has taken her will keep her alive for one month . . ."

"Well, that's good news, it gives us . . ." Parker cut in, instantly relieved.

"That's not all," Wyatt interrupted. "He also left us a list with nine clues. Each clue represents a woman . . ." he trailed off again. Then uttering a deep sigh continued, "He's going to kill one woman every two days unless we can solve his riddles, figure out who they are, and save them."

"He's gonna do what?" Wyatt's words sounded like nothing but gibberish to his brain.

"There's still more."

Parker put the window back up, suddenly ice cold, and ran a hand through his thick black hair, preparing himself for something he wasn't sure he was ready for. "Go on."

Casting a glance at him, Wyatt continued, "If we save the women on the list, then he kills Janice Peters."

* * * * *

11:00 A.M.

Running through the rain Tessa Micah took deep breaths and pushed herself to keep up the pace. Tessa went running every day regardless of the weather. Rain, hail or shine, she never let anything interrupt her schedule. You never knew when that blue moon would come along, she told herself wryly.

She always ran in the exact same spot. The woods surrounding her house, an estate she had inherited from her father's parents. The property was huge, incorporating a large mansion, a cottage, stables, an orchid and acres upon acres of wild woods.

Tessa had never felt comfortable here. She hated the huge, pretentious main house and had not been inside it since moving here after college, preferring instead to stay in the cozy little cottage. The only reason she stayed here at all was because of the remote location. Tessa loved the quiet, tranquil woods. She had fallen in love with them ever since she had read Laura Ingalls Wilder's *Little House in the Big Woods* at the age of four.

Passing the large mansion, she shuddered at its blank, empty windows that seemed to stare back at her. Vines crept over the huge, stone walls, the place looked cold and creepy. As a little girl she had hated visiting her grandparents here, had lain awake each night listening to the old house creak and moan, imagining bogeymen creeping through the halls coming to get her.

Crossing the lawns behind the mansion, she slowed as she reached the woods again. The cottage was set just inside their limits in a small clearing. Upon seeing her tiny cabin, Tessa felt herself relax, just as she always did. Bright flowers surrounded the small house, shining happily through the rain. Welcoming her home.

Pulling open the back door, Tessa almost tripped over as her two dogs ran at her, begging for their lunch. Securing the three locks on the door she laughed as she patted each dog's head, "hey Buttercup," she smiled at the golden retriever. Unhappy at not being the centre of attention the Dalmatian nudged the other dog out of the way and nuzzled her nose in Tessa's hand. Turning to the other dog Tessa patted her too, "I didn't forget you Ladybug."

Flipping on the TV, which was set on a shelf in the corner of the kitchen, she set about feeding the dogs. Filling the bowls with water, she grabbed the giant bag of dog food, which lasted her two hungry pets all of about a week, from its place in the locked cupboard under the sink. It had remained locked ever since the day she had come home to find her dogs lying miserably on the kitchen floor. They had gotten into the cupboard, pulled out the bag and gorged themselves.

About to pour the food into the dog's bowls when suddenly her head snapped up and she froze. "A shocking abduction overnight has police baffled. Janice Peters was taken from her home . . ." the too tanned news reporter continued in her falsely somber voice. Her overly made up eyes betraying her glee, but Tessa was no longer seeing or hearing her. She couldn't move. She couldn't breathe.

The perplexed dogs whined and pushed at the bag in her arms. Sucking in a shaky breath, she let go of the dog food sending it scattering across the floor. The delighted dogs raced to track down every piece they could find, as though if they weren't quick enough it would disappear forever.

Tessa barely noticed as she struggled to remain standing, her legs had turned to wobbly jell-o and threatened to collapse at any moment. Reaching a trembling hand for the phone. Dialing a number she knew by heart, she tried to calm her uncontrollable shaking as she waited for the phone to be answered. When the person on the other end picked up she spoke without preamble, uttering the words both of them dreaded hearing and that chilled them each to their very core.

"He's surfaced."

* * * * *

11:24 A.M.

Climbing from the car, Parker pulled his bright red scarf tighter around his neck and did a visual sweep of the apartment building. Despite the fact that it was the middle of the day, and that the rain persisted in its deluge, the sidewalk was filled with people who had stopped to see what all the commotion was.

"It's an old building," he observed, half to Wyatt half to himself, surveying the huge red brick structure. "Could have made it easier for the intruder to get inside."

Despite its age the apartment block looked fairly well maintained, there was a security door and intercom, but no door attendant. Two huge steel doors, one at each end, provided access to the underground garage, admission was by a keypad entry system. Huge windows covered the front of the building, staring out at the world like giant sleepy eyes.

There was any number of ways that the intruder could have got inside Janice's apartment. "Any signs of forced entry in her apartment?"

"Might have got in through a window off the fire escape."

"CSU finished up there?"

"They finished in the apartment, they're checking out the rest of the building, garage, lift, hallways."

Climbing large stone steps they entered the big brick building, Parker paused to gather Janice Peters' mail, flipping though it he saw nothing but bills.

"Anything?" Wyatt asked.

"Just bills."

Throwing him a quick glance, "Elevator or stairs?" his partner asked.

After being locked in a closet as a child Parker now suffered from claustrophobia and could only tolerate confined spaces when he was calm and relaxed. Now was not one of those times. "Stairs."

They took the stairs two at a time, quickly reaching the fourth floor, and headed down the hall to Janice Peters' apartment, where a young officer stood guard at the door. Walking inside they found themselves in an open and airy living room, a small kitchen to their right. The walls of both rooms were painted a soft peach color, the curtains at the living room windows were the exact same shade. The kitchen had no windows, the bench tops and cupboard doors were a thick mahogany wood.

The apartment was furnished in a mixture of cheap, well-worn pieces and exquisite antiques. The couches were covered in a scruffy, cream material, but were arranged around a beautiful, very old and expensive looking table. A gorgeous grandfather clock stood next to the door, beside it laid a stack of papers, a pair of high heels and a handbag.

There were no photos or personal items around either room. There was no TV in the living room, no DVD player or iPod either. The entire place was in perfect order. The books in the bookshelf arranged in alphabetical order, the pile of magazines on the coffee table were aligned precisely in its middle. The kitchen was just as perfectly organized and as spotlessly clean and tidy, the only thing lying on the benches were two grocery bags.

Everything in the apartment had a place and everything was in its place. There was nothing anywhere to indicate that there had been a struggle.

One of the CSU guys approached them, "Wyatt. Parker, good to have you back," he nodded at each of them.

"Hey, Marty," Parker greeted him. Marty Jenkins was the best in the business. In his mid-fifties, he reminded Parker of a bird. Tall and thin, with greying black hair, a narrow, angular face and a sharp beak-like nose, his beady grey eyes were always hidden behind thick black-rimmed glasses. A widower for almost fifteen years, had no children, was a no nonsense guy who took his work very seriously, and as far as anyone knew he had no outside interests. "Looks like a hotel in here, I thought there was a struggle. What can you tell us?"

"Looks like he got her in the bedroom, it's a mess in there," Marty headed down the hall as he spoke. Trailing along behind him they entered the bedroom and surveyed the scene before them. An antique bureau lay on its side, cosmetics littered the floor, sheets lay in a tangled mess next to the bed, a mahogany four poster, and a robe lay in front of a full length mirror. All the furniture in the room matched, and had been chosen with great care, and Parker suspected that Janice Peters had begun her redecorating in here, and then moved on to the living room. Unfortunately there was a high probability she would never get the chance to finish it.

"Clothes were on the floor in the bathroom, so we're thinking he got her as she came out of the shower," Marty told them, using his typical hand gestures as he spoke.

"Signs of sexual assault?" Wyatt asked, gesturing at the pile of sheets and robe on the carpet.

"No sign of recent sexual activity on the bed."

"Any blood?"

"We didn't find any but we did find this," Marty handed Wyatt an evidence bag containing a white handkerchief.

"What is it?"

"It's soaked in chloroform."

"That's how he got her out," Wyatt commented to no one in particular, as he was in the habit of doing. "You find a computer or cell phone anywhere?"

"No. Nothing."

"What young woman doesn't have a cell phone?"

"We checked the whole place . . ."

"The car?" Wyatt interrupted

Marty hated to be interrupted, and frowned his disapproval. "Yes, we checked the car. Again, nothing."

"Maybe he took it with him."

"Maybe," Marty sounded unconvinced.

"But you don't think so."

He shrugged, "We didn't find anything to suggest that she owned either. No chargers, no USB memory stick."

Parker was only half listening to them talk as he surveyed the room, trying to visualize the scene that had taken place in here just hours ago. The young woman accosted in her own bedroom, struggling against a madman who would abduct her and leave a list of riddles threatening nine others. Shaking his head, even after all these years as a cop the criminal psyche still sometimes baffled him. "You got the note?"

Marty nodded and retrieved the note, enclosed in an evidence bag, from his case and handed it to Parker. Holding it so that both he and Wyatt could read it.

My name is Janice Peters the man who has taken me will keep me alive for twenty days. If you don't find me within this time he will kill me.

Here are nine clues. Each one represents one woman. The man who has taken me will kill one of these women every two days unless you can solve the clues and find them in time.

1. What sparkles brightly and is a flower in a field?
2. What is a satellite and a ruler?
3. What is a comic opera and a state of place?
4. What is an ancient town and a way to go?
5. What is dark and dances and flies high in the sky?
6. What is a film of horror and is small and round?
7. What is a universe in time and a man of many colors?
8. What is a rocket with eight ways of living?
9. What is a novel and is old at thirty-three?

If you solve the clues and save these women then the man will kill me.

Please help me.

The three of them stood staring in disbelief at the note. Reading it over and over again as if that would somehow change what it was telling them.

"It's handwritten we thinking our guy brought it with him?" Parker finally asked breaking the silence.

"We'll get someone to check it against a sample of her writing back at the lab, but . . . I'd say he made the victim write it herself."

Wyatt and Parker exchanged a look then turned to Marty in surprise, he was never one to jump to conclusions that were not based on irrefutable scientific fact.

"Hey, Jenkins!"

All three turned to see Maisy Wallace gesturing at them excitedly as she hurried down the hall towards them. Maisy was new to the CSU team. She was a young redhead, bright, bouncy and absolutely bursting with enthusiasm.

"What'd you find, Maisy?" Marty asked, removing his glasses, taking a handkerchief from his pocket and starting to clean the lenses.

"Hey, Parker, Wyatt," she greeted them with a beaming smile before turning to her boss, "We found some blood in the garage. Looks like maybe she cut her foot on something on the way from her car to the elevator." Her excitement getting the better of her Maisy was on a roll, "maybe she got spooked by the guy in the garage, and maybe he follows her up, breaks in while she's in the shower, maybe . . ."

"That's a lot of maybes there, Maisy," Marty interrupted, returning the glasses to his face and giving her a stern, reproachful frown. He was a science and facts guy, who liked to leave the speculating to the police. "We don't do conjecture, we simply collect the evidence."

Maisy was not deterred, simply flashed a winning smile at her boss, her warm hazel eyes twinkling merrily, "Sorry, Marty. See you later guys," tossing her red ponytail over her shoulder she hurried back down the hall.

Marty rolled his eyes and was about to comment further on his young colleague's zeal but was interrupted when a young officer tentatively approached them. "Detective Bell, Detective Wyatt," he began nervously, "I was . . . ah, I was assigned to canvass the neighbors . . ." he trailed off his eyes bouncing back and forth between the two detectives like he was watching a tennis match.

"And . . ." Parker prompted impatiently, waving his hand to hurry the man up.

"Well, I was talking to the guy who lives downstairs, right below her, ah Janice Peters. He's a retired biology teacher, he says he was out shopping last night, and that he saw, I mean he says he ran into the victim, I mean the . . . the . . ." again he trailed off.

"Has this story got a point?" Parker snapped at the flustered cop.

The young man bobbed his head up and down, his face an identical shade of red as his hair. "Yes, sir."

"He saw Janice Peter's last night?" Wyatt interjected with more patience than Parker could muster.

The young officer nodded emphatically. "Said he saw her in the garage and that she looked real jumpy. And I thought, I thought you might, maybe, you know, want to talk to him."

"Thanks, Officer Landry," Wyatt smiled encouragingly. "Great job."

The young man smiled back gratefully. "Oh, he's also the neighbor who called it in," he added, then took off towards the door, to continue talking to the apartment building's other occupants.

Parker rolled his eyes at the officer's retreating back and Marty laughed. "New guys," he said as he started to gather his evidence to take back to the lab.

"Hey we were all new one day," Wyatt told them reproachfully. "You two should learn to be more patient."

"I'm plenty patient," Parker huffed as both Wyatt and Marty laughed. "That guy's just too nervous," he complained.

"Cut the guy a break, Parker, this is his first big case. He was the first officer on the scene, he found the note."

"I just hope he didn't put his hands all over it," he muttered, huffing again, but feeling guilty for being too judgmental. Thinking back to his own first big case, where his over enthusiasm had almost let a murderer go free. He was not usually so rough on young officers, but it had been a really long and exhausting couple of months and he was worn out. Turning to leave he called over his shoulder, "Come on lets go see the retired biology teacher."

Wyatt followed and shot him another reproachful glance. "What's with you?"

"Nothing," Parker snapped back, and then sighed, relenting. Wyatt was his best and oldest friend, more like the brother he had never had, and he was only looking out of him. "This case. It makes *me* nervous. I feel like we need to hurry, that if we don't get this guy soon then the whole thing is gonna blow up in our faces."

Cautiously, "Parker, if you're not ready to be back, it's understandable after everything that happened, I can work the case myself."

"No," he could not stand another day cooped up in his house, with nothing but his thoughts for company. "I'm fine. Honest," he added upon seeing Wyatt's unconvinced look. Parker couldn't blame his partner, he wasn't sure whether he would ever be 'fine' again.

* * * * *

11:52 A.M.

Grinning to himself Dylan Riley stretched back in his chair and enjoyed the sunshine that had just broken through the clouds. Lingering raindrops glittered in the bright sunlight, and people hurried to make the most of the sunshine while it lasted. Winter was on its way.

He waved his hand at the waitress signaling for the bill, and reached into his pocket, pulling out the credit card that corresponded with today's identity. In the ten years since he had been forced to leave this place, Dylan had created at least five aliases, each complete with driver's licenses, credit cards, family histories, and disguises.

Passing a credit card with the name *Peter Daniels* on it to the young waitress, he could barely contain his glee. He couldn't remember when he had last had such fun. No that wasn't true he told himself. He could remember all right, it had just been a really, really long time. Ten years to be exact.

He'd been pleased with the media coverage the abduction had gotten. It had been on every station, they hadn't mentioned the note, but that was fine he was sure that his message had reached its intended recipients as soon as they heard the name of his victim.

"I just need your signature, sir," the waitress announced from beside him, he looked up and shot her a flirty smile, taking note of the name on her badge.

"Sure thing, darling," he drawled in his best southern accent. Hiding a smile as the pretty, young girl blushed. She was young, with black curls that framed her freckled face, and brown eyes that shone with youthful energy.

Handing her back the pen and paper, she passed him his credit card. He always thought it best to make a good impression on strangers. You never knew when a pesky cop was going to latch onto you, start checking into the places you've been and the people who've seen you. Nobody suspected the friendly old southern gentleman who flirted with the pretty waitresses.

"Have a nice day," she smiled shyly at him.

"I will if I come back here for dinner, Susie," he grinned, throwing in a light chuckle for good measure, and watched as she blushed again then hurried away.

Laughing to himself at the unbelievable naïveté of young girls, his thoughts returned to Janice Peters. She was stowed safely away, somewhere where nobody would think to find her. Nobody except Tessa Micah.

She would figure it out. It might take her a little while, but she was a smart girl, she'd get there. And when she figured it out nothing would stop her from coming after him. When she came, he'd be ready. He'd been waiting a long time.

Cautioning himself to put Tessa out of his mind for the time being, he had to remain focused on the task at hand. Glancing over at the hairdressers across the street from the café where he was enjoying lunch, he saw his next victim blithely leaving the building. Carefully closing the door behind her, and setting off down the street, she had absolutely no idea that she was being watched, followed, stalked.

Putting down his newspaper he got up to follow her, slipping sunglasses on he waved to Susie the waitress, and sauntered off at a leisurely pace in the same direction.

Tiffany Poppy didn't know it yet, but she only had two days left to live.

* * * * *

12:01 P.M.

"Here you go," Mr. Pickering set the tray down on the table and began to hand out cups of tea and coffee. The cups and saucers were all from the same set, the teapot, little jug for pouring milk and the sugar bowl also matched, as did the tray.

Despite his seventy years, Ted Pickering was lean and fit, with smooth skin, a full head of thick silver hair, and clear ice blue eyes, which were now red rimmed. It was clear that he had been crying earlier, but he had composed himself before they arrived and seemed eager to help them in any way he could.

"You have a beautiful home," Parker commented glancing around the roomy apartment, which was filled with antique furniture. He and Wyatt were in the apartment below Janice Peters, they were seated side by side in a soft leather sofa, Mr. Pickering was opposite them in a matching armchair. Looking around Parker noticed an ornate lamp stand that was identical to one he had seen in Janice's living room.

Mr. Pickering beamed proudly. "Collecting used to be our hobby, back before Katherine was diagnosed. After the kids grew up and I retired we started visiting antique stores." He swept an arm around the room, "we amassed this collection over the last twenty years."

"Is your collection worth a lot?" Wyatt asked, he and his wife had recently bought a new house and were in the middle of renovating it. They were also in the middle of disagreeing about almost every decorating decision that came along. Casey wanted to go modern, while Wyatt preferred a more traditional style.

"Some of the pieces are very rare," Mr. Pickering's face became animated as he talked about what was obviously his passion. "Others are more common, so they're not as valuable.

Once you start visiting antique stores you start to get a feel of what a good price is for certain types of furniture."

"Maybe you could give me some pointers in getting started."

Having heard more than enough about interior design to last an entire lifetime, Parker gestured at the lamp and steered the conversation towards Janice, "I saw one like this in Janice's apartment."

Nodding slowly Mr. Pickering sobered instantly, a sad smile crossing his face. "We got her interested in collecting antiques just after she moved in. That was the first piece she bought, we saw them the first time we went antique shopping together. They were a pair. We took one each. It was Katherine's idea."

"I'm sorry, Mr. Pickering, but we're probably going to ask you some questions that you've already answered for the other officers, so try to bear with us," Wyatt told him with a sympathetic smile.

Mr. Pickering nodded, face pained but focused. Parker had to admire the old guy. He was obviously shaken about what he had found in his young friend's apartment, but he was holding it together better than many cops Parker knew.

"You spent a lot of time with Janice?" Wyatt asked.

"Yes. Again, it was Katherine's idea. She was lonely after our kids moved out, and she had no one left to fuss over, we still see them regularly but it wasn't the same and Janice lives right upstairs."

"How many children do you have?" Parker asked, keeping the conversation as non-threatening as possible to keep the old man at ease.

"Three daughters." He gave a rueful laugh, "Daughters are a father's worst nightmare you know."

"Tell me about it," Wyatt sighed. "My daughter Stacey's four going on fourteen."

Mr. Pickering laughed, "Janice was such a lovely girl, but she didn't have many friends, she seemed so lonely."

"What about family?"

"She never talked about her family. I asked her once but she changed the subject and wouldn't give me an answer. We felt sorry for her, we didn't like her to be alone, so we had her over for dinner at least once a week, and on holidays."

"What about a boyfriend?"

He shook his head thoughtfully, "I never saw one around, and she never mentioned one to me. She might have said something to Katherine, but I doubt she'd remember if Janice had told her anything. She's not doing so good these days."

"Is your wife here now?"

"No, she's spending the day with out oldest daughter, gives me a bit of a break," he said sadly. "After I went to Janice's apartment this morning and found it all messed up I called Candice, asked if she wouldn't mind looking after her mother today. I couldn't face telling Katherine about Janice yet."

"You've known Ms Peters a long time?" Parker asked, blowing on the steaming coffee to cool it, and steering the conversation slowly back towards the abduction.

"Two, no it must be three years now. The year Janice moved in was the year my Katherine was diagnosed with Alzheimer's." He trailed off as he picked up a photo of himself and his young bride and gently stroked his wife's face. He stared at the picture wistfully, his eyes glazing over as he remembered happier times when they had been young and invincible, with the whole world at their feet and their whole lives ahead of them.

"Mr. Pickering" Wyatt began gently.

"Ted," he corrected, looking up from the photo, "Janice is such a nice girl. Always coming over to check on Katherine, sits with her, listens to her stories, gives me a bit of a break." He smiled sadly as he replaced the photograph on the table, "I can't believe she's gone, that someone would hurt her."

"Did you hear anything last night? Any noise coming from her apartment?"

"No. Janice was always very quiet. I had to go out to the store, I got held up, it was late by the time I returned. I got Katherine's dinner and we both had an early night."

"You saw her last night, is that right?" Parker asked.

Ted nodded, "Down in the garage, I startled her I'm afraid. She dropped her keys I thought she heard me but I guess she was distracted."

"Did she say that?"

"She said she was on edge, and that she hadn't been sleeping well the last few nights."

"What time was that?"

Mr. Pickering thought, "About eight, I think."

"Did you see anyone in the garage, someone who shouldn't be there?"

"No, just Janice," he paused and scrunched up his face in thought.

"What is it, Mr. Pickering? Did you see someone down there?" Wyatt pressed gently.

Shaking his head slowly. "Not someone, something. There was a car, a car I've never seen before. I used to be a mechanic," he clarified upon seeing their puzzled expressions. "I've always been interested in cars. I know every one of the cars each of the residents here owns. I do a bit of work on them now and then. But last night there was a car I'd never seen before, I think it was a Citroen. Blue if I remember correctly."

"Do you remember where the car was parked?" Parker asked, shooting Wyatt a glance, this could be their first solid lead.

Pausing to think then nodding, his intense blue eyes sparkling as he realized that what he was saying could save his young friend. "It was parked right near Janice's car," he told them triumphantly. "I remember because it was right where I found her keys." He beamed when he saw their hopeful faces, "Do you think that might help you find her?"

"Maybe," Wyatt told him giving him a reassuring smile.

"Did you see the license plate?"

His eyes dropped, "No, I'm sorry," his face flashing disappointment as though he had let Janice down. "I found the keys and I wanted to get to her before she got up to her apartment. So she didn't have to come all the way back down looking for them."

"Had you seen this car around before, maybe parked out the front of your building? Or maybe seen someone hanging around that shouldn't be here?"

"No, I'd never seen it before. Do you really think that car has something to do with Janice's kidnapping? Do you think that someone followed us up to Janice's apartment? Do you think someone was stalking her?" The old man was firing questions at them, overcome with guilt about not protecting his young friend.

"There was nothing you could have done," Parker assured him, feeling his own heart tighten as he felt the man's pain. "Can you tell us exactly what you saw when you went to her apartment this morning?"

Clearing his throat, Ted took a long drink of tea and then began. "As I said, I wanted to check on her because she seemed so upset last night. When I got there, I knocked and knocked, even called out, but there was no answer. I have a key, so I let myself in. The first thing I noticed was the microwave beeping, and I knew right then that something was wrong. I called out to her, but . . ." he shrugged helplessly. "I went down to the bedroom and when I saw it . . ." his hands were shaking as he set the teacup down. He closed his eyes to steady himself and when he opened them, tears were shining. "I left immediately and called the police."

"Can you think of anyone who would want to hurt Janice?"

"No, she was such a sweet girl. I wanted her to come over for dinner last night," Ted's eyes brimming with tears, he stared off into space, his voice dropping to a mere whisper. "I should have insisted, she was obviously worried about something, I should have pushed her to tell me. I should have insisted," he whispered softly to himself as though he had forgotten that they were still in the room.

Parker glanced at Wyatt and gestured at the door, Wyatt nodded. "You've been very helpful, Mr. Pickering. I'll leave you my card, please call us if you think of anything else, however unimportant you think it might be."

Standing they each shook Mr. Pickering's hand, and Wyatt passed him a card. "We'll see ourselves out," Wyatt told the devastated old man.

Ted Pickering nodded without looking up. They were almost out the door when he spoke, his voice heavy with despair, "She was like a daughter to me detectives, please find her and bring her safely home."

They nodded encouragingly at him, but Parker knew that the chances of this girl being found alive were slim to none.

* * * * *

2:12 P.M.

Parker pushed the drawer closed and yanked open the next one. The papers inside were neatly stacked, just like everything else in Janice's life, and as he shuffled through them, he saw that they were all work related. "You find anything on the computer?" he asked as he slammed the drawer in frustration.

Looking briefly up from the computer Wyatt shook his head. "There's not one personal thing on here. No photos, no documents, nothing. She hasn't used this computer for anything other than work."

They were in Janice Peters' office, looking for something that might give them some clue as to who this woman was and who might have had reason to abduct her. After leaving the Pickering's apartment they had stopped for a quick lunch then come straight here, only to find that Janice's office was just as impersonal as her apartment had been. It was like the young woman had hardly existed.

At least the rain had lifted while they had been inside Janice's apartment building. As the sun shone, making the world shimmer and sparkle, it had served to slightly brighten his mood on the ride over here. People were out enjoying the sunshine, happily going about their business with no idea that a monster was lurking in the midst of their community. Any cheerful thoughts that might have emerged from under his own dark cloud had quickly fled during the fruitless search of Janice's office.

Thumping his fist against the desk in annoyance, Wyatt jumped and turned back to look at him. "What is it with you today?"

"We have nothing. The woman's a shadow. If we can't find out anything about her we're never going to find who took her," Parker ranted. He was tired and angry, and he detested feeling helpless. "And as if that's not bad enough we have nine women who are walking around with no idea that some maniac is planning to kill them. This is personal, he chose her, all of them, for a reason, the only way we're gonna find Janice is if we find the connection."

Wyatt raised an unconvinced eyebrow. "And" he prodded.

"That's not enough?"

"It is, but it's not all that's bothering you," his partner replied mildly, completely un-rattled by Parker's temper tantrum.

Sighing irritably, sometimes Parker hated it that Wyatt knew him so well. Wyatt was a great friend and a great partner and usually he loved having someone to bounce ideas off, or to confide in, but right now Parker was in no mood to discuss his feelings.

"It's the O'Hara case, isn't it? You did the right thing, Parker," Wyatt eyed him carefully.

Parker felt his heart freeze and his breath catch in his throat at the mention of the name, but was spared from having to give an answer when there was a tentative knock at Janice Peters' office door. They both turned as the door opened a crack to reveal a timid young woman with long chestnut hair cascading down her back and nervous brown eyes staring back at them.

"Lilly Michaels?" Wyatt asked. The woman nodded but didn't move. "Come in."

Lilly moved slowly into the office, gingerly closing the door behind her, as though she were afraid that she would shatter if she made any noise. Wyatt gestured at the two couches facing one another at one end of the office, before taking a seat on one of the couches himself. Parker watched as the tense young woman crossed the office and sat down on the edge of the couch, then pulled the desk chair towards them, spun it backwards and sat down.

Lilly's red-rimmed eyes darted from him to Wyatt and back again as she waited for one of them to start talking. She was dressed in a professional grey suit, a pale pink blouse and matching pale pink heels. She kept her knees pressed tightly together, hands held stiffly in her lap, she clutched them together so tightly Parker wondered if she would break her own fingers.

Wyatt glanced over at him and raised an eyebrow, Parker nodded slightly. It was their unspoken way of deciding which of them would lead the interview.

"Have you worked here long, Ms Michaels?" Wyatt began.

Nodding stiffly, "Almost six years, and you . . . you can call me Lilly." She spoke so softly it was almost impossible to hear what she was saying.

"Three years before Janice Peters started here?" Wyatt clarified.

Again, she nodded stiffly, but said nothing.

"Are you and Janice friends, Lilly?"

"Yes," she whispered. "Yes we are, we've been . . . we've been friends since she started here. We, we . . ." she trailed off as she started to cry. "I can't believe this is happening. Who would do this?"

Parker reached for the tissues on the side of the desk and passed them to Lilly. "Can you think of anyone who would want to hurt Janice?"

Lilly looked at them with desperate eyes, as though begging them to wake her up and tell her that this had all been just a horrible nightmare. She shook her head slowly, "I can't think of *anyone* who would want to hurt her," she whispered emphatically.

"Can you tell us a bit about Janice? Help us get to know her?"

"Okay," Lilly wiped at her eyes with a tissue then twisted it in her hands as she spoke, her voice growing stronger. "Janice and I hit it off right away," a sad smile lighting her face as she remembered happier times. "Janice is great, she's a really good listener, and she loves to help others, but," Lilly faltered and looked guiltily away from them.

"What is it, Lilly?" Parker asked.

"It's just that," she sighed unhappily and wouldn't meet their eyes.

"Lilly?" Wyatt prodded gently.

"Janice is really great," she clarified, looking at them as though daring them to disagree. "But she doesn't have a lot friends. She doesn't like to open up to people. She closes herself off. She's nice and polite and thoughtful, but it's always about others, never about herself."

Parker frowned. "Being nice, polite, thoughtful and not talking about herself stopped her from having friends?"

"Not exactly," Lilly whispered forlornly, staring out the office's small window, Parker and Wyatt waited patiently for her to continue. After almost a minute of uncomfortable silence, Lilly sighed and continued, "Some people thought she was a snob. She didn't like to go out, always turned down invitations to go anywhere with us. She was always all about work. Some of the other women here didn't understand that. They thought she was standoffish."

"But you understood her?" Wyatt interjected.

Lilly nodded sadly, "Yeah I did. Janice was the sweetest person I ever met, she helped me through a really hard time," her voice faltering. "She was really wonderful," she sniffed and tears started to slide down her cheeks again.

"What else can you tell us about her?"

Wiping at the tears on her cheeks, she resumed twisting the tissue in her hand. "She loves old movies, anything in black and white, it's what we usually do when we hung out together. She's really, really smart, she has an IQ of 125, she loves puzzles, any kind of, of puzzles," she cleared her throat, "We used to do them together in our lunch break."

"Does Janice have a cell phone or a laptop? Maybe do puzzles online?"

"Janice doesn't really like technology, she uses the computer here at work, but in her personal life she doesn't have one. And she doesn't have a cell phone, she doesn't like to be reachable all the time, she likes her privacy." Parker opened his mouth to ask another question but Lilly cut him off, anticipating his question, "Oh and she doesn't use the internet except for work, so you won't find anything personal on her work computer."

"Does Janice have a boyfriend?"

"No," Lilly looked thoughtful for a moment as she dropped the twisted tissue onto the table in front of them and pulled another from the box, delaying answering their question for as long as possible. "Janice was really weird around men," she began eventually. "Shy and uncomfortable. I asked her about it once, I thought that maybe she uh, she had a bad experience once."

"You thought she might have been raped?" Parker asked, this would certainly give them a direction to move in.

Lilly looked embarrassed but continued, "Maybe. Or I thought that maybe she might have been in a bad relationship at one time. I asked her about it, I thought that maybe she might have told me, opened up to me . . ." Lilly trailed off and wouldn't meet their gaze.

"Because you were in an abusive relationship? Is that what Janice helped you with?" Wyatt questioned gently.

"Yeah," Lilly's voice faltered again, her cheeks reddened slightly, and she still wouldn't meet their gaze. "I married my high school boyfriend right after graduation, it uh, it didn't go well. Anyway Janice helped me to divorce him, to get away, that's why I thought maybe she'd open up to me."

"She never said anything?"

"She never said anything," Lilly echoed, her eyes tearing up she stared vacantly at the wall. "Maybe if she had told me I could have helped her, maybe this never would have happened. I should have pushed her to tell me," she whispered softly to herself.

Blame went hand in hand with trauma. Friends and family of a victim always seemed to blame themselves. If only they'd done this or that, or said this or that, then maybe everything would have been okay. Maybe the loved one would still be here.

It was a feeling that Parker understood all too well. But life just didn't work that way. He knew that but it didn't stop him, and it didn't stop the people he encountered in his job, from thinking these thoughts just the same.

Wyatt laid a comforting hand on her knee. "This isn't your fault, Lilly."

"What can you tell us about her family? So far we haven't been able to locate any next of kin," Parker asked, deciding a change of topic was in order.

Lilly sniffed and wiped at her eyes, focusing herself. "She was an only child and she never really got along with her parents, they died when she was in college. Her parents were really wealthy they left her a huge inheritance, that's how she was able to afford that awesome apartment she lives in. I think she has a cousin that she saw from time to time, I think she lives in California, but I don't know her name."

"We'll look into it," Parker said, making a note on a pad.

"Was Janice having any problems with anyone here?"

"No, she was doing really well here, she was in the middle of her first really big sale." Lilly gave a proud, albeit sad, smile, "It might have gone national."

"Have you noticed anyone hanging around the building, or maybe Janice might have mentioned someone following her around, any unusual phone calls?"

"She never said anything." Her eyes going vacant again, she whispered, "Do you think she's still alive? He's, he's probably killed her already," her voice rose, her eyes going wild as she became panicked. "Why would he keep her alive? He's killed her, I'm sure he's killed her!"

"We're going to do everything we can to find her," Wyatt said soothingly, patting her on the shoulder. "Thank you, you've been very helpful, Lilly."

She nodded dully, her breath coming in gasps, and rose unsteadily to her feet, Parker rose with her and put a steadying hand on her elbow, guiding her to the door.

Opening the door Lilly paused and turned clutching desperately at him. "Please, please find her," she sobbed.

Parker watched her go then closed the door behind him and leaned wearily against it. "This is a nightmare," he said, rubbing his eyes tiredly. He had only been back at work for one day and already it felt like a lifetime. "Who's next on the list?' he asked looking over at Wyatt.

Consulting his notebook, "Roger Heart, Janice's boss."

* * * * *

10:26 P.M.

Wind whipped around him, thick fog obscured his view, and he wasn't sure where he was.

Parker looked around. "Hello?' he called, his voice muffled by the fog.

A noise sounded behind him, turning he took a few steps forward, but froze as a person emerged from the mist.

"No, you're dead," Parker whispered.

The man said nothing.

"You can't be here," Parker insisted.

Still the man said nothing, just stared back at him with calm eyes as another figure stepped out from behind him. A teenage girl. Parker stared at her in disbelief. Closing his eyes, he shook his head as though that would make her go away.

The man and the girl stared back at him with unblinking eyes. Then in sync they glanced down at his hand. His eyes followed theirs and he was surprised to see a gun in his hand.

Looking back up he saw bullets flying towards the girl, little red dots appearing on her chest. Her eyes remained locked on his own, and he was unable to break away. Watching, riveted, as her eyes opened wide in surprise and she fell to the ground in slow motion.

Startled by the sound of gunfire he tore his eyes away from the motionless teenager and turned to see a tiny little girl standing beside him. A little girl he knew. When he looked back at the man, he saw what he knew he would, red dots appearing on his chest. The man dropped to the ground alongside the teenager.

Crying echoed behind him and he turned back to see the little girl curled up on the ground, knees pulled up to her chest, arms wrapped tightly around them. She rocked slowly backwards and forwards as she cried. As he reached down to comfort her, she disappeared beneath his hand, a child sized hand. Glancing around for her, Parker saw that the two bodies were standing on their feet staring at him with blank, empty eyes. Mocking him. Taunting him.

"You killed us," their monotone voices droned together. "You killed us, you killed us, you ..."

Parker woke in a panic. Drenched in sweat, his breath coming in ragged gasps, his pulse racing. It took him a moment to realize that he was in his bedroom, in his bed, he'd just been sleeping.

The dream was back.

* * * * *

11:01 P.M.

Moaning softly Janice felt like there was a hammer thumping inside her head. She tried to open her eyes but her eyelids felt like they were weighted down with stones. Next, she tried rolling over but was overcome by waves of dizziness and nausea. Lying still she took several deep breaths and tried to settle her stomach and her head.

Becoming aware of something cold and hard beneath her Janice tried to move her hands to feel what it was but found that she couldn't. Tugging her arms, she was again rocked by dizziness. Lying still she wiggled her fingers just a little and felt something rough tied around her wrists.

Trying to focus her swimming head, she attempted to remember where she was. Janice didn't think that she could be in her apartment, but she couldn't actually remember anything after getting in her car this evening to drive home. At least she thought it was this evening.

Janice pushed herself to concentrate, taking another deep breath to quell the queasiness rumbling in her stomach. She put all her effort into concentrating on just opening her eyes. As she slowly raised her eyelids, at her first her vision was nothing but a blur. Blinking her eyes to clear them, the world slowly stopped spinning, and she found herself lying on the concrete floor of a small, dark, windowless room. A single candle glowed in the corner. Her wrists were tied together with rope and chained to the wall, making it impossible for her to sit. She was also naked.

Terror taking over she struggled wildly, ignoring the waves of dizziness and nausea that still coursed through her body. Sobs catching in her throat she choked them back and screamed as loudly as she could, her voice echoing in the small room. Strength failing, she lay still resting her head on the cold concrete floor and closing her heavy eyes.

No one answered her screams for help.

Not that Janice really believed anyone would.

A face flitted through her mind and her memory came back with a flash. She'd been in her apartment, a masked man in her bedroom, he had grabbed her, dragged her to the mirror, where she had seen the face of her nightmares. He had held a cloth to her face, her mind fading to black as she had collapsed into his arms. She remembered nothing else until she awoke in this dungeon.

Something fluttered through her mind and she struggled to hold onto it. Before he drugged her, he had made her do something. Latching onto the memory, Janice now knew for a fact that she was not getting out of this alive. Recalling the letter he had made her write, telling the police that he would let her go alive if they didn't find his other intended victims. Janice knew that was a lie. He would never let her go. He would kill them all. Except maybe Tessa.

Exhaustion overwhelmed her, and she let it take her out of this dank cell and into the beautiful oblivion of unconsciousness.

* * * * *

11:57 P.M.

Parker sat on the stoop outside his backdoor looking up at the clear black sky. The rain had stopped and the clouds had dissipated as he was driving home earlier, the sky was now clear and the stars twinkled brightly.

Setting his water bottle down on the ground, he stood and paced up and down his backyard. He was still on edge from his nightmare earlier. He hated the feeling of waking breathless and sweaty, and rather than lie and toss and turn in bed, unable to go back to sleep for fear of his nightmare returning, he had decided to get some fresh air.

Standing out here always brought back memories from his childhood. He and his sister running and playing, the swing set where they had spent hours seeing who could go the highest. The huge oak tree where his dad had helped him build a tree house that he and his friends had used to hold their 'secret' club meetings.

His sister's playhouse, from which he had been banned after he'd beheaded her dolls as a joke, still sat in a corner of the yard. Mattie hadn't seen the humor in his joke and had retaliated by fiddling with his bike, causing the front wheel to come off. He'd gone flying through the air and into the fence, cutting open his head in the process, he still had the scar. Parker wondered where his twin sister was right now. What she was doing, *how* she was doing, and whether she thought of him as often as he thought of her.

It had been a long day, a long and stressful day, it was to this that he decided to attribute his nightmare and resulting reminiscent moroseness. He and Wyatt had interviewed Janice Peters' colleagues until nearly nine o'clock. They'd learnt nothing new. Nobody knew much about Janice's personal life or her family and most of them had echoed the same sentiments as Lilly Michaels. Although not all of them liked her as much as she did, many took her reluctance to talk about herself as a sign that she thought she was better than them.

Arriving home, he'd skipped dinner and gone for a run around the neighborhood, spent some time pondering over the clues to the nine women's identities, before falling into bed. Where the nightmare had found him. A nightmare that dated back to his childhood, and that he had had hundreds of times before. It had ceased for a while, after he joined the police force, but had come back with a vengeance after the Gina O'Hara case.

Taking a deep breath of the cool night air, he enjoyed the tingle of the cold breeze on his flushed skin, pulling off his t-shirt to soak in more of the night. Parker loved the freedom the dark afforded, the way the shadows danced in the moonlight, the quiet. The darkness hid everything so completely that it made him feel safe. When he had lived in foster care he often used to sneak outside after everyone had gone to bed and sit for hours watching the stars twinkle and the moon move slowly across the sky. It was the only time he had felt truly happy.

Pushing his own problems out of his mind, his thoughts turned to Janice Peters. He wondered if she was out there somewhere, alive and praying for someone to find her and save her. His gut told him that this guy hadn't killed her, at least not yet. His gut also told him that there was no way this guy was going to let Janice go alive, even if he was able to fulfill his plan and kill the other nine women.

His thoughts straying to Gina O'Hara, he felt his stomach drop and his heart tighten, the same way it always did when he thought of her. He'd tried to help Gina, to save her, and he had failed. There was no way he was going to fail Janice. He would save her no matter what.

NOVEMBER 22ND

7:31 A.M.

Tiffany Poppy wrapped herself up in her favorite pink coat. It had been a present to herself after a particularly rough patch she had gone through a few years ago. Slipping on matching mittens and a scarf, tucking her short blonde hair under a hat, and then braving the cold to head out the door.

Whistling to herself, a habit she had picked up many years back, she started down the sidewalk towards the elementary school a few blocks from her house where she was a second grade teacher.

Her parents would have been thrilled with her chosen career. Her mother a high school math teacher and her father a university lecturer, had always instilled in her the joys of working with kids. Of teaching them and watching them grow.

Deliberately pushing the thoughts away, it was not a good idea to bring up bad memories on today of all days. With everything that she was going through at the moment, with all the inner demons she was fighting, she did not need to be remembering her family.

Hand straying to the locket that she always wore around her neck, it had been a wedding present from her father to her mother. Stored safely inside was a picture of her parents on their wedding day, and one of her and her brothers when they had been small.

Instead of reminiscing she attempted to focus on the day ahead, of the lessons on time and adjectives that she and her class would be covering throughout the day.

Hard as she tried Tiffany couldn't quite keep her mind from wandering back to yesterday's events. Ever since she had received the phone call at lunchtime the day before, she had been unable to think of anything else. Going through the rest of the day in a haze, barely registering anything that was going on around her, she was sure even her second graders must have noticed her disconnect. After work she'd gone straight home and spent the night viewing the news and reading the papers. Desperately hoping that somehow what she was watching and reading would suddenly change.

A car horn honked and Tiffany's head snapped up as a car whizzed past her, she had been about to walk straight onto a road. Making herself concentrate on her surroundings she continued carefully across the road. Try as she might all she could think of was Janice. If she wasn't dead already she soon would be. Then he would come after the rest of them, of that she was certain.

A gust of strong wind knocked her hat off her head, sending it flying behind her. Turning quickly to grab it before it blew onto the road she paused as she thought she saw a figure duck into a storefront. Studying the shop anxiously, considering backtracking to see if there was indeed someone following her. Deciding against it, she had to get a grip, what had happened to Janice was making her paranoid.

Setting the hat back on her head she set off resolutely down the street, determined to think only of the day ahead. Unable to shake the feeling that she was being watched, Tiffany ignored the urge to turn and check behind her. He was out there. Watching her. She knew he was coming, she had always known he was coming. She had made her peace with it a long time ago, it was only the when and where that still scared her.

As she continued down the street, the figure crept from its hiding place and continued to follow her.

* * * * *

44

8:40 A.M.

Parker paced uneasily up and down the hallway of his house. The house he had lived in for two thirds of his life. He and his twin sister, Matilda, had grown up in foster care. Their mother was a drug addict who had lost custody of them, when they were only three months old, after she got arrested robbing a gas station in the middle of the night with them in the car. A runaway, from the age of fifteen, their mother had lived on the streets, or with a string of boyfriends, when she wasn't in jail on drugs and robbery charges.

Their mother had not known who the father of her twins was, so with their mother in jail and no family to take them in, he and Matilda had entered the foster care system. They had been bumped from home to home, some of which were a living nightmare, before being adopted by Luka and Laura Bell at the age of ten. The Bell's had lost their only son, Taylor, to cancer. He had been only seven.

Life for Parker had improved dramatically after moving in with the Bell's. At first he had been angry and withdrawn, not really believing that things would work out with his new family. Luka and Laura had been patient and loving, taking every opportunity to make sure he and Mattie felt like they belonged. Their support, and his friendship with Wyatt, had eventually broken down his defenses and he had started to feel comfortable. His grades and behavior in school improved and he was happier than he had ever been.

Caterina Matilda Landston appeared only once more in her twin's lives. Reappearing suddenly just before their fourteenth birthday, eight years after being released from jail. His life on track, Parker had refused to spend any time with her, angry at her abandonment, and not fooled by her desperate pleas that she had changed.

His sister, however, had never recovered from her experiences in foster care. She remained quiet, distant and introverted, even after years spent in the Bell's stable family environment. When their mother had reappeared Mattie had latched on to her, clinging desperately to her and becoming even more distant from him and their adoptive parents. Matilda had been devastated when Caterina had been arrested for selling drugs to the kids at their school.

A horn honked outside, yanking him out of the past and back to the present. Wrapping a blue and purple woolen scarf around his neck he headed outside. Parker possessed a huge collection of scarves, they filled a whole cupboard in his spare bedroom. They were his signature item of clothing, when the weather got cold he never went anywhere without one. Some were brightly colored, some were striped, others patterned. His very first scarf had come from the Bell's the first Christmas he had spent with them. He still had it packed safely away.

Outside the sun was shining but it was bitterly cold, despite the chill Parker would not wear a jacket. He had a whole box of unused suit jackets tucked away in a corner of his attic. When the weather was cold, he wore a woolen sweater with his shirt and pants, but he refused to wear a jacket or coat. It was one of the reasons that he had begun wearing and collecting his scarves.

Climbing into Wyatt's car, he slumped tiredly down in the seat.

"You get any sleep last night?" Wyatt asked, handing him coffee.

Ignoring the fact that the coffee was white, and steaming hot, he pulled off the lid and drank several mouthfuls of the burning liquid. "Not much. You?"

"Some," Wyatt answered reversing down the driveway. "Sam was up sick half the night, Casey and I took turns sitting with him." Sam was Wyatt and Casey's eight-year-old son. Casey was Wyatt's high school sweetheart. After high school she had gone off to college to study history, while Wyatt had gone to the police academy. They had married after she graduated and were celebrating their thirteenth wedding anniversary this year.

They had been through their ups and downs. Several years ago, following their daughter's death, Wyatt had almost given up his career as a police officer and Casey had sunk into a deep depression. They had fought their way back. The birth of little Sam had helped, giving them both something to focus on. Although they still did, and always would, miss Serena, they had managed to move on with their lives and be happy again.

"You okay?" Wyatt asked looking over at him.

Blinking, Parker realized that he had zoned out, he sighed and rubbed his heavy eyes. "Yeah."

"You had the dream again." It was a statement not a question.

Parker nodded.

"The man and Gina O'Hara?"

Again, Parker nodded.

"You had no choice, you know that right?"

Parker disagreed but he wasn't in the mood to argue so he told Wyatt what he knew he wanted to hear. "Yeah, I know."

Wyatt sighed, and Parker knew that he didn't believe his lie, but his partner didn't push him, instead opting to change the subject, "You go over the list last night?"

Nodding wearily. "Yeah. Those clues are gibberish, they don't mean anything, they're never gonna help us find those women."

"We have to do something and so far it's the only lead we've got." Hearing his stomach growl Wyatt glanced over at him, "Wanna stop for breakfast?"

Smiling for the first time in days. "Bacon, eggs, sausages, tomatoes, mushrooms and pancakes."

"Who's buying?"

"You are," Parker grinned. "It's my welcome back breakfast."

* * * * *

10:31 A.M.

Consciousness came swirling back slowly, as Janice once again became aware of her surroundings. Head still pounding, stomach still queasy, she realized that she was lying on something different, something soft. Forcing her eyes open she saw that she was no longer in the small dungeon.

Taking in her surroundings, she was now in a bedroom, a child's bedroom. The walls were covered in pink striped wallpaper and thick pink carpet covered the floor. She was lying on a four-poster bed, her hands and feet tied to the bedposts, with a warm woolen blanket, pink again, covering her. Hanging on the walls were pictures of baby animals and ballerina's, a teddy bear and some dolls sat in an armchair by the window, and a bookshelf filled with children's books took up most of one wall.

Tall trees were visible through the open window, stretching their branches up to the clouds. Other than some birds chirping, there was not a single other sound. It was light out now, but she couldn't be sure how long she had been unconscious. The thought of his hands on her, touching her, carrying her, made her feel physically sick, and she fought back the urge to throw up.

Janice felt her mind start to fade again, but pushed herself to fight it. If she was going to get out of here alive then she had to stay alert. Realization dawning she remembered being in this room before. Maybe not this exact room, but one that looked exactly like it. Unfortunately her mind was slushy and refused to work properly, she tried to hold onto the thought but it moved tantalizingly out of reach.

Hearing a noise outside the door, she quickly closed her eyes, and tried to breathe deeply to convince him that she was still unconscious. A key turned and the door creaked as it opened. Footsteps sounded as he moved towards her and stopped beside the bed. Her heart thumped in her chest and she felt herself shiver involuntarily at having him so close to her after all these years.

A hand gently stroked her hair and Janice couldn't control herself any longer. Her eyes flew open and she flinched away from him. The face that hovered above her was the same one that haunted her dreams. It was a little older, the reddish brown hair was streaked with some grey, a few wrinkles marred the once tanned, smooth skin, but the evil hazel eyes and smug smile were exactly the same as she remembered.

"You'll never get away with this," she whispered, her voice hoarse from lack of use.

He just laughed, maddeningly. "Of course I will. The police have no reason to suspect me and your friends will never say anything."

Wiggling as far away from him as she could with her wrists and ankles restrained, when he sat beside her on the bed. "Someone will find me." Catching the desperation in her voice.

"You haven't figured out where we are yet?" he smirked.

Her mind was still swimming from the drugs he had given her earlier. She tried to think of a place from their past that held some significance but came up empty so she shook her head.

Laughing again he grinned at her, brushing his hand lightly across her cheek, and again she tried desperately to recoil from his touch. "You'll figure it out eventually. It's somewhere quiet, somewhere deserted, somewhere where no one will think to look for you."

Unconsciousness ebbing at her mind, Janice shook her head to clear it and tried to keep him talking, hoping that he would give away something that would help her escape from this place. "Why didn't you just kill us all, why the note? We both know there's no way you're letting me out of here alive."

Giving her a self-satisfied smile, he laid his hand on top of her stomach, and Janice had to force herself not to throw up at his touch. "You're smart, not as smart as Tessa, but then she was always the pick of the litter. This way is much more fun, the other's will be working themselves into a panic, wondering what

I'm up to and when I'm gonna strike."

"Who's next on your list?"

"Tiffany."

Janice thought of Tiffany. Of all their friends, she and Tiffany had been the most alike. Both had been quiet, sensitive and completely lacking in self-confidence. Both of them had been quietly envious of the confident, self-assured Tessa, she was smarter, prettier and more in control than either of them could ever hope to be. Janice knew that there was no way Tiffany could escape her fate, none of them could. They had known what would happen from the moment they had made their decision all those years ago.

"You'll never get what you want, Tessa will kill you first," she whispered, hoping that Tessa had figured out what was going on. She was sure that someone from work would have reported her missing by now, they would call the police and they would find the note. She was sure that her abduction would be on the news. Tessa would see it and figure out what had happened. Janice was sure that Tessa would stop at nothing to protect their secret.

"On the contrary, my dear, Tessa will come after me and I'll have everything I ever wanted," he told her, his horrible conceited smile mocking her.

"Not everything," she whispered back just as mockingly.

His face darkened instantly, his familiar rage vibrating through every pore of his being. "Tell me where they are and I'll let you go."

"I'd rather die."

"And you will," he murmured, his hazel eyes clearing and his sardonic smile returning as quickly as it had disappeared. He was even crazier than he had been back then.

Fatigue was pulling her under again and this time she couldn't fight it, her vision blurring she looked up to see him preparing a syringe. "What's that?" she whispered her voice slurring, and her eyes fluttering closed against her will.

"Something to help you sleep," he grinned, then pulled back the blanket that had been covering her. "You didn't see your surprise," he said with mock disappointment.

Forcing her eyes back open, she glanced down at herself, her body convulsing in shock as she saw what he had dressed her in. She felt the sharp stab of the needle in her arm then her horror dissipated as she sunk once again into blissful unconsciousness.

* * * * *

1:11 P.M.

"What do we have so far?" The question came from their boss, Lieutenant Jacob Jacobson. He was a big bear of a man, towering over almost everyone at close to seven feet tall, weighing nearly three hundred pounds, with a thick, bushy beard and moustache.

Looking up from the note in front of him Parker gave a shrug. "Not a lot." Besides himself, Wyatt and the lieutenant, Marty Jenkins and Elisabeth Bennett, the criminal profiler and psychologist they consulted with, were also present for the meeting.

J.J. frowned. "That's not good enough, people," he hollered. Jacob Jacobson, or J.J. as he had been called since he was a child, had beaten the police force divorce rate statistics and was still happily married after almost thirty-five years. He and his wife Linda were the proud parents of four children and the proud grandparents of twelve, with another two on the way. He had joined the police academy right out of college and had risen up the ladder quickly. Sighing, J.J. ran a hand through hair that was still as thick and brown as it had been the day he entered the academy. "Start at the beginning."

They were seated in J.J.'s cramped office where every spare bit of wall, desktop and cupboards were covered with picture's of his children's accomplishments. From preschool swimming certificates, to college graduations, from wedding pictures, to photos of newborn grandchildren, it was like a complete catalogue of his life.

"The victim is Janice Peters," Wyatt began. "Twenty-five years old, brown hair, grey eyes. Last seen in the elevator at her apartment building at approximately eight o'clock on the night of November 20th by her neighbor Ted Pickering . . ."

Interrupting Wyatt J.J. asked, "Are we thinking he got her right away or broke in later to abduct her?"

"Officer Landry, the first on scene, reported that when he arrived at her apartment the microwave was still beeping, there was a frozen dinner inside. And her clothes were still in a pile on the floor in the bathroom, her bathrobe was on the floor in the bedroom. Grocery bags were still on the kitchen counter. So it looks like he got to her not long after she arrived home," Wyatt continued.

"We don't know whether he kept her in her apartment for a while or left with her straight away," Parker interjected. "Or how he got her out."

Glancing over at him, J.J. sighed again. "No-one saw a stranger leaving the building carrying a giant bag?" he asked half-heartedly. "Marty you got any good news for me?"

"We found no physical trace evidence anywhere in the apartment. No hairs, no fibers, no fingerprints, no blood or other fluids. Nothing."

"You found a handkerchief though, with chloroform on it?" J.J. persisted, brown eyes boring into the CSU tech, as though through sheer force of will he could make evidence appear.

"Yes," Marty responded giving a sharp nod.

"And . . .?" prodded J.J. impatiently. He was a good cop, confident, fair, a good judge of character and he cared about the victims and their families, but he had a tendency to lose his temper at the drop of a hat. With his wild hair, wild eyes and wildly unpredictable temper he could have an almost manic air about him. Any criminal or negligent cop that was unfortunate enough to get caught up in one of his tirades could attest to that.

"And in and of itself that's not very helpful. If you find this guy I might be able to match the chloroform's composition to anything he might have on him, but it's not something that is going to help you find him."

"What about the note? Please tell me it sheds some light on the situation."

"No forensics indicating that anyone other than Janice Peters touched the note," Marty jumped in first.

"The handwriting confirmed that Janice wrote it?" Parker asked.

Marty nodded in the affirmative.

"The press don't know about it yet?" J.J. asked.

Parker shook his head.

"Good, let's keep it that way for now. Where are we on identifying the women from the list?"

"Nowhere," Parker began, continuing immediately when he saw the look on his boss' face. "The problem with the note is that there are too many possible outcomes. The clues aren't too narrow, they're too broad, we've already come up with hundreds of possible matches."

Taking the information on board and jumping onto the next topic, J.J. moved on, "Do we know how he got in?"

"Picked the front door lock," Wyatt replied.

"You've been very quiet over there, Elisabeth, tell us what you're thinking," J.J. pounced on the psychologist.

"Maybe we should consider the possibility that the whole situation was faked by Janice," Beth suggested.

For a full minute they all stared at her in shocked silence. None of them had considered that possibility. Elisabeth always provided a unique perspective on any case they were working, which was one of the reasons Parker loved to work with her. She had also helped him a lot after the Gina O'Hara situation. At first he had been reluctant to talk with her, but she had been patient, and eventually he had started to open up to her.

Beth was in her forties and had recently become engaged to her long-term boyfriend, whose cancer had recently gone into remission. She had dark brown hair that reached all the way down her back, and eyes that were so dark they were almost black. A bright red scar stretched across Elisabeth's left cheek marring her smooth olive skin. An identical scar crossed her stomach. Almost a year ago Beth had been attacked by a violent psychopath, who had slashed her face with a knife, then plunged it into her abdomen in an attempt to escape from police custody.

"There's no evidence of anyone else being in her apartment . . ."

"What about the car Ted Pickering saw in the garage that night?" Parker interjected.

"We don't know that had anything to do with the case," Beth pointed out. "Maybe the car was rented by Janice herself."

"By the way where are we on the car?" J.J. directed the question to the room, tapping his fingers on the table in frustration.

Wyatt shrugged, but Parker answered, "There are only a handful of blue Citroen's in this area, and one was reported stolen two weeks ago."

His eyes lighting up, "Anything suspicious on the report?" J.J. asked.

"Sorry, nothing. The car was stolen overnight from the home of its eight-five year old owner, there were no leads." Parker felt like he was drowning in this case, there was nothing to hold on to, no solid lead. It was too much too soon.

Focusing on Beth's voice as she resumed presenting her theory, ". . . there was no sign of a struggle in any of the other rooms of the apartment. Nothing was touched, nothing was stolen."

Interjecting Parker argued, "If he was there for the girl he wouldn't take anything."

Nodding agreement Beth continued, "Yes, but so far we haven't been able to find anyone that seemed to know the real Janice Peters. Everyone you've interviewed has said that Janice is intensely private, she doesn't socialize very often, she doesn't have a boyfriend. She might have thought that faking her own abduction was an easy way to escape from her life. She didn't hurt herself, there was no blood in the apartment . . ."

"What about the blood Maisy found in the garage?" Wyatt asked.

"We confirmed that it was Janice's blood," Marty told them.

"It could be related to the abduction or it could be a coincidence," Beth shrugged.

"I don't know, Beth, that sounds a bit farfetched," J.J. looked unconvinced.

"I'm not saying it is what happened, I'm just laying it on the table as a possibility."

"How would the note fit into that theory?" Parker asked her, glancing at the copy that lay on the table in front of him.

"Could be a way of deflecting attention away from herself, the note was written by her remember," Beth suggested.

"He forced her to write it," Parker muttered defensively, he couldn't deal with another victim that turned into a perp.

J.J. raised a hand to calm him. "Let's just assume for the moment that we're dealing with an actual abduction and nine other potential victims. Care to shed some light on what kind of maniac we're looking for?"

"Well a serial killer," Beth began, "Which is what this guy is claiming that he's going to be, is usually a white male between the ages of eighteen and thirty-two, and probably came from an abusive family. Most likely he's an organized offender, with a high IQ. He's planned his crimes methodically, he'll be following the media coverage carefully, and he's probably got a good social life, possibly a girlfriend, maybe even a family."

"We got any idea on a motive?" Wyatt cut in.

"Power, control, maybe lust, but I'm thinking he has a specific mission in mind. He's choosing these particular women for a reason," Beth looked thoughtful.

Parker nodded in agreement. "This feels personal. He has a grudge against them, he knows them, he's come across them some time in his past. If we can find where he knows them from then maybe we can find the other women before he kills them."

"We have to figure out the clues on his list," J.J. interjected.

Beth shook her head. "You'll never figure them out. I studied them all day yesterday, they don't mean anything, we're not supposed to solve the riddles. He wants to kill them all, he has no intention of letting any of them live."

"Why leave the note at all? What's its point?" J.J. bellowed, he hated not having the answers to every possible question.

Shrugging a shoulder, "Control, ego, fun, a distraction, just to annoy us, who knows."

"He says he'll let Janice go alive if he kills the other nine women. Do we believe him?" Wyatt asked.

"He's not going to let her go alive. Your only hope of stopping this guy is to figure out why he chose these particular women, what links them all together."

"The only way to find the link is to wait and see who his next victim is," Parker said softly. His mind clouding over at the thought of a young woman walking around with no idea that she was in the sight of a vicious murderer.

"I know," Beth nodded, her face grim.

* * * * *

9:56 P.M.

The thrill of the chase was making his stomach twitch in delightful, nervous anticipation.

The night was dark and clear, after a beautiful cloudless sunny late fall day. A strong wind had picked up in the evening, which meant they would be in for a storm tomorrow. Dylan thought that was very poetic, he remembered the night of the accident, the night that they had taken from him what was rightfully his. It had stormed that night and he hoped the storms lasted until he was finished.

Tessa thought that she had outsmarted him. She hadn't thought that he would figure it out. It had taken ten years but he had not rested until he had discovered the truth. Now it was time to reclaim his prize. And to make those girls pay for what they had done. He felt his anger bubbling up at the thought of all that had been ripped away from him. Tessa was going to pay if it was the last thing he ever did.

He thought of Tessa's childhood, of the dominating role that he had played in it. He thought of how she had grown, in intelligence, in intuitiveness, in her ability to read other's body language. Without him, she would never have become so proficient in these skills.

Thoughts tumbling slowly to his own horrible childhood.

There had been no one to guide him, no one to teach him the skills that he would need to face a tough and heartless world. His mother had left when he was four, leaving him with but a few fleeting memories of her, tucking him into bed at night, singing to him, reading to him.

After she had left, taking her money and the security that brought with her, his once loving father had turned into a drunken idiot. He had dragged young Dylan all around the country, latching onto one wealthy young woman after another. Some had paid no attention to the quiet, withdrawn little boy, but others had become like real mothers to him. It had broken his heart each time they had been ripped away from him, upon finally coming to the realization his father was nothing more than a drunken gold-digger.

Moving constantly, from house to house and from school to school. Back then he had hated the lack of control he'd had over his own life. He never stayed in one place long enough to make friends, the other children thought that he was weird, his intelligence making him a misfit. Luckily, he had always preferred his own company to that of inferior beings, as he had thought of everyone with an IQ lower than his own 155.

Tessa should have been grateful for all that he had done for her. It was because of him that she had grown into the woman she now was. She, however, did not see it that way. She thought that he had ruined her life. That he deserved to die for what he had done to her and her friends.

Forcing himself to calm down he took a deep breath, now was not the time to become distracted by past injustices. A movement at the door caught his eye and he felt his spirits lift as Tiffany left the library. Huddling into her coat and bending her head against the wind as she headed towards her house.

Pulling up the hood of his black sweatshirt, he slipped into the shadows to follow Tiffany from a distance. She walked quickly, glancing around her nervously as though she sensed his presence. Her unease making the chase all the more fun as he dodged into another driveway to avoid her gaze. He knew that she knew she was being followed, she knew about the abduction of Janice, and that he was back.

He remembered following her earlier in the day, she had almost seen him when the wind had blown her hat from her head. He'd run a few errands this morning but spent most of the day outside her school. Following her to the gym during her lunch break, and even calling her cell phone a couple of times. It had been a struggle not to laugh as her terrified voice had called down the phone line, growing increasingly anxious at the silence that was her only answer.

Nearing Tiffany's house he decided it was time to make his move, he was going to grab her as she was entering her front door. Just when she thought she was home safe. Quickening his pace as she reached her front gate, she hurried down the path and fumbled with her key at the door.

She heard him as he climbed the front steps, opening her mouth to scream, but he was too quick. One hand clamped over her mouth, the other snapped around her waist, pinning her arms to her side, he pushed her inside the house, kicking the door closed behind them.

Holding her tightly, he enjoyed the way she squirmed and thrashed in his grip, her breath coming in gasps, her chest heaving, he felt tears drip onto his hand.

"You know who I am don't you?" he snarled close to her ear, and felt her shudder and try to pull away from him. Receiving no answer, he shook her making her whimper pitifully. "Don't you, Tiffany?"

Nodding, she tried to wiggle free as he maneuvered his hand so that it now covered both her mouth and her nose. She writhed wildly, her hands clawing at her face as he released his grip from her waist, trying desperately to draw a breath.

Loosening his grip, he whispered in her ear, "Tell me where they are and I'll let you go."

Despite her terror, Tiffany valiantly shook her head.

"We're gonna have some fun before you die. It'll be just like old times." His hand tightened once again, preventing her from breathing, and she struggled vainly beneath him, until her hands eventually dropped to her sides and she went limp.

Lowering Tiffany's unconscious body to the floor, he tied her up, then threw her over his shoulder. Carrying her through the house and into the garage where he had parked his van earlier in the day. Flipping the trunk open he lay her inside and climbed into the car, ready to exact his revenge upon one of the people who had conspired to ruin his life.

NOVEMBER 23RD

Mark and Marley Sutherland snuck into the empty office building.

Marley giggled nervously. "Our parents are gonna freak."

Grinning back just as nervously, Mark pushed her against the wall. "I can't believe we really did it," he pressed a kiss to her lips.

"We really did do it, we're really married." Marley couldn't believe that they had actually gone through with it. Her parents were gonna go ballistic when they found out. They did not approve of her dating Mark, much less marrying him, they had forbidden her to see him after the two of them had almost been arrested for shoplifting. Mark was a high school drop out, with no job, no money, and as far as they were concerned nothing to offer their baby girl.

Yesterday had been her eighteenth birthday. Tonight, after her parents had gone to sleep, she had crept out her bedroom window and she and Mark had gotten married. She gazed at her new husband and wished her parents could have seen him like this, all dressed up in a pale blue shirt, and a bright blue tie that perfectly matched his dreamy blue eyes.

Mark pressed another kiss to her lips and she ran her hands through his thick black hair as his hands reached up and started to undo the buttons of her blouse. A blouse that had cost her an entire months pay cheque. It was silk, in the most beautiful magenta color, she had fallen in love with it the moment she had seen it, knowing it would be the perfect thing to wear for this particular occasion. Marley could not believe that she was about to lose her virginity to the handsomest most wonderful guy in the whole entire world.

Something bumped somewhere in the supposedly deserted building and Marley pulled away. "Did you hear that?"

Shrugging Mark continued to unbutton her top, but Marley pushed him away. "I'm serious, I heard something. I thought you said the security guard left at one."

"He does, there's no-one here, Mar," he kissed her again, and after a moments hesitation Marley kissed him back. Mark was right, there was no one there, she was just nervous about what they were about to do. Running her hands up and down his back, she slid them down to his pants and slowly begun to unbuckle his belt.

A door slammed somewhere in the building and they both jumped. "Okay I definitely heard that," Mark said, struggling to re-buckle his belt with twitching fingers. "Wait here."

Grabbing his torch from where he had dropped it on the floor when they had started making out he headed towards the noise. Marley watched him go, looking around nervously, "Wait up," she called running after him, buttoning her blouse as she went.

Catching up to him he whispered, "I think he went out the back." Mark gestured for her to stay behind him as they made their way slowly down the hallway.

Passing an open door Marley paused as she saw something in the room. "Mark, stop, there's something in there."

Shining the flashlight into the room they saw something swinging from the ceiling. "What is that?" Mark asked frowning in confusion.

Moving slowly into the room he switched on the light and Marley heard someone screaming.

It took her a while to realize it was herself.

✶ ✶ ✶ ✶ ✶

3:50 A.M.

It was close to four am by the time Parker arrived at the office building, almost an hour after Tiffany Poppy's body had been discovered. The parking lot in front of the building that should be empty at this time of night was instead filled with police cars and CSU vans.

Finding a spot near the door, Parker climbed out of his car and walked into the office building, nodding to the officer who stood guard. He had not been asleep when the call had come in. Having spent the rest of the previous afternoon going over the list trying to make sense of the riddles, he had gone home around midnight and gone straight to bed. Awakening an hour later after another nightmare. It was always the same dream. After so many years he knew it by heart.

Reaching the end of the hall he came upon Maisy, dusting the door for prints, she looked up at him grimly as he approached. For once she was without her bright smile and sunny disposition. It was not the first time Parker had worked scenes with her in the middle of the night, so he knew that lack of sleep did nothing to waver her always-positive attitude. Whatever was in there must be pretty horrific if it could wipe the smile off Maisy Wallace's face.

"It's horrible in there," she told him, her hazel eyes, usually bright and cheerful were now haunted, and she shuddered as she spoke. Maisy looked away as he opened the door, and he found himself shuddering at the sight before his eyes.

Hanging from the ceiling was the body of Tiffany Poppy. A rope around her neck, blank, empty eyes staring down at him, she was swinging from side to side almost hypnotically.

Marty Jenkins stood when he entered the room, his gaze bleak, he had completed his initial sweep of the crime scene. "From the amount of blood on the table it looks like she was alive when he did it," he said in way of a greeting, with a gesture at the ceiling.

Following his stare, Parker shifted his gaze to look once again at Tiffany's body hanging above the conference table then lowered it to the table below. Blood pooled in a large circle beneath the body and arranged at each corner of the table were Tiffany's arms and legs.

"She was alive when he did . . ." gesturing at the table, "This?" Parker found himself struggling not to throw up at the thought of someone cutting off the arms and legs of another living, breathing human being.

Nodding solemnly, Marty resumed taking photos of everything in the room, ready for the medical examiner to come and remove the body.

"He leave us anything?" Parker asked, dragging his eyes from the repulsive yet mesmerizing swinging body.

"There's a shoe print in the blood on the table," Marty replied as he continued to snap away. "We haven't found anything else yet."

"How do we know this is one of our girls," Parker asked. That was the way he had come to think of the nameless women on the list, as 'their girls'.

Handing him a piece of paper encased in an evidence bag. "This was taped to her body."

Gingerly taking the bag from Marty's outstretched hand, Parker almost couldn't bear to look at it, but commanded himself to read it anyway.

My name is Tiffany Poppy and I'm dead because of you. You didn't figure out the clue and find out who I was and now I'm dead. You have only two days before the next woman will die.

Parker felt his chest tighten, another young woman dead because of him. The room spun around him, as he clutched the note tightly. A hand on his shoulder made him jump.

"It's not your fault, Parker. There was no way we could have figured out who she was." Marty was studying him, his eyes concerned, and Parker forced himself to relax.

Letting out a shuddering breath. "He made her write it."

Marty nodded. "Probably, but we'll need to confirm it with a sample of her handwriting."

"Did he grab her here or just kill her here?"

"She was definitely killed here," Marty moved away replacing his camera in its bag. "And as far as we know she had no reason to be here, so I'm guessing he abducted her somewhere else then brought her here to kill her."

"How do we know she has no reason to be here?"

"Someone got in contact with the company that rents the building and got a list of all employees. There's no Tiffany Poppy on their list."

Glancing at the young woman's deathly empty face. "Are we sure this is Tiffany Poppy?"

"Oh yeah." Marty ferreted around in his box and dug out another evidence bag, tossing it over to him. "He also left us this."

Studying the driver's license, he compared it to the body swinging from the ceiling. Even with her face bloated and distorted in death, Parker conceded that it was the same person. "Wyatt and I will go visit her house after we finish up here," he said taking note of the address on the license. "Where are the kids who found the body?"

"Out back in a patrol car," Marty answered, then called through the closed door, "Maisy, I need you in here."

The door opened slowly and Maisy peeked warily inside. "You need me in here?" she asked deliberately avoiding looking at the body or the dismembered body parts.

Marty ignored her and began what would be a long and tedious search of every inch of the room, in the desperate attempt to find anything that could point them in the direction of their killer. Maisy sighed and reluctantly entered the room to help him.

"I'll see you two later," Parker said, heading out the door and closing it behind him, grateful to be out of that room, but feeling a little guilty that Marty and Maisy had to remain.

Leaving the building through the backdoor, he met Wyatt in the rear car park, climbing from his car. His partner waved at him and he headed over. "Is it as bad as J.J. said over the phone?"

Grimacing and trying to block the image of the bloody room from his mind, Parker nodded. He now had another image to haunt his dreams. "It's worse. I was on my way to speak to the kids who found her." Wyatt followed him as they both rounded the building and headed to the patrol car. "Sam feeling better?"

"Yeah. Casey let him stay home from school today, uh yesterday," he corrected checking his watch. "By lunchtime he was playing video games and reading comic books."

News of the crime had spread quickly and news vans had been added to the throng of vehicles surrounding the place. Reporters, wearing falsely grave and anxious faces, were busy exaggerating the few facts they had. Cameras flashed wildly and video cameras rolled, as the vultures hoped to get a shot of anything even remotely morose. Several officers stood behind the police tape to keep the crowd in check, their expressions bored.

A couple of yards in front of them were two kids, standing alone amidst the flurry of activity in front of the building. Heading towards the shaken teens, Parker noted that both were pale and both were shaking. "Mark? Marley?" he asked them.

In unison turned in his direction and nodded, nervous eyes darting between him and Wyatt, the reporters and the office building.

"Why don't we go somewhere a little quieter, where we can talk," Wyatt suggested.

"I'm not going back in there," the girl blurted out, wrapping her boyfriend's jacket tighter around her shoulders, and shooting them a defiant stare.

"We'll use one of the rooms at the front of the building,"

Wyatt assured her calmly, as they gently herded the terrified teens towards the building. "Don't worry we won't go near that room."

The four of them walked in silence, Mark and Marley's steps slowing the nearer they got to the door. Inside they led the teens into a vacant room, Parker gestured for them to sit, and pulling their chairs close together they complied, perching nervously on the edges of their seats. Wyatt and Parker took the chairs opposite.

"Alright, why don't you start at the beginning?" Wyatt gently prompted.

Exchanging glances Marley gave Mark an almost imperceptible nod, and he began to speak. "We're in love," he began defensively, as though challenging them to disagree.

"We're not interested in your love lives," Parker told them, impatient to get to whatever these two had seen or heard.

"My uncle owns this building, we came here to . . . to . . ." Mark trailed off.

"To consummate our marriage," Marley supplied, slipping her hand into Mark's.

"So you broke in here to make out?" Parker asked.

"We didn't break in," Mark whined, once again defensive, seeing the world only from his own point of view as only a teenager can. "I have a key," he pulled it from his pocket and jangled it at them.

Parker was ready to shake the kid, but Wyatt cut in, "Did you see anything out of place?"

Mark shook his head quickly but Marley looked thoughtful. "Did you see something, Marley?" Wyatt asked gently.

She nodded slowly, "Yeah, I did." Mark looked at her, confused. "It was while you were disarming the security system," she told him. "I was nervous, I'm a . . . a virgin, and I was kinda jumpy, excited though," she said with a reassuring smile at her new husband. "While I was waiting I was sorta looking around, and I saw a car. I thought it was weird cos this place was supposed to be empty, that's why we were here."

Exchanging a glance with his partner, Parker could barely contain his excitement. "A blue Citroen?"

"No, a white van," Marley told them.

Parker had to rein in the urge to throw something. The car had been a solid lead, now it was nothing.

"So you came inside . . ." Wyatt pressed.

"Yeah, we were in the hall," Mark resumed the storytelling. "We were . . . you know, and then Marley said she heard something."

"What did you hear?" Parker interjected.

"It was kinda like a bump, like maybe something falling."

"Then what did you do?"

"Well Mark said it was nothing, so we kinda kept going, but then we heard a door slam, so we stopped, and Mark grabbed his torch. He told me to wait, but I was scared on my own so I followed him and . . ." she trailed off as she started to cry.

Mark wrapped a comforting arm around her shoulders and she buried her face in his neck. "Then we found the body, the blood." Mark too looked like he was about to cry.

"Did you see anything, anyone?" Wyatt persisted gently.

Shaking his head. "Just the body," Mark whispered.

"Did you call 911 right away?" Parker asked, trying to establish a timeline.

Mark nodded but said nothing.

Parker glanced at Wyatt and shook his head, they weren't going to get anything else out of these two, they were still in shock, and Parker wasn't even sure that they'd seen anything else of relevance. "Alright, you two have been very helpful, here's my card, call us if you think of anything else, however small." Parker gestured at an officer at the door, "Officer McIntyre will take you home."

Helping his new wife to her feet Mark kept a supportive arm around her shoulders as the two of them left the room quietly.

Parker watched them go and rubbed a hand over his tired eyes. "Breakfast then Tiffany's house?" he asked Wyatt.

"Sure. But this time you're buying. If you've started eating as much for breakfast as you had yesterday you're gonna send me broke."

*　*　*　*　*

5:15 A.M.

Consciousness came slowly as Janice tried to roll over. Her body wouldn't obey and she remembered that she was tied to a bed in the house of a maniac who was just biding his time before killing her. Fighting through the fog in her brain, she realized that she felt a little better. Her stomach was not so queasy and her headache had eased to a dull throb.

Shuddering as she looked down at herself and saw the clothes that he had dressed her in were still there. She had thought, albeit half-heartedly, that maybe she had just dreamed them up, that they were just a figment of her over-worked and over-drugged imagination.

Janice realized that she was not afraid anymore.

Now she was just angry.

Angry for everything that he had done to her and her friends in the past. And angry at everything that he was planning on doing to them now. Frustrated she thrashed wildly against her bonds, and let out a bloodcurdling scream.

Frowning she remembered something that he had said to her earlier. He had asked her if she had figured out where he had her stashed. At the time, she had thought he was just telling her that there was no one nearby to help her. But now that she thought about it, she realized he must have meant something else.

Dylan Riley was a very egotistical man. Everything he did, he did for a reason. He had planned this all out, down to the smallest detail. He had chosen this place for a reason, it held some significance to their past. If she could figure out where she was being held then maybe she did have some chance, however small, of getting out of this alive.

* * * * *

8:46 A.M.

"This is it," Parker pointed at a street on their left.

They had dropped his car off at his house then gone for breakfast together in Wyatt's car. They always went in Wyatt's car. He was their designated driver.

Several years back, while Casey had been pregnant with Sam, their three-year-old daughter Serena had been abducted by a killer with a grudge against Wyatt. Following Casey to a gas station the killer had stolen her car with Serena still inside. A high speed police chase had ensued ending in Casey's car, with both the killer and the little girl still inside, slamming into a concrete wall, killing both of them on impact.

Following Serena's death, Wyatt had been unable to face getting in a car. For a time it had crippled his life. It wasn't until Casey had gone into labor with Sam and he had been forced to drive her to the hospital that he had finally faced his fear. Now he drove all the time as a sort of therapy, a way to prove to himself that he was able to continue with his life without his daughter.

On their way to Tiffany's house, they had stopped to grab something to eat. Keeping the conversation focused on family and sports during breakfast, the case off limits by mutual, although not voiced, agreement, they had both needed some time to clear their heads.

Turning into the street Wyatt drove slowly down it. "What's the number?"

Consulting the copy of Tiffany's license. "83. There's 57."

They continued on slowly until Wyatt announced, "There it is."

Parking the car in front of a small two-story weatherboard house. It was painted a bright and sunny yellow, a lone oak tree stood in the front yard, and bright flowers were overflowing from window boxes. The lawn was green, neatly mowed and trimmed around the edges, along the fence line, and the stone path that led from the sidewalk to the front door.

The sun that had shone so brightly the day before, was now hidden behind the clouds that had blown back up some time during the night, giving the setting a gloomy overtone, which certainly meshed with its owner's brutal murder.

Climbing from the car, they walked down the path, Parker found himself in a pessimistic mood. "We don't even know if this is where he abducted her."

"We know she went to work yesterday, and that she was at her book club meeting at the library last night," Wyatt reminded him patiently.

Jiggling the doorknob Parker half smiled as the door swung open, "It's not locked."

Finding themselves at one end of a short hallway, a living room on the right, a dining room on the left, a closed door at the hallway's other end. Immediately in front of them was a bag, presumably Tiffany's, on the floor, the contents spilled out, keys and makeup lay scattered across the floor by the door.

Bending Parker pulled a pen from his pocket and poked through the items, looking for anything that could point them in the right direction. Coming across nothing useful he stood, "I'll get CSU over here, see if he left us anything. You want upstairs or down?"

"I'll take up."

Wyatt headed up the staircase next to the front door, while Parker headed into the living room on his right. The room was small, the walls painted bright blue, a lounge set in the same shade as the walls took up most of the room. A desk was crammed into one corner and Parker made a beeline straight to it. Pulling open a drawer, he felt like an intruder in Tiffany's life as he rifled through her personal papers and belongings.

Finding nothing of interest in the living room he headed across the hall and into the dining room. A beautiful table with ten matching, velvet seated chairs, filled the space, an ornate vase overflowing with flowers was set in the middle of the table.

An open fireplace covered most of the far wall, with a few old photos dotting the mantle. Crossing to look at them, he saw photos of a young Tiffany with her family. There were pictures of her at the park surrounded by her parents and two grinning little boys, of a teenage Tiffany sitting on a horse, with her family at one of her brother's high school graduations, on holidays at the beach and skiing.

Each of the photos depicted a young Tiffany, the catalogue of her past seemed to stop when she was about fifteen. There was not a single picture of an adult Tiffany.

"Parker." Hearing Wyatt call his name he left the room and met his partner at the bottom of the stairs. "I found a laptop," Wyatt grinned heading into the living room, Parker followed and they settled on the couch and switched on the computer.

"It's probably password protected," Parker muttered.

"You are certainly in a cynical mood today," Wyatt commented, looking at him out of the corner of his eye.

"I've been used and fooled a lot lately, it tends to make one a little cynical," he grumbled back.

Apparently refusing to get sucked into another argument with him about whether or not he had done the right thing in the O'Hara case, Wyatt ignored his comment and focused instead on the computer. Which surprisingly, started without a hitch and they searched through her documents, finding nothing but a manuscript for a book she was writing about gardening. They searched her Internet history but found nothing except that the only sites she had visited were book discussion groups and gardening sites.

Closing the computer's lid with a sigh Parker stood up and began to pace. "Well this was another waste of time."

"What do you want to do now?"

"I guess we go back to the list, try and come up with some possible victims, and hope that Marty brings us some good news."

* * * * *

4:18 P.M.

Hours later Parker and Wyatt were sitting at their desks back at the station. They'd spent the majority of the day looking for any connections between Janice Peters and Tiffany Poppy.

So far they had found nothing.

Seemingly, someone was very enthusiastic about Christmas this year and had already set up a small Christmas tree on a table in the corner of the squad room. Tinsel and twinkling lights were strung up around the windows and criss-crossed the ceiling. Mistletoe hung from every available doorframe.

Leaning back in his chair, Parker propped his feet up against his desk, closed his eyes and blocked out the noise of the busy room. His mind swirled with thoughts of Janice, alone and scared. Of Tiffany's final moments of terror as she was grabbed entering her own home. Of the eight remaining women going about their lives unaware that they had only days left to live.

Then his thoughts returned, as they always did, to Gina O'Hara. The way she had been the first day he had met her. That was the way he preferred to remember her, before everything had fallen apart. She had been vulnerable and afraid, cowering in the back of her boyfriend's truck, having just witnessed him murder her father in a fit of drug induced rage. She was also seven and a half months pregnant.

Gina had been terrified but willing to testify against her boyfriend. Parker had spent hours with her, reassuring her, comforting her, trying to help her. She had latched onto him as a replacement father figure, calling him up at all hours of the day and night, sobbing in his arms as she tried to decide whether or not to keep her baby. He had sat and listened to her talk about how utterly alone she felt, a feeling that he himself was all too aware of.

He had continued to believe in her even when she held a gun on him, her newborn daughter in her arms, used as a human shield. Gina had been eerily calm, describing how she had killed her own father because he wanted to raise her baby, then drugged her boyfriend and manipulated him into thinking he had committed the crime. Parker had still believed he could somehow get through to her, help her, save her, make her see reason, right up until the moment she had turned the gun on the tiny infant in her arms.

He had been a fool.

He'd empathized too closely. It had blinded him.

It was a mistake he did not intend to repeat.

A file dropped onto his desk startling him out of his recollections. Looking up to see Marty Jenkins staring down at him, a gloomy look on his solemn, narrow face.

"He raped her," Marty announced with a disgusted frown.

Wyatt sighed. "Please tell me he left behind something that will help us find him."

Perching on Parker's desk, Marty fiddled with his file, flipping through it aimlessly. "Nothing. Other than the shoeprint, which is only helpful for a comparison, he left nothing."

"No sperm?"

"Nope, he wore a condom. There were no fibers or hairs . . ."

"Nothing? What about from the people who work there?" Parker cut in.

"The cleaners go in at eight and are done by ten. Tiffany left her book club at nine thirty, so he couldn't have got to the office building until after ten thirty. I checked and security does a final sweep at one so he probably went in after that. The call came in about three so that left him about two hours to cut her up and kill her. I do have some good news though."

With hopeful faces Wyatt and Parker waited for him to continue. "She was unconscious when he cut off her arms and legs."

They both let out a thankful breath that at least Tiffany had been spared that pain. "He knocked her out first?" Wyatt asked.

"Yeah, drugged her, then got her up on the table, amputated her limbs then hung her from the ceiling."

Breathing easier, it was the best news that he had heard in days. "Any idea what he used to do it?"

"Marks on the wounds indicate he used a saw . . ."

"Something rare?" Parker cut in hopefully.

"We're still doing comparisons but I think we'll find it's a common, buy at any hardware store, saw." Marty looked just as dejected as himself and Wyatt. "You guys find anything linking her with Janice Peters?"

"Nope." Parker got up and went to fill his coffee cup with the grey sludge that passed for coffee around the station. "They live in different neighborhoods. They have completely different jobs. Different interests and hobbies. As far as we can tell, they have absolutely nothing in common. However this guy is choosing them is still a complete mystery."

NOVEMBER 24TH

8:09 P.M.

Lying on the bed staring aimlessly up at the ceiling, Janice glanced towards the door when she heard a sound on the other side.

He was back.

He'd been gone for hours. The sedative he had given her earlier had worn off ages ago and she'd been lying here with nothing to do but watch the sun slowly set until it was pitch black outside. She'd been trying to figure out where they were.

As the key turned in the lock, she closed her eyes, determined not to give him the satisfaction of a conversation. Light spilled into the room, adding to the light of the small lamp next to the bed, and she felt his presence move towards her.

"I have a surprise for you, Janice."

Ignoring him, she turned her head away, but he grabbed her chin and forcefully turned her face in his direction. "Believe me it's something you'll want to see."

Whimpering emanated from next to the bed and Janice's eyes sprang open, then widened in shock. "Bianca?"

A gleeful smile crossing his face, "I knew you'd be pleased," he singsonged. "I'll leave you girls alone for a few minutes. To say goodbye."

Pulling the gag from Bianca's mouth, he left the two of them alone, locking the door behind him.

"You're still alive," Bianca whispered, struggling to wiggle herself into a sitting position, her wrists and ankles bound. "We saw on the news that you'd been abducted."

"Did they mention the note?" Janice strained against her own bonds so that she could see her friend.

Confused Bianca shook her head, then grimaced and closed her eyes.

"He drugged you too?" Janice asked, a dull ache still throbbing inside her own head.

"Yeah," Bianca sighed tiredly then focused, "What note?"

"He made me write a note to the police telling them that he was going to kill all of you . . ."

"The police have our names?"

"No, he made me write clues, for the police to figure out, you know how he is," she said rolling her eyes. "He had me write that if the police find you and save you, then he kills me."

Bianca raised an apprehensive eyebrow and began tentatively, "You know he's uh . . ."

"I know," Janice cut in. "He's gonna kill me anyway."

"You scared?"

"A little, you?"

"Yeah, but not surprised, we always knew this day was going to come sooner or later. My head is killing me," Bianca moaned. "Is there any way the police are going to solve those clues?"

"No, they're just gibberish. Do the others know?"

"Yeah we all know," Bianca told her. "But no one's going to say anything."

"He's going to kill us all, except maybe Tessa," Janice commented and Bianca nodded her agreement. "Have you talked to her?"

"Yeah. And yes she called and warned them."

Sighing in relief. "So they can be prepared . . ." breaking off as she heard the key rattle in the lock again. "He's coming."

"Janice?" Bianca whispered.

"Yeah?"

"If I had to do it all again I'd do it the same way."

"Me too."

The door opened. "Having a good time, ladies? Sorry to break up the party but Bianca and I have a date."

Taking a syringe from the bedside table, he filled it and plunged it into Bianca's arm. Janice watched as her friend's eyes fluttered closed and her body went limp. Hoisting her up into his arms, he shot her a wicked grin. "Two down, seven to go."

Watching him go Janice felt helpless anger bubbling up inside her, determined that the very least she could do was make sure that he got absolutely no pleasure from killing Bianca. "You can kill us all but you'll never get what you really want," she taunted.

He stopped, his smile fading into a frown, he snarled at her, "They'll come. When they find out you're all dead, they'll come."

"Keep telling yourself that," she mocked.

Pure rage flashed in his eyes, he opened his mouth to respond but apparently thought better of it, instead he said nothing, just carried Bianca through the door, slamming it behind him and locking it once again.

Satisfied that she had indeed succeeded in ruining his perfectly planned night, Janice closed her weary eyes. Trying not to think of the horrible things that he would be doing to Bianca. Or of the horrible things that he would soon be doing to her.

Clearing her mind, she drifted off to sleep.

* * * * *

11:57 P.M.

Slowly she became aware of a tapping sound somewhere near her head. Trying to open her eyes to see what it was, but it felt as though they had been glued shut.

"Bianca. Wakey, wakey," a voice singsonged.

Forcing her sticky eyes open Bianca found herself lying at the bottom of a giant glass box. They were outside, it was dark, but a huge spotlight beamed down on her, making it even harder for her tired eyes to see.

He was there, sitting cross-legged beside her glass cage, tapping merrily on the side, a manic smile on his face. Shuddering she pushed herself up, closing her eyes against the swimming in her head, and pulled her knees up to her chest she rested her chin on them.

"Where are we?" she asked, voice coming out all croaky.

Standing he began to circle around and around her, adding to the dizziness that threatened to make her pass out again. "The pool," he answered as he switched off the spotlight, plunging them into darkness.

Looking out, her eyes adjusting slowly to the dark, she could just make out the huge waterslide that she had watched her friends slide down time and time again in the summer, back when she was a teenager. The kiddie pool still had its tiny elephant slide. The lap pool was right next to them, a huge cavernous hole, drained for the long, cold winter.

There would be no one coming to this deserted place to save her.

The light flashed back on, once again temporarily blinding her, and she pressed her eyes closed against its glare. "What are you going to do to me?" she asked, knowing that nothing he could do would make her tell him what he was so desperate to know.

Instead of answering she heard him dragging something across the concrete. Tentatively opening her eyes she saw that he was setting up a ladder next to her small prison. "What are you doing?"

Again, he didn't answer, simply walked to his van, parked just a few feet away, and pulled out a hose. Hooking it up to a tap by the wall of the snack shop, he unrolled it as he slowly made his way back to her. Standing she balanced herself against a side of the box and looked up, the top was about two and half feet above her head. The lid was padlocked closed and next to it was a funnel, and she knew instantly what he intended to do.

"You're going to drown me," she commented, struggling to stay calm. It was not death that scared her, she had made her peace with that a long time ago, but this particular death. Bianca had hated the water ever since she had almost drowned in a swimming pool at the age of three.

Making herself remain calm, to keep her breathing even. He was going to kill her, there was nothing she could do about that, but she could make sure he got not an ounce of pleasure out of doing it.

Climbing the ladder, he silently put the nozzle of the hose down the funnel and released the catch, sending freezing water pouring into the glass cage. Bianca sucked in a breath as the cold water showered down upon her, her body reflexively trying to get away from it but there was nowhere to go. Blinding terror threatening to overwhelm her and for a moment she didn't think she could go through with it.

Abruptly the water stopped and he peered down at her. "Tell me where they are and I won't kill you," he told her, his voice eerily calm, but his eyes wild.

Managing to regain control of her fear Bianca shook her head, she knew it was a lie. "You'll never let me go. And even if you would I'd still never tell you." She wanted more than anything to be anywhere but here. She could face any death but this. And yet she knew without a doubt that even this would never make her tell him what he wanted to know.

Shrugging he turned the tap back on, the icy water rising from just above her ankles to her waist. Shivering she sucked in her stomach against the cold.

Forcing herself to keep taking deep, calming breaths as the water slowly rose over her, lapping unpleasantly against her skin. As terror threatened to overwhelm her, she made herself think of the reason she was here. Of the people who were counting on her.

Once again the water stopped. "Last chance, Bianca. Tell me

where they are and I'll let you go.

She said nothing just glared defiantly back up at him.

"You know you may think you're ready for death, but in a minute the water is going to be over your head. I know that thought scares you."

Still she said nothing, the cold was starting to numb not just her body but also her mind.

Again the water started to pour back down over her head like a frosty shower. It seemed to rise in slow motion, like she was trapped in some sort of weird movie. It rose from her waist to her shoulders, then to her mouth, and she had to start treading water, rising closer and closer to the top of the box.

Head bumping against the glass lid the water stopped one last time, the water up to her chin. She was close to him now, their faces separated by nothing more than the smooth glass.

"You were right," his frenzied grin beaming at her. "I would never have let you go even if you'd told me."

Turning the tap on one last time, he pressed his face against the glass in front of her and watched, as though he were an inquisitive child doing nothing more than a harmless science experiment.

Water rising quickly, Bianca hardly even noticed the cold anymore. Twisting her head back so that her face was still out of the water, her mouth desperately sucking in air as her hands clawed fruitlessly at the locked lid. Horror overwhelming her as water completely filled her glassy coffin, cascading down the outside.

Holding her breath as long as she could, her chest burning for air, she finally choked and water flooded into her lungs.

The last thing she saw was his malevolent smile, distorted through the running water, mocking her as she crossed from life to death.

NOVEMBER 25TH

9:14 A.M.

The wind whipped through his sweater as though it were not even there. Parker's choice of scarf today was an orange one that was covered in dancing red and yellow dogs. He always wore this particular scarf when he needed to lift his spirits, it had been a present from his sister before she had skipped town.

Overnight the rain had started up again. As the sun had gone down the skies had opened up, once more sending sheets of freezing rain pouring down on the barely dried out world.

He and Wyatt had spent the day before interviewing the devastated friends and workmates of Tiffany Poppy. None of them had ever heard Tiffany mention a Janice Peters. They had learnt that Tiffany was a quiet, shy young woman, a sensitive and caring teacher who loved small children, and that she had been orphaned at the age of fifteen when her parents and brothers had been killed in a car accident.

An hour ago they had received the call that another body had been found. The killer had got his next victim. Bianca Kingston. Her body had been found at the local pool, closed for the winter, a security guard had found her body floating in a huge glass box. Stuck to the front was another note.

The deserted and empty pool had a creepy and unnatural feel to it, like an amusement park at night after everyone had left. The large glass box with a corpse inside didn't help.

My name is Bianca Kingston and I too am dead because of you. Two down and seven to go you have only two days

before the next woman will die.

Along with the note had been a copy of her driver's license, which had confirmed her identity. He and Wyatt had interviewed the guard, who had not seen or heard anything unusual, and were now waiting for CSU to work their magic. Marty had arrived just minutes after them, setting up a tent around the body in the box, to prevent the press from snapping pictures.

Waving at them from across the pool Marty yelled, "Hey, guys, I found something."

Exchanging a smile, both of them hurried around the empty pool, and into the tent. Bianca's bloated naked body was still floating in the giant glass box filled with water, her empty eyes staring lifelessly out at them.

Avoiding her gaze he focused on Marty, "What did you get?"

Beaming uncharacteristically at them, his small eyes practically aglow, Marty held up an evidence bag containing a single hair. "I found this right by the water box."

"We can get DNA from it?" Parker asked cautiously, not quite ready to believe that things were finally looking up.

Nodding vigorously Marty grinned at them, then nodded to the officer at the tent's door, "Tell Zak we're ready for him."

"Zak do Tiffany too?" Wyatt asked.

Marty nodded as the flap of the tent opened and Zak Fenton, the chief medical examiner, entered. He was in his early thirties, he was a genius who graduated top of his class in medical school, and he was an ex-model. He had smooth cocoa skin, short fuzzy black hair, and the largest eyes Parker had ever seen. He wasn't married, much to the joy of every one of the single women on the force, the CSU team or who worked at the medical examiner's office. He had plenty of offers, but dated only from time to time, he was very picky about the women he got involved with.

"Hey, Parker, Wyatt, long time no see," he gave them one of his winning smiles, and Parker had to refrain from rolling his eyes.

Zak was good at his job, but he tended to get on Parker's nerves with his smug smile and arrogant attitude that came from knowing he was good looking. Zak sobered as he turned to look at Bianca Kingston's body floating in her watery grave. "We going anywhere on this case yet?"

"Not quickly," Parker muttered. "She alive when he put her in there?"

Zak and Marty exchanged glances then, "Autopsy will confirm it but . . ." Zak trailed off uncomfortably, dark eyes looking everywhere but at Bianca's body.

"But," Marty supplied, "I don't see why he'd go to the bother of putting a lock on the top of the water box unless he was going to put her in there alive."

Forcing himself to look carefully at Bianca's watery grave for the first time he noticed the glass cage was huge, at least eight feet tall. Besides the lock on the top that Marty had mentioned, there was also a funnel through which the killer could fill it with water.

He winced as he thought of Bianca's final moments of terror, trapped inside her glass coffin with no means of escape, as the water level slowly rose. According to her driver's license, she was only five foot two, she would have tried to tread water as she watched her tormentor slowly pour in more and more water. Inside his head he could see her, turning her head to desperately suck in air as he added the last of the water, clawing at the lid trying franticly to escape.

"He wanted her to suffer," he said softly.

The others said nothing but the horrified looks on their faces told him they agreed.

"This box," Wyatt gestured at it without looking at it, "He put it together here?"

"There's no way to know for sure," Marty replied.

"It's huge, if he brought it with him he has to have a van or a truck or something big enough to transport it," Wyatt said hopefully. "And the kids who found Tiffany said they saw a van, this could support that. Prove that he actually owns one and didn't just steal it like the car from Janice's apartment building."

Parker jumped as his iPhone chirped in his pocket, pulling it out and sliding to answer. "Parker." He listened as Victoria Baker gave him the news that they had all been waiting for, he could barely keep a grin off his face.

"What?" Wyatt asked as he hung up his phone.

"They found a connection between Bianca Kingston and Janice Peters."

Wyatt, Marty and Zak all stared at him expectantly.

* * * * *

11:00 A.M.

"Look we can do this the easy way or the hard way," Wyatt said, somehow managing to keep his voice calm, when all Parker wanted to do was punch the smug 'Fitness and Fun' gym manager in the face.

"I'm not sure the owner would want his gym associated with a string of murders," Greyson Wade the pimple faced, forty-year-old manager whined. He seemed too skinny for someone who worked in a gym.

Parker, near to the end of his rope after the last few months, almost imperceptibly raised his fist. Noticing, Wyatt jumped in before he could do anything he'd later regret. His partner was always ready to diffuse any situation. Parker had always thought that a police officer was an unusual job for someone who hated confrontation as much as Wyatt did.

"We can get a warrant if we have to. It might take a while though," Wyatt continued, then to Parker, "I guess we can just hang here until it comes through. Talk to some of the clients, see if they know Janice or Bianca, see if they've seen anyone suspicious hanging around, or . . ."

"Okay, okay," Greyson sighed. "If I give you the client list you'll go away?"

"We'll need somewhere to go over the list," Parker muttered through clenched teeth, willing to play nicely now that they finally had a lead, but eager to get going and run with it. Seven women were depending on them.

Nodding reluctantly, "I'll take you to one of the offices," he started to lead them through the 'Staff Only' door. "It might take me a while to get the list printed," he whined, his greasy face glistening unpleasantly in the light.

"No problem, we'll wait," Wyatt said cheerfully.

Leaving them in the office, Greyson spun on his heel and with an irritated humph, departed. At the far side of the room two young gym instructors sat, heads bent over a magazine, deep in conversation.

Parker nodded at Wyatt and then looked over at the young women, and pasted a smile on his face. "You two got a minute?"

The two young girls stopped their conversation, and faces lighting up with flirty smiles came over, swinging their hips and tossing their hair. Refraining, with difficulty, from rolling his eyes, Parker kept the smile on his face. "I'm Detective Bell and this is my partner Detective Wyatt. Mind if we show you a couple of pictures, see if you know these women?"

"Sure," the younger of the two grinned up at him, her wavy brown hair in pigtails, she couldn't be more than about eighteen.

"Are you here about Janice? Cos we heard about what happened to her. Everyone here is talking about it," the other girl gushed, she looked only slightly older than her friend.

Parker nodded and pulled out Janice's picture from the file Wyatt handed him. "Do you know Janice?"

"Yeah I know her, she comes to my Saturday morning step class," the brunette nodded enthusiastically.

"What about her?" Parker held up Bianca Kingston's picture.

Barely glancing at the picture the older of the girls twisted her blonde ponytail between her fingers and looked up at him with big doe eyes. "Is this girl dead?"

"Do you know her?" he repeated, voice kept calm with an effort. The girls waited for him to elaborate, when he didn't they shrugged and turned to the picture.

This time the brunette shook her head. "Di, you know her?"

Frowning in concentration, Di eventually broke into a smile. "That's Bianca, Bianca Kingston, she comes to my spin class."

Figuring he had nothing to lose by showing them Tiffany Poppy's picture, despite the fact that they had not found any evidence that she attended this gym. "One more."

Holding up Tiffany's picture both girls nodded immediately. "Tiffany," Di told them.

"Tiffany Hendrickson," her friend added.

Frowning, "This woman's name is Tiffany Poppy."

Smiling at Parker, Di explained patiently, "That's right, she started using her husband's name a year ago. Before that she was Tiffany Hendrickson, that's the name on her gym membership."

"Tiffany's married?" Wyatt asked confused.

Faces instantly donning identical sorrowful frowns, Di explained, "They were only married for a month, then he died in a boating accident."

Groaning softly to himself Parker wondered how they'd missed that, filing away his annoyance, he made a mental note to track down her late husband's family. "Do any of these women attend the same classes?" Parker asked.

"Tiffany comes to one of my spin class," Di told them. "And I think she goes to one of yours too doesn't she, Tash?"

Tash nodded, "My Tuesday night class."

"Not the same one as Janice?" Wyatt confirmed.

"No, I'm sorry," Tash replied.

"Do Tiffany and Bianca go to the same spin class?" Wyatt asked hopefully.

Di thought for a moment and then shook her head slowly.

"No. Tiffany goes to the Monday morning class."

"As far as you know do any of these women know each other?" Parker felt the buzz that had seemed so promising earlier slowly start to fade.

"I've never seen them together," Tash said, looking to Di for confirmation, her friend nodded in agreement.

"Is there anyone else you can think of that any of these women are particularly friendly with?" Parker hoped that for once they could get ahead of this guy and perhaps even pre-empt his next kill.

Both girls thought for a moment. "They're all kinda quiet. They don't really socialize with any of the other people in their classes," Di told them.

"Is there anyone who's a regular client who hasn't been in for a while?" Wyatt asked.

The girls thought, then exchanged glances and answered simultaneously, "Tessa Micah."

Surprised, "You came up with that name pretty quick, any reason why?"

"Tessa has a . . . presence," Di replied.

"She's really pretty, really rich, and she comes here at least three or four times a week," Tash expanded.

Wyatt subtly raised an eyebrow at him, Parker nodded, they'd gotten everything out of these girls they could, and they had a lead, a potential victim to go and see. Turning to the young woman, keeping his smile pasted on. "Thanks, Tash, Di, you've been really helpful."

They both grinned at him enthusiastically, excited to be part of a real life police drama, then sobered, again simultaneously, as though they were robots linked to the same system. "Tiffany and Bianca were the girls from the news weren't they?" Tash whispered wide-eyed.

"The ones who were killed by the serial killer, the one who abducted Janice," Di continued.

Parker muttered under his breath, he always deliberately avoided the news. He hated the false and sensationalized way in which reporters presented things. Their uncaring and self-centered attitudes. He hated the way they took people's pain and used it to further their own careers, with seemingly no comprehension that it was people's lives they were so carelessly playing with. He also hated the way that reporters had no regards for the facts. They twisted things and blew things out of proportion, always to their own ends, with no regards for a police investigation.

"Do you think that he's after Tessa now?" Tash asked, her and Di's brows wrinkled in identical worry.

Ignoring the girl's questions he struggled to keep his voice light. "Thanks girls."

Disappointment on their faces they reluctantly bounced out the door, letting it swing closed behind them. When they were gone, Parker turned to Wyatt who was rummaging through the papers in his arms. "Well?"

Wyatt said nothing, but finding the page he was looking for leaned over one of the tables and ran his finger down the sheet. "There it is. I knew it," giving a triumphant grin.

"What are you talking about?"

Waving him over Wyatt gestured at the list of clues given to them by the killer to identify the nine women he planned to kill. Wyatt pointed at the last clue on the list 'a novel and old is thirty three'. "That's Tessa Micah, I'm sure of it. *Tessa* is a book, used to be my grandmother's favorite, and Micah is the thirty-third book of the Old Testament. That's gotta be her."

"How do you know that?"

Wyatt shrugged, he had more useless trivia stored in his head than anyone else Parker knew. Raising a doubtful eyebrow Parker wasn't convinced. "I don't know . . ."

"Come on, Parker, think about it. The clue fits and she attends the same gym as our three other victims."

"Yeah, but she doesn't know any of them. And Beth said that we weren't supposed to be able to solve the clues," Parker reminded him.

"I'm sure that's true, but he wasn't expecting us to find a link between them . . ." Wyatt trailed off as the office door opened.

Greyson Wade entered, a stack of paper in his arms. "Here you go," he muttered dumping the pile on a desk then turning and stalking towards the door.

"Mr. Wade?" Wyatt called.

Turning to face them with a scowl on his face. "Yes?"

"We're also going to need a list of all employees."

Greyson's greasy face turned bright red and he spluttered, so angry he could barely speak. "What?" he finally managed to spit out.

"We are going to need a list of everyone who works here," Wyatt repeated calmly, and Parker choked on a laugh.

"Mr. Kendall is not going to like that," Greyson Wade snarled, enunciating each word.

"We're in the middle of a murder investigation, Mr. Wade, surely Mr. Kendall would want to be seen to be doing everything within his power to co-operate with the police," Wyatt kept a friendly smile on his face.

Unable to speak Greyson turned and left, slamming the door.

Parker laughed then pulled out his phone. "Lets go make a house call."

* * * * *

12:23 P.M.

Weaving down the long, tree lined driveway a huge stone mansion appeared in front of them. "Those girls were not kidding. Tessa Micah must be super rich if she lives here."

Nodding in agreement Wyatt parked the car at the end of the

driveway. Climbing out, Parker noticed that the temperature had dropped several degrees and it had started to snow, the first flakes of the season.

Awed by the sheer magnitude of the place, at least twenty windows peeked from the front of the house, several marble steps led up to the wide veranda that appeared to circle the entire way around. Ten intricately decorated stone pillars, five on each side of the front door, held up the second storey balcony. Vines and ivy had grown over most of the lower section of the house, giving it a distinctly country air. The largest place he had ever lived in was a dilapidated farmhouse, of which you could probably fit about fifty inside this mansion.

Passing two overly ornate lion statues standing guard at the bottom of the steps, which were tiled in geometric patterns, on their way up to the large wooden door. There was no doorbell just a massive wooden knocker in the shape of a lion's head.

"These people sure love lions," Parker muttered as he lifted the heavy knocker and banged it briskly against the door.

They waited in silence for the door to be opened, probably by a butler, he mused, but there was not a sign of life from within. After almost two minutes, Wyatt tried again, but still no one came to the door.

"Maybe she's out," Parker suggested moving from window to window, trying to peer through. But it was dark inside and the thick lacy curtains made it even harder to see anything.

"May I help you?" a voice enquired sharply from behind them.

Spinning around his heart skipped a beat as he stared in stunned silence at the beautiful young woman standing at the bottom of the steps. Her skin was white like porcelain, her hair the kind of white blonde that was usually only found on small children. She was dressed in pink sweats, with a Golden Retriever and a Dalmatian bounced wildly around her legs, clearly annoyed that their jog had been cut short.

Finally finding his voice, "Tessa Micah?"

She nodded slowly, sending the curls that had escaped her ponytail bouncing wildly around her thin face.

Descending quickly down the steps and crossing over to her, Parker saw that she was small at least a whole foot smaller than his own six foot frame. Everything about her was petite, she was like a pixie, with tiny hands, thin limbs and a delicate face sprinkled with freckles.

Taking a deliberate step away from him, the eyes that stared back up at him seemed to be both blue and green at the same time, yellow flecks around the pupils. Hands on her hips. "And you are?" she asked.

Her voice was sweet, melodic, she reminded him of the pictures of angels that had decorated his Bible when he had attended Sunday School as a child. Clearing his mind he gave her a reassuring smile. "I'm Detective Bell and this is Detective Wyatt," he gestured to his partner who had joined them on the driveway.

Narrowing her eyes suspiciously at them. "And you're here because . . .?"

"If we could go inside then we'll explain why we're here," Parker told her gesturing at the mansion.

Studying him with a carefully blank gaze, revealing nothing that was going on inside her blonde head, and Parker found himself instantly put on guard. Reminding himself not to be taken in by her angelic looks, he forced himself to remember Gina O'Hara. He had been fooled by her. He was not going to let that happen again.

"I don't live here," she told him, brushing snowflakes from her cheek.

Exchanging a confused glance with Wyatt. "We were told that this was your address."

Shuddering involuntarily as she looked at the mansion, a flicker of distaste flashing through her eyes, it was gone as quickly as it had appeared. "I hate that house, I haven't spent a single night in there since I inherited this place. I live in the cottage around the back."

Without another word Tessa Micah turned and began to jog around the house. The two dogs bounding after her, twisting in and out of her legs, it was a wonder she didn't trip over them.

Startled by the strange young woman they both watched her go.

"Well she knows something," Wyatt said as they started to follow her. "Did you see her eyes?"

"We don't know that," Parker shot back, for some reason feeling an unexplainable need to defend her.

"Parker," Wyatt warned. "Don't go getting yourself personally involved with her. Don't forget . . ."

"I know," Parker cut in, irritated.

Rounding the house they saw Tessa crossing the smooth, green lawn, she didn't look to see if they were following, sure that they would be, and Parker found himself intrigued by her self-assured confidence. Reaching the woods, she followed a narrow pebble path through the trees.

Following her across the lawn and down the path, that opened onto a small clearing in the centre of which sat a small cottage. The place was made of stone, just like the main house, but somehow it had a lighter, warmer feel to it. Two dormer windows peaked out of the slate roof, a huge stone chimney on one side, and it was surrounded by an array of bright, cheery flowerbeds. Tessa had left the door, painted a warm cream color, open for them.

Brushing off the snow that lightly dusted their clothes they entered, finding themselves in a small cozy room. Despite the fact that Tessa Micah was clearly very wealthy, the place was simply and unpretentiously adorned.

The dogs lounged on a thick, bright rug in front of a roaring fire in the huge open fireplace that took up most of one wall. A cream colored leather lounge set was grouped in front of it. Two matching bookcases stood guard on either side of the fireplace, the books inside perfectly arranged.

A small kitchen took up most of the other side of the room. A staircase was by the back door, and another door at the end of the kitchen led to a small bathroom. A country style wooden dining table, with matching chairs, covered with a red-checked tablecloth, was in the middle of the room.

The furnishings were expensive, but simple, giving the place a warm, homey feel. The floor was wooden boards, polished and buffed until they gleamed, the walls were painted a warm bright yellow. There were no photos in the room, but several paintings hung on the walls, houses, animals, people, all were brilliantly life like.

Everything in the small cottage was perfectly organized, there was nothing lying around on the floor, nothing left out on the kitchen benches or the table. The place reminded him of Janice Peters' apartment and wondered what else the two girls had in common.

Tessa was busy in the kitchen. "Tea? Coffee? Soda?" she asked as she heard the door close behind them.

"I'll take coffee," Wyatt said.

"Soda for me."

"Hang up your coats," she ordered pointing over her head at the coat rack by the door. Wyatt shrugged out of his coat and hung it up, Parker unwound his scarf and draped it over a hook.

"Take a seat," she gestured at the couches, but again didn't bother to turn and look at them.

Taking a seat in front of the fire they waited while Tessa finished in the kitchen then carried over a tray with their drinks and a plate of home made chocolate chip cookies.

Surprised, "You bake?" Parker asked her.

She frowned back at him as if he were an idiot. "Of course. Make yourselves comfortable, I'm just going to go and change," she gestured at her snow covered sweatpants and hooded sweatshirt.

Watching her as she disappeared up the stairs Parker shook his head. "Rich people are weird. Did you see how many locks she has on her door?" He'd counted three, including two deadlocks and a padlock, plus a chain.

"Windows too," Wyatt commented pointing to the kitchen windows.

"She's afraid of something, or someone." Surveying the room, the closer you looked the more like a fortress it appeared. Parker wondered just what this beautiful, intriguing young woman was scared of.

Studying him closely. "Parker, you like her," Wyatt sighed in a bemused whisper.

"I do not," Parker glared back at him.

* * * * *

12:40 P.M.

Tessa took her time changing, listening to the conversation from downstairs over the intercom. She had always been paranoid, with good reason she reassured herself, and had installed an intercom system linking the living room with her bedroom as soon as she had moved into the cottage.

Choosing her outfit carefully, she pulled on a pair of tight jeans, and a turquoise sweater that perfectly matched her eyes. She pulled her hair from its bonds and sighed as her curls sprung free, framing her face in a wild blonde mass. Sliding her feet into her turquoise sneakers, she smiled as she listened to the discussion going on downstairs.

It seemed that Detective Bell might have a little crush on her, she could definitely find a way to use that to her advantage.

If she was honest with herself, and she always was, she found him very attractive too. He had thick, wavy black hair, amazing caramel colored eyes with the longest lashes she had ever seen. He also had a wonderfully toned body. She felt herself blushing as she remembered the way his muscled arms and chest had looked straining against his sweater. And the cute scarf that he had been wearing with dancing dogs on it hinted that he had a sweet, soft side.

Shaking away these thoughts, she had to focus on the task at hand. There was no time to fantasize about a cute cop she was never going to have. She had pegged them for cops the moment she had seen them pull up the driveway in their department issue car. She had stayed out of sight and observed them as they stood outside the mansion's door.

She didn't know how they had figured out her connection to the disappearance of Janice and the deaths of Tiffany and Bianca. Fighting back tears at the thought of what had happened to her friends, when she got back down there she would not be able to show any emotion. The lives of three people depended on her and her remaining friend's ability to keep the secret that they had vowed to take to their graves ten years ago.

Taking a deep breath, she readied herself to go back downstairs, making sure that her face was a blank mask, her eyes carefully devoid of any emotion.

Taking the stairs slowly, the detectives ceased their conversation the moment they sensed her presence. She could feel their eyes on her as she poured herself a glass of water before crossing to sit with them on the couch. Keeping her eyes carefully blank she looked up at them. "Why are you here, detectives?"

They exchanged glances and she caught the almost imperceptible nod that passed between them, from Detective Wyatt to Detective Bell, presumably to indicate that he should be the one to lead the interview. In order to keep control of this discussion she would have to pay close attention in order to learn their individual body language and their personal form of non-verbal communication that any two people who spent any time together inevitably developed.

"What do you do, Ms Micah?" Detective Wyatt asked her with a warm smile meant to put her at ease.

"I'm an author," she took a long drink from her glass. "I write children's books."

"You do the illustrations?"

"Yes, it was the drawing side that got me interested in children's books in the first place." She wanted to stick to the truth as much as possible.

"Did you do those," he pointed to the paintings that hung on her walls.

"Yes, I did."

"They're good, you're very talented."

"Thank you."

"Ms Micah . . ." Detective Bell began, ready to get down to business.

"Tessa," she interrupted, she was happy for them to call her by her first name, to put them more at ease, but she intended to refrain from using their names. Calling someone by their name held a sense of familiarity, of closeness, and Tessa had learnt a long time ago that relationships only ever led to pain and hurt.

He nodded, smiled. "Tessa. We wondered if we could show you some photos. See if you recognize these women. Is that okay?"

Going for wary and distant, "Sure."

Holding up a picture of Janice. "Have you seen her before?"

He would be expecting her to acknowledge the news story. "Isn't she the lady on the news who was kidnapped?"

In order that he might keep control of the conversation, Detective Bell refrained from answering and instead held up another picture. "What about her?"

Tiffany's picture was next and Tessa had to struggle to keep control of her emotions. "I think I saw her on the news too. She was murdered. Right?" Looking from one to the other, her face a mask of innocence. Once again, neither offered any answer.

"Last one," Detective Bell told her, she mentally prepared herself to see Bianca's face.

As far as she knew news of Bianca's death had not yet been released, she'd seen nothing about it on TV or in the papers. The only reason Tessa herself knew that she was dead was because she had figured out his plan. His one mistake was always underestimating her. She frowned and shook her head as she examined the picture. "No. I don't know her. Sorry."

The two detectives exchanged looks, silently deciding whether or not they believed her, while she waited patiently for them to tip their hand.

"You've never seen any of them before anywhere else?" Detective Wyatt repeated.

So they knew about the gym. But if they knew that she went to the same gym as Janice, Tiffany and Bianca then they also knew that she did not attend any of the same classes. "I don't think so." She frowned in confusion, "Should I have?"

"They all go to the same gym as you," Detective Bell told her, lapsing into silence, waiting for her to fill the gap with something incriminating. It was an old technique, one that she herself had learnt and mastered many years ago. An excellent way to get someone to tell you something they otherwise wouldn't was to sit quietly and wait. Most people felt uncomfortable with silence and filled it with information they would otherwise never share. Tessa herself was an old hand at this technique, and waited patiently for him to continue, never once breaking eye contact.

After almost a minute of silence he cleared his throat and continued, "You've never seen them there?"

It was best to say as little as possible, so she simply shook her head.

Raising an eyebrow at her. "You haven't said much, Ms Micah."

Phrasing it so it sounded like both a question and a statement he was still trying to trick her into giving something away, unfortunately for him she was not that easily manipulated. "Tessa," she corrected again. "I guess I'm just not that curious. Anyway I assume you'll be getting to the point any minute now," she replied calmly.

Momentarily startled by her candor, neither of them spoke for a moment. Recovering Detective Bell frowned then nodded. "Fair enough. There's something that hasn't been released to the media yet. When Janice Peters was abducted the man who took her left a note saying that he was going to kill nine women, he left clues so we could identify them . . ."

Of course he did Tessa thought to herself, she had figured that out the moment she heard Janice had been taken. He was nothing if not predictable, arrogant, and always melodramatic.

" . . . the note said that if we find out who the women are then he'll kill Janice. But if we don't find them, and he kills them all, then he'll let Janice go alive . . ."

Yeah right. That was a lie. There was no way he would let Janice or any one of them go. She hoped the police were at least smart enough to figure that out.

". . . when we found the bodies, the two women in the pictures, there was a note attached identifying them as his victims . . ."

A look of something flashed quickly across his face as he mentioned Tiffany, Bianca, and the notes. If she knew their killer, and unfortunately she did, then in his notes he would have blamed the police for the deaths of his victims. For some reason this bothered Detective Bell, he actually felt like he was to blame. She filed this information away for future use.

". . . we think that you might be on this guy's list," his beautiful amber eyes unable to hide his worry.

Going with irritated disbelief, "You think what?"

"We think that you might be in the sights of a killer," Detective Wyatt told her, placing a comforting hand on her shoulder.

She shrugged him off. "Are you crazy? You think that a serial killer is after me because of some weird list of riddles?"

"Is there anyone from the gym that you can think of that might want to hurt you?" Detective Wyatt asked.

Pushing to her feet. "I think you should go now."

"Tessa, we want to put an officer on your place, make sure that you're safe," Detective Bell told her.

She cold see that he meant this sincerely, he felt a genuine desire to protect her, to keep her from harm. The irony being that if she had ever had a man in her life who had been there to protect her then she would never have gotten stuck in this mess in the first place. Now it was too little too late.

"Ms Micah," she spat out frostily. "And I think I'll be fine without the useless but good looking soap opera police at my door." Walking to the front door and throwing it open. She could see hurt flash across Detective Bell's face, apparently he was self-conscious about his good looks, very endearing.

Putting aside his annoyance in order to do his job, he followed her to the door. "Maybe you could take a look at the list of clues, and see if anything on there reminds you of someone you know . . ."

"I am not on any list. I do not know anyone on any list. You have got the wrong person. Now please just go!" she screamed, throwing her hands up in the air in annoyance. She had no time for this now, she'd played along long enough, but she had things that needed to be taken care of. Her dogs bounded to their feet at the sound of her distress and came to stand protectively at her side, growling softly at the detectives.

Eyeing the dogs warily, Detective Bell looked like he was a hairsbreadth away from slinging her over his shoulder and throwing her in the back of his police car. However, he restrained himself with an effort and attempted to reason with her. "There could be a serial killer who's already kidnapped one woman and killed two others who's just biding his time before he kills *you*."

"There is no serial killer after me," she shrieked. "Now get out!"

Reluctantly they left.

Detective Bell still looked like he wanted to lock her away someplace where he could keep an eye on her. She watched them go and let out the shuddering breath she had been holding. Barely noticing the tears streaming down her cheeks as she rifled through one of her kitchen cupboards, upon finding her disposable cell phone she made a call.

* * * * *

1:01 P.M.

Sitting in the car as they rode back down the driveway of Tessa's estate, Parker hit the dashboard in frustration. "Well she definitely knows more than she's letting on. Let's run her phone, see who she's been in contact with lately."

"Maybe she's scared," Wyatt replied.

"Maybe she's an idiot," Parker huffed.

"I thought you liked her."

"Then you're an idiot too." Turning down the window, he watched as the snowflakes fluttered gently into the car. Snow had always had a calming effect on him, ever since he was a child. Now it seemed to do nothing to calm his frazzled nerves. "Well I guess the girls from the gym were right, she certainly does have a presence." He groaned irritably, "If she knows something why wouldn't she just tell us."

"If she knows who the killer is he might have threatened her," Wyatt reasoned.

But Parker was in no mood to be reasonable. He hadn't felt this way about a woman in a very long time, especially a woman he didn't even know, and the fact that there was no chance of anything happening with her only served to fuel his annoyance. "I don't get her. Those blank eyes and her cool, calm confidence . . ."

"Don't forget how she didn't fall for your fill the silence trick," Wyatt added with a grin. "Just admit it, you've got a crush on her." Growing serious, "You should be careful, Parker, you know what happened last time you got involved with a victim. If you're going to do anything, at least wait until we find this guy and everything blows over."

Holding up a hand to emphasize his point "One, this is completely different from the situation with Gina. Two, I don't like Tessa Micah. And three," he stared sullenly out of the window and balled his hand into a fist, "She called us the soap opera police."

"Yeah but on the plus side she said you were good looking," Wyatt laughed.

NOVEMBER 26TH

9:34 A.M.

"They just brought him in," Wyatt sat down on the edge of his desk.

"Marty find anything else at the pool?"

"Just the hair," a smile spreading across his partner's face, his green eyes twinkling merrily. "Although that's all we'll need to convict this guy."

Parker wanted to smile back, but something about this just didn't sit right with him. After leaving the gym the day before they'd faxed both a copy of the gym's client and employee lists back to the station. While they'd been talking with Tessa Micah, other detectives had been going through the employees list looking for anyone with a criminal conviction.

They'd hit the jackpot with Owen Unger. He had spent thirteen years in jail for rape, released three years ago, he'd been working at the gym for the last eighteen months. Everyone was convinced that this was their guy. Everyone except him.

Sticking his head through his office door. "He's ready for you," J.J. called out to them.

Making their way to the interview room that held Owen Unger, Parker stopped at the door, deciding to voice his doubts to his partner. "I don't think this is our guy."

Wyatt frowned. "What? Why?"

"Owen Unger is a pervert who grabbed women going home late at night, raped and beat them. He just doesn't strike me as the kind of guy who does," shaking the papers in his hand, "This."

"Maybe he branched out after prison, learnt some new tricks

while he was in there," Wyatt suggested. "Let's not count him out just yet. We'll do the interview, and Marty will do a DNA comparison and then we'll know for sure."

When they opened the door, Owen Unger looked up at them with nervous brown eyes. He had changed a lot since he had been arrested sixteen years earlier. Back then he'd been stick thin with long stringy brown hair, and impossibly smooth skin. Now he was big and bulky from years of working out in the prison exercise yard, tattoos weaved up and down his arms, and his head had been shaved bald.

He watched them closely as they took their time settling into the chairs across the table from him. Keeping him on edge, Parker rifled slowly through the folder.

"I didn't do nothing," Unger finally muttered defiantly.

Giving him a sharp look. "That's a double negative, it means that you did do something," Parker explained.

Beside him Wyatt snorted back a laugh while Unger gave him a blank look. "Huh? Whatever, man. Look whatever you think I did, I didn't."

Parker said nothing just lay the photos down side by side in front of him. Unger twitched nervously but refused to look at them. Waiting a full minute, making sure that Unger was good and anxious, he thumped the table with his fist. "Look at them," he bellowed.

Jumping, the big man's hands trembled as he picked up the pictures, dropping one on the floor he fumbled to pick it up. His eyes flicking from the picture of Janice, to Tiffany's, and Bianca's, and back to him and Wyatt.

They both stared stonily back at him, he twitched and sweated before finally giving in. "These . . . these are those women from . . ." his pink tongue darting out to wet his lips. "These are the women from the news that were murdered. You don't think . . . you don't think I killed them. I didn't. I swear I didn't."

"We do think you killed them," Wyatt told him calmly.

"I didn't. I swear I didn't. I've been clean since I got out of jail. I swear," Unger repeated nervously, aware that things were not looking good for him.

"We want to help you out here, Owen, but we can't do that unless you start telling us the truth." Wyatt always played the good cop. "Have you ever seen these women before?"

Unger took his time looking at each photo, then laid them all back on the table. "I've never seen them before."

Standing up so quickly his chair toppled backwards, Parker put his hands on the table and leaned across so that he was right in Unger's face.

Cringing as far back in his seat as he could, Owen's beady black eyes darted around the room, looking anywhere except at Parker.

"You're lying, Unger. We know that you know them. They all attend the gym where you work," Parker spat out at him, enjoying watching the man squirm. He may not be their guy but he was definitely a scumbag.

"Oh I uh, I didn't notice, maybe I should look again," he fumbled for the pictures, "oh yeah now I remember them."

Parker rolled his eyes and righted his chair, sitting back down, as Wyatt gave Unger a sympathetic smile. "So you've seen them around the gym?"

Helpful now he nodded eagerly. "Yeah I've seen them around a lot. They all take some classes there . . ."

"You like to watch women working out, Owen, it turn you on?" Parker cut in.

Nervous again. "I uh, I mean . . ." he looked to Wyatt for assistance.

"You've just seen them around while you're working," Wyatt supplied helpfully.

Relieved Unger nodded, head bouncing up and down so frantically it looked like a ping-pong ball. "Yeah that's right."

"Have you ever spoken with them, asked them out, maybe

slept with them," Wyatt kept his voice calm and non-judgmental.

"No," he said vehemently. "I've never slept with any of them, I've never even talked to them. I promise," he looked from one to the other to see if they believed him.

"Okay, I believe you, Owen," Wyatt patted his hand comfortingly. "Have you maybe seen someone suspicious hanging around the gym, someone who shouldn't be there?"

Back to helpful, he frowned in concentration. "I don't think so. I can't think of anything."

"You know what would really help us out, Owen. If you were to give us a DNA sample, you know so we can exclude you as a suspect."

Practically falling over himself with enthusiasm, "Yeah sure, whatever you want, I didn't kill those women. Whatever gets you off my back."

Parker felt Wyatt deflate beside him, if Owen Unger had agreed to a DNA test so readily it was highly unlikely he was their guy. This may have turned out to be a dead end concerning their case, but he at least he had enjoyed the chance to get some of the pent up anger out of his system.

"Wait here and someone will be in to do a swab," Wyatt told him, as he and Parker stood, gathered their papers and moved to the door.

Pulling open the door Parker paused, "One more question, you know a Tessa Micah?"

Owen Unger's face went bright red. "Whatever she said is a lie, man."

Closing the door behind them Wyatt leaned wearily against it. "You were right, Parker, he's not our guy."

"Yes and no, he didn't kill our girls, but I'm sure he did do something."

* * * * *

10:57 P.M.

Another night, another chase.

Unfortunately, his night with Bianca had been ruined.

It had been a mistake to let the girls see one another, he was man enough to admit it. They had drawn strength from each other. Even at the point of death, Bianca had not given in to the panic that he was sure had been coursing through her every fiber.

Then there was Janice's stupid comment. He was sure he was right. When the others found out what was happening they would come. They wouldn't be able to help themselves. She had been right about one thing though. Tessa would eventually come after him. She couldn't help herself. She would do whatever she had to in order to protect her friends.

Gently sliding up a back window of Dorothy Dallas' house, he climbed soundlessly inside, and eased the window closed behind him. He knew the layout of the house by heart, having visited it many times while Dorothy was out at work. Dorothy's taste in interior design was distinctly different from most of the rest of her friends, who preferred older, wooden furniture, antiques, whereas Dorothy, and Michelle, were distinctly modern girls. However, one trait they all had in common was the complete lack of personal items displayed in their homes.

Slipping down the hallway towards her room. He had been watching her house for hours, waiting patiently until all the lights had gone off and she was safely tucked away in bed.

Opening the bedroom door he stood still for a moment, watching as her chest rose and fell calmly in her sleep. Nothing was going to ruin tonight.

Taking a step into the room he found himself tripping and falling to the floor, something clattering down around him.

A light flicked on, temporarily blinding him. "I've got a gun," a voice called from the bed.

"A booby-trap, very inventive Dorothy," he said as he rose to his feet. "Your idea or Tessa's?"

Taking a step towards her, her panicked blue eyes following his every move. "Don't come any closer," her voice shook.

Pleased that this was turning out to be a most entertaining evening. He had been momentarily stunned tripping over the wire that had been placed strategically across the door. However, now that he thought about it, it actually made things all the more fun.

Giving Dorothy a bemused smile. "I must admit I underestimated you," taking another step towards her. She kept the gun pointed at him, but her hands trembled violently, he knew she didn't have it in her to shoot him. "You've changed a lot, Dorothy, you used to be such a timid, mousy little creature." Continuing to move towards her until he was standing right next to the bed.

"It's over," she whispered.

He watched her closely, her wobbling lip, the tears that she blinked back, her shaking hands. "I think not, dear."

Before she had a chance to fire the gun, he moved to the side and swung his fist at her temple, hard enough to stun her but not knock her out. He chuckled as she moaned, and pried the gun from her hands, tucking it into his pants and leaning over her, "I thought you would have learnt by now, I always get what I want." Blood dripped down her face, but she looked up at him with defiant eyes. "If you tell me where they are I'll let you live," he whispered in her ear.

She said nothing and for a second he thought that she was going to tell him, but then her eyes clouded over and she raised her hand to slap him. Gripping her wrist, he stopped her hand inches from his cheek. "That was a mistake, Dorothy," he fought the urge to hit her again, to beat her and beat her until she was nothing but a bloody mess. Taking a deep breath he restrained himself, he needed her alive.

At least for the moment.

"Let's go, Dorothy," he started to bind her wrists.

"I'm not going anywhere with you," she struggled wildly beneath him, but the blow to her head had weakened her.

"It wasn't a question." Tying her ankles and adding a gag, finishing up, he hoisted her into his arms. "I thought we'd take your car." He grabbed the keys from the dresser and hummed to himself as he headed for the garage.

NOVEMBER 27TH

Switching the TV on and setting the disc inside the DVD player Parker sat back down beside Wyatt. "He left this instead of a written note," he explained to J.J. who had joined them to watch the recording.

"How'd he kill this one?" J.J. asked despondently, for once his wild eyes were oddly despairing.

"It's on the disc," Wyatt told him.

J.J. took a deep breath and ran a hand through his beard, his usual gesture when he was stressed. "Do we at least get a good look at him?"

"Nope, we only see the back of his jacket. A plain black leather jacket," Parker added anticipating his boss' next question. "And his gloved hands."

"She was found dead in her car this morning?" J.J. confirmed.

"Yeah. He filmed the video, then killed her in her car and left her."

"Media's linking the cases together, the murders and the abduction," Wyatt told him. "But they still don't know about the note. They're just warning all young women to be careful. And clutching at straws to come up with a 'reason' why this guy's roaming the city looking for vulnerable girls to kill."

"Roll it," J.J. commanded pointing to the TV and muttering under his breath at the exploits of the media.

Parker pressed play and the TV sprang to life. Forcing himself to stay and watch the death of yet another woman whom he had failed to save when all he wanted to do was flee the room.

Dorothy Dallas appeared on the screen, she was seated in the driver's seat of her BMW convertible, the top was down. She was dressed in pale pink flannel pajamas, her shiny black hair hung in a tangled mess around her head, her blue eyes were focused on the filmmaker. She had a huge gash across her right temple, and blood streaked the right side of her face, her wrists were tied to the steering wheel.

Shivering involuntarily at the eerie feeling that flowed through him as he listened once again to Dorothy's voice coming to them from beyond the grave.

"My name is Dorothy Dallas. And just like Tiffany and Bianca, I too am dead because of you. Six clues remain on your list and six women will soon be dead. Unless you find them and save them. Janice Peters is still alive, if you don't find the other women then he will let her go free."

Dorothy held in her bound hands a time-dated photo of Janice Peters, lying tied to a bed, as proof that she was still alive. The date on the photo indicated that it had been taken at seven o'clock the previous night.

They all watched in helpless silence as a figure in black came into view, leant over Dorothy and proceeded to strangle her to death. Her wrists bound to the steering wheel prevented her from fighting back. But it did not stop her from squirming and wiggling desperately as her life was choked from her.

After what seemed like an eternity, her body went still, her blue eyes taking on the glassy, lifeless stare of death. Their killer kept his back to the camera as he moved out of view, and then a moment later the screen went black.

For a long minute none of them moved. Finally J.J. spoke, "She was reading from a script."

"Makes sense since he told the others what to write," Wyatt agreed.

"Did she attend the same gym as the others?"

Wyatt shook his head. "We're still waiting to confirm DNA with Marty, but we don't think that Owen Unger is our guy."

"She wasn't scared," Parker interjected softly. He had been watching Dorothy's eyes while she had been reciting her lines and in them he had seen no fear.

They both turned to look at him. "What?" J.J. asked.

Skipping back through the disc to the beginning and pausing it so that they could all look. "The way she looked at him, she wasn't scared, just angry. She didn't look terrified or even surprised. She looks almost resigned, as if she had been expecting this. She definitely knew this guy."

"That settles it." They all turned as Marty barged through the door to J.J.'s office. "DNA from the Bianca Kingston crime scene does not match Owen Unger."

"He's not our guy," Wyatt sighed, disappointed, even though this was the news they had been expecting.

"No. However we did find out that Unger had a camera hidden in the women's locker room at the gym, he'd been secretly videoing the women in there. And he tried to rape Tessa Micah. Apparently she fought him off in the gym's underground car park, gave him a broken nose and a dislocated kneecap."

"Little Tessa fought him off?" Wyatt looked surprised and impressed.

"Good for her," Parker agreed. Himself awed and amazed, and surprised at the rush of pride that splashed through him at the knowledge that Tessa had successfully fought off someone more than twice her size. Parker had to remind himself that nothing was going to happen with her.

"She tried to report him," Marty continued. "But he denied it and the gym had no proof so they couldn't fire him. Several other woman came forward when they found out he'd been arrested and admitted he tried to rape them too. At least he's back in jail now, where he belongs."

"Well at least we had one happy ending to all of this," Parker muttered. Trying to be pleased that they had gotten a rapist off the streets but unable to muster a single positive vibe.

"You get anything from Tessa Micah?" J.J. asked.

Feeling Wyatt's eyes on him, Parker knew his cheeks were blushing red. Clearing his throat, "Uh no, we didn't. She flipped out on us when we suggested that she may be in the sights of a serial killer."

"Does she know our victims?"

"She said she doesn't," he replied.

"But she was extremely careful to keep her expressions blank and neutral, giving away nothing," Wyatt added.

"Which doesn't mean she knows anything," Parker countered. Then once again had to remind himself that he and Tessa were not involved, nor were they ever going to be.

"She's scared of something though," Wyatt continued. "If she knows who the killer is, and what he's capable of doing, it would certainly be a reason to keep her mouth shut."

"That the DVD?" Marty had been the one who found the disc, tucked into a pocket of Dorothy's pajamas.

"Yes."

"It shows him killing her?"

Three somber heads nodded, and Marty shook his own in shocked disbelief. "I didn't find any physical evidence at the scene."

"He rape her too?" Parker asked. The post-mortem on Bianca Kingston had showed that, like Tiffany, she too had been raped before being drowned.

"Yeah he did."

"Parker, Wyatt," Victoria Baker rushed into the room. "I found another connection between them. All five of them."

"Five?" J.J. frowned, confused.

"Including Tessa Micah," Victoria explained.

"What is it?" Parker hoped that this lead turned out to be more helpful than the last one.

"They all attended the same private school."

* * * * *

10:31 A.M.

At last, her stomach full, Janice was able to concentrate. He had left a while ago, to kill another of her friends she presumed. They were prepared for his coming, but there was not a lot they could do about it. If she was honest, it was more like there wasn't a lot they *would* do about it.

They had made a vow ten years ago to keep this secret no matter what the cost, even if that meant giving their lives to keep it. They may have been only fifteen when they made their vow, but they had known even then that someday it would come to this. Nothing and no one would make her friends tell their secret because other people's lives depended on them.

Janice had long ago given up on her initial plan of finding a way to escape. Now she almost welcomed death. Her life was miserable, she was tired of being alone and yet she would not embark on a relationship, she did not deserve one. She had never been the same after what he did to them.

Thinking back over her life. At the things she would change if she could. Her relationship with her parents would be number one on her list. At the time of their death she had thought she'd made her peace with their past. They had never been good parents, they had never wanted a child, she had been an accident and they had taken every opportunity to make that very clear to her.

She and her friends had all grown up in wealthy families, with parents too busy to spend any time with their children, raised by strings of nannies. That was why she had grown to rely on her friends so heavily. Why they had become so close. It was not just because of what they had gone through together, it was also because they were all lonely. They had never had anyone else to rely on so they had learnt to draw strength from one another.

As she lay in her small, pink prison, her mind wandered once again back to what he had said to her earlier. He had dared her to figure out where she was. She knew that she was in the middle of the woods, in the middle of nowhere. She'd thought she heard voices outside earlier, but he'd had her so drugged that she couldn't be sure.

Wherever they were, it had to have something to do with Tessa.

Everything he did somehow revolved around her. He was obsessed. Janice strained to think of a place significant to Tess, but sighed and gave up. She had never been good at figuring out what was going on in that warped mind of his, that had always been Tessa's job. She was brilliant, always seeming to know, to anticipate, what everyone else was thinking.

Exhaustion washing over her again Janice frowned in annoyance, the drugs that he kept pumping through her system left her drained. As she drifted off a thought whispered in her mind, nagging insistently at her. Something that had happened to Tessa a long, long time ago. Something that she had never shared with a single living soul.

* * * * *

2:00 P.M.

"Janice Peters, Tiffany Poppy, Bianca Kingston, Dorothy Dallas and Tessa Micah were all in the same class?" Parker couldn't believe their luck. Once again, things were starting to look up and he hoped that this time they were about to catch a real break.

After Victoria had found the connection between their girls and the private school, Harlwood Academy, he and Wyatt had made an appointment with the school's headmistress. Amazingly the same one that had been here when the girls had attended the

118

school. Then they'd jumped in Wyatt's car, grabbed some lunch and driven out to the school.

Arriving at Harlwood Academy, they'd found it was comprised of five enormous brick buildings nestled deep in the woods. Inside the school looked just as old as it had from the out. The long hallways through which one of the seniors had led then were painted in dark colors. Framed paintings of past school principal's staring imposingly down at anyone who dared to walk by.

Now they were seated in the fancy, old worldly, office of the sixty-five year old principal. Tabitha McKreeney was well preserved for her age, her silver hair was pulled back into a neat bun, blue eyes still sparkled merrily, her face was mostly wrinkle free with just a few laugh lines around her eyes.

"Yes," she nodded. "They graduated eight years ago."

"Were the girls all friends?" Wyatt questioned.

"Yes," she smiled. "They were all in the advanced class. They're all very smart girls," she said proudly, as she stood and began rifling through a drawer.

"We heard that Janice Peters had an IQ of 125," Parker looked for confirmation. Fighting the urge to squirm, sitting in a school principal's office made him feel like he was thirteen all over again.

"Yes that sounds about right. She actually had one of the lower IQ's of the group, if I recall correctly, Tessa Micah had an IQ of 178. Ah ha," pulling a photo triumphantly from the drawer, "I knew it was in there somewhere."

Returning to her desk she passed them the photo. "There they are. Tessa, Janice, Bianca, Tiffany, Dorothy and the rest of their friends, all eleven of them."

Parker frowned, "Eleven of them? There's only ten names on our list, including Janice." The photo showed eleven girls of about twelve, posed with their horses. Parker could pick out Tiffany from the photo's he had seen in her house, and the girl in the middle had to be Tessa. The teenagers smiled at the camera with their mouths, but their eyes were eerily blank.

"What list?" Mrs. McKreeney asked them.

J.J. had given them clearance to share limited information with the headmistress. "You've been following the news?"

She nodded gravely. "Yes, it's awful."

"Didn't you think it was strange that four of the girls who attended your school, and were all friends, had been either abducted or killed?"

"I'm afraid my memory is not what it used to be, and I've never been great with names. I'm afraid I didn't put it together until you called."

"When Janice was abducted the man who took her left a note claiming that he was going to kill nine women, instead of giving us their names he left us riddles." Parker left out the part about how he claimed he would let Janice go if they didn't save the other women. "So far we haven't been able to identify any of the women on the list except for Tessa Micah, who wasn't entirely convinced . . ."

"That sounds like Tessa," Mrs. McKreeney cut in with a smile.

"But there are only ten women on the list, if we include Janice, who's the eleventh girl?"

"That would be Chelsea Ward," her smile fading. "Chelsea and her boyfriend Jasper Connor killed themselves when they were fifteen. They drove their car off a cliff, their bodies were never recovered."

"That had to be hard on her friends. Something like that happening when they were so young," Wyatt said sympathetically, and Parker remembered that Wyatt's best friend from high school had killed himself.

"It was. It came at the end of a very long few months for the girls. Tessa was involved in a horrible accident, she was in the hospital for three months, she almost died. And then about six months later Chelsea . . ." she trailed off unable to finish her sentence. "It was a very hard time for everyone here at Harlwood."

"Can you tell us who the other girls are in the photo?"

She took the photo back and looked at it closely, before sighing, "I'm sorry. It's been a long time . . ."

"You remembered that they were friends," Parker interjected.

"Only after you reminded me of them. You've got to understand detectives that we have almost ten thousand students from pre-K right through," Mrs. McKreeney defended herself, fiddling nervously with the buttons of her pale blue suit.

"You seem to remember a lot about Tessa," Wyatt commented.

"She's not someone one forgets easily. You've met her, you know. And she and her friends were not ones who got in trouble often, they were good girls."

"You'd have records though, of all the girls in that year?"

"Yes, but it was eight years ago, so it might take a little while to locate them, we don't have these things computerized," she told them apologetically.

"Is there anyone here who might remember them?" Parker had come here for names and he wasn't leaving without them.

Mrs. McKreeney thought for a moment then her eyes lit up, "Mary Abbott. She was in the same year as the girls, and she recently started here as a middle school math teacher."

"We'll need to speak with her."

"Yes, of course, I'll go and get her," she hurried from the room.

Wyatt followed, closing the door behind her. "Well we're making some progress," he said hopefully.

"We still don't have any names," Parker muttered back sullenly.

"But we have the photo, and we have Tessa. Now we know that she was lying to us before. We were right about her, she did know more than she was letting on."

Sighing, "I'm suspicious of everyone now."

"Parker, you tried to help Gina, she didn't deserve it. You did what you had to do. She was going to kill her own baby. You have got to move on . . ." Wyatt stopped abruptly as the door opened and a pretty young redhead stuck her head in.

"Detective Bell? Detective Wyatt? I'm Mary, Mrs. McKreeney said you wanted to talk about Tessa?"

"Come in, grab a seat," Wyatt gestured to the seat the principal had just vacated.

"I've been a teacher here for two years and I still get nervous in the headmistress' office," she gave them each a warm, confidant smile, shook their hands, then pulled over another chair. "You're here about what happened, about Janice and those other girls," her serious hazel eyes stared steadily at them.

"Did you know Janice or any of the others?"

She shook her head. "There were about seven hundred girls in my year level, I don't remember a lot of them. But it's gone all over the school since you got here. I guess no one realized at first that all of those women went here."

"You said that you didn't know those girls, but you do know Tessa?" Parker was starting to wonder what it was about this woman that she seemed to stick in everyone's mind.

"Everyone knew Tess. You've met her right? She looked like an angel with the blonde curls and those big blue eyes, and she acted like one too, she was really sweet. She was also a real live genius."

"Did you ever spend much time with her?"

"Not really. I mean we were both here since pre-K, but we were never really friends. She mostly hung with the other girls in her advanced class."

"If we showed you a picture of Tessa and her friends would you be able to identify any of them?"

"Maybe," she said doubtfully. "But like I said I didn't really know them." She took the photo from Parker's outstretched hand and studied it carefully, her freckled face frowning in concentration. Finally she shook her head, and handed the photo back. "I'm sorry, other than Tessa the only one I recognize is Chelsea . . ." she checked to see if they knew about the suicide. "You know what happened right?"

Wyatt nodded. "Mrs. McKreeney told us."

Mary sighed in relief.

"What can you tell us about Tessa?"

"Well, like I said she was really pretty, really smart and really nice. All the boys had crushes on her . . ."

"I thought this was an all girls school?" Parker interrupted.

"It is, but we do a lot of stuff with Hendlewood Academy, the boys school, it's not far from here. Even though boys really liked her and she got a lot of offers, Tessa never dated. Tessa was kind of . . . well she . . ." Mary trailed off.

"Whatever you can think of might be really helpful, Mary," Wyatt said softly.

She nodded. "Tessa was always really sad, her eyes were always carefully empty like she didn't want anyone to know what was going on inside her head." Parker remembered Tessa's blank eyes staring back at him, as though she could see what was going on inside his head, but giving nothing away about what going on inside her own.

"Do you know why she was so sad?"

"I know that she didn't have a really happy family life. I mean most of the girls here didn't too. A lot of us lived here, only went home for the holidays. Tessa was a day student, she had an older brother, but I don't know a lot about him. Her father was away a lot for work, her mom suffered from depression, I think she was really hard on Tess."

"But she had a lot of friends?"

"Yeah. From what I could see she really loved her friends, those girls were really close. Tessa was like their leader. A lot of her friends were really shy and self conscious about their intelligence, Tessa kinda held them all together. Anyway after the accident . . . you know about that right?"

"We know that Tessa was in the hospital for three months and that she almost died." Parker felt a tightening in his chest at the thought of Tessa at death's door, but determinedly pushed the feeling away.

"Well there was a rumor going around the school that it was her friends that hurt her."

They both stared at her as she looked around the room as though checking to make sure no one was listening. Then began to elaborate, "They were out one night on one of their school work camp things, they used to go on them a lot. Anyway apparently she fell down some stairs, broke her arm so badly the bone went through the skin. It was hours before they got her to the hospital, her arm got infected, and she got really sick. Everyone thought her friends did something to her, she didn't have any other injuries like she would have if she fell, and if they had nothing to hide why'd it take them so long to get her to a hospital."

"I thought you said she and her friends were close, why would they hurt her?" Wyatt asked, confused.

Mary shrugged. "I'm just telling you the rumor."

"Did Tessa know what people were saying?"

"Tessa knew everything. She was like a mind reader, she always knew what people were going to do before they did it. It was kind of creepy," Mary shivered involuntarily.

"What about her friends did they know what people were saying about them?"

"Yeah, I think so. And then Chelsea died, it was a really rough time for them."

"Did you think they hurt her?"

"I . . ." she shook her head slowly, "No, I didn't."

Shaking his head in irritation at the silliness of teenagers Parker asked. "Why didn't someone just ask Tessa?"

"She wouldn't talk about it. And . . ." again Mary looked around nervously, "And people were kinda afraid to talk to Tessa after what happened to her."

"You mean the accident?" This tale was turning into a soap opera story.

"No I mean what happened to her before, when she was little." Looking from one blank face to the other. "No one told you?"

"We have no idea what you are talking about," Wyatt told her.

"When Tessa was eleven she and her friend Eleanor Matthews went missing one weekend, only no one knew they were gone until after."

She paused, they waited for her to continue, when she didn't Wyatt prodded gently, "After what, Mary?"

"Tessa was found two days later covered in blood at the side of a road miles from her house. Eleanor was never seen again."

Staring at her in shocked silence for a moment. "What happened?"

Shrugging, "I don't know, no one does. After she was found, Tessa didn't speak to anyone for months. I remember she was out of school for ages, then just before she came back they sat us all down and gave us a talk about being really nice to her."

"Did people think Tessa . . .?" Parker could hardly finish the sentence, the idea of anyone thinking Tessa had killed someone unbearable.

"No," Mary jumped in. "Of course not, she was only eleven. People thought that someone took them, and . . . you know . . ."

"Raped them?" Parker supplied, his gut tightening.

"Yeah," Mary wouldn't meet their eye.

"Can you think of anyone that might want to hurt Tessa or any of her friends?" Wyatt asked, looking to wrap things up.

"I can't think of anyone who would want to hurt them. But Tessa had a lot of secrets, so . . ."

"Thanks, Mary, you've been really enlightening," Parker told her. His mind already wandering, forming a mental list of question he intended to ask Tessa.

"I hope it helps, sorry I couldn't help you figure out the names of her friends," Mary stood, shook their hands again and hurried out the door.

Watching her go. "We're going straight to Tessa's to get some answers. Even if I have to drag them from her pretty little mouth."

Wyatt barked out a laugh, Parker turned to glare at him. "What?"

"You just said she had a pretty little mouth."

* * * * *

5:20 P.M.

It was just starting to get dark as they pulled down the driveway of Tessa's estate, the snow had stopped but the sky was still heavy with clouds and it was bitterly cold out. Parking in front of the mansion, they climbed from the car, stretching their stiff legs. They had been cooped up in the car for almost two hours, buying dinner on the way but eating it on the road. Parker had tried calling Tessa several times but had gotten no answer.

Looking up at the dark windows of the huge stone house Parker felt himself shiver. "Tessa is right this place is creepy." For a moment he thought he saw a shadow flit silently across one of the third storey windows. But upon closer inspection he saw that it had been nothing more than his tired and over-active imagination.

The huge open property reminded him of the last foster home that he and Mattie had lived in before going to live with the Bell's. It had been by far the worst of all the foster homes they had lived in. There had been up to twenty children staying there at any one time. The middle aged foster parents were in it only for the money, their only biological son enjoyed nothing more than tormenting the younger children.

126

Sniffing the air he turned to Wyatt, "Do you smell something?"

Wyatt sniffed too. "I don't smell any . . ." stopping he looked back to Parker.

"Smoke!" they both said at the same time.

Without a word, they took off towards the little cottage behind the big house. As soon as they were around the mansion, they could see the orange haze emanating between the trees surrounding the cottage. The air shooting from his lungs as though he'd been punched, Parker forced himself to suck in a nauseous breath, if Tessa was in there he'd get her out. The thought of losing her, even though he knew that he didn't have her, was unbearable.

Crossing the huge, green lawn in seconds, through the woods that glowed an eerie orange, reaching the front door they found it locked. Wyatt called for backup while Parker threw a rock through the window next to the door so they could get inside. Pure blinding terror overwhelmed him, not at the thought of his own safety, but of Tessa, alone, inside this burning coffin.

"She might not even be in there, Parker," Wyatt cautioned hanging up his phone. "Or we could be too late."

"If there's even a chance she's in there . . ." he cast his friend and partner a look, "You don't have to come, you've got kids to think about."

Wyatt said nothing, just rolled his eyes and followed Parker inside the smoldering inferno.

Flames licked at the outside of the building as though someone had poured an accelerant around the perimeter then set it alight. Fire had not yet reached the inside of the house, but it was thick with smoke.

"Tessa!" Parker screamed as he searched wildly around the living room, looking for any sign of her. Heart thumping furiously, seeing nothing he turned to Wyatt, "She could be upstairs."

Taking off up the stairs, Wyatt at his heels, they were met with three closed doors. Choking on the thick smoke, he tried the first door, it opened into a home office and art studio. It was empty.

"Parker, this one's locked." Wyatt was trying to knock down the middle door, thumping it with his shoulder.

"Stand back," Parker called running over to him. Slamming a practiced foot into the door, it cracked and splintered down the middle, another kick and the door flew open.

It was Tessa's bedroom and she sat in the centre of the room. She was tied to a chair, a gag in her mouth, blood streaking her face, her head hanging limply against her chest.

Dashing to her and dropping to his knees at her side, Parker saw her eyes were closed and felt his chest tighten in panic. Pressing two fingers to her neck, relieved to find a weak pulse. Attacking the tape on her wrists, it didn't budge.

"Ambulance is on its way," Wyatt said coming up behind him.

"I need something to cut the tape," his voice already hoarse from the smoke, his lungs burning.

As Wyatt ran to find something sharp, Tessa moaned above him, her eyes fluttering slowly open. Reaching up to pull off the gag. "Tessa, can you hear me? It's Parker, Detective Bell, everything's gonna be okay. Just hold on."

Her eyes glassy, pupils dilated, she tried to speak but choked on the smoke. "Don't try to talk," he cautioned, stroking her cheek to calm her. Her eyes slid closed again and he gently tapped her face. "Tessa, hey, honey, stay with me. We're gonna get you out of here, but I need you to stay awake for me, okay?"

Obediently her eyes struggled back open, dazed with pain and panic.

"You with me?" he asked, working to keep his own panic in check. She nodded slowly, coughing. Taking her face between his hands, Parker examined the wound to her head, hoping she didn't have a concussion on top of the smoke inhalation.

"Wyatt!" he yelled over his shoulder, keeping one hand pressed gently to Tessa's neck, reassured by the weak but steady beating of her pulse.

"Here," Wyatt dropped down beside him, passing him a knife. Immediately he started to saw at the tape on her wrists, while Wyatt did her ankles.

"Tessa, you still with me?" he asked, not slowing from his task to look up.

"Yes," she managed to croak, before dissolving into another coughing fit.

"We're almost done, just hang in there a little while longer," he reassured her, freeing one of her hands he moved on to the other.

Finishing with her ankles Wyatt crossed to the window, looking down at the flames below. "They're blocking the door now, Parker," he whispered, coming back over to them.

"We'll go out a window then." Tessa's other wrist came free, and Parker stood, once again taking her face between his hands, "Hold on tightly okay?"

Nodding compliantly, albeit tiredly, Tessa struggled to keep her eyes open as she wrapped her thin arms around his neck. Lifting her gently into his arms, Parker was surprised at how light she was, she couldn't weigh more than about eighty pounds. And at how right it felt to be holding her.

Following his partner back down the stairs, they found the living room now so full of smoke it was almost impossible to see more than a couple of inches in any direction.

"There's no way out, the fire's everywhere," Wyatt called to him from the other side of the room.

Mesmerized by the dancing red flames, that leapt and twirled merrily around the house, the smoke was making him tired and he struggled to concentrate. Lowering Tessa down to the floor, where the smoke was thinnest, he shook her gently. "Tessa?" Her blue eyes shone brightly in the eerie orange glow, blinking slowly and focusing on him. "Do you have a fire extinguisher?" Wracked by fits of coughing she was fighting to remain conscious. "Come on, Tessa, stay with me, I need you to think."

Struggling to breathe, her lips moved but he couldn't hear what she was saying. Leaning over, his ear above her lips, he could just make out her raspy voice, "Kitchen . . . stove."

"Under the stove," he yelled to Wyatt.

Retrieving the extinguisher, Wyatt smashed open one of the kitchen windows near where the flames surrounding the house seemed to be at their smallest and began to attack the fire, eventually carving out a safe passage from the burning inferno.

"Okay," Wyatt called, climbing through the broken window.

Lifting Tessa's limp body up into his arms, Parker carried her quickly to the window, passing her through it and into Wyatt's waiting arms. Pulling himself through behind them, carefully avoiding the shattered glass.

Wyatt gently lowered Tessa to the ground, shrugging out of his jacket to cover her. Choking on the fresh air, Parker dropped down at her side, his fingers once again checking for her pulse.

"You okay?" he asked Wyatt.

Coughing too much to speak, his partner just nodded.

Taking several deep breaths, Parker fought to get his own breathing under control.

"I'm gonna go wait for the ambulance," Wyatt wheezed, heading off at a slow jog back down to the driveway.

Leaning over Tessa, who was struggling to breathe, unable to get enough oxygen into her smoke filled lungs. Her eyes were open and filled with panic as she desperately sucked in a shuddering breath, she stared up at him silently begging for help.

Ignoring the burning in his own lungs, Parker covered her mouth with his own and forced air into her lungs. "Stay with me, Tess," he begged. "Please."

Snow started to fall once again, the flames flickered and curled behind him, sirens sounded in the distance.

Help was on its way.

NOVEMBER 28TH

9:17 A.M.

It had been a long night, but, Parker mused, not an altogether unpleasant one.

The sirens had brought with them fire fighters who had immediately begun to attack the flames and paramedics who had intubated Tessa so they could breathe for her, then quickly bundled her into an ambulance and rushed her to the hospital.

He and Wyatt had also been brought to the hospital. They had been treated and released fairly quickly, suffering only mild smoke inhalation. They'd been inside the burning cottage only a couple of minutes, although at the time it had felt like hours. Tessa however had been in the house much long, her smoke inhalation had been more severe, it had been touch and go for a while but she was now stable.

While he'd been sitting around the hospital, he had begun to daydream about a life with Tessa. Parker had never had a serious relationship, he'd always been afraid that he was genetically predisposed to fail at relationships. As much as he loved his adopted parents, and the stable family they had given him, he always thought that the damage had already been done before he went to live with him.

Over the years, all through high school, college and the police academy, he had actively avoided any hint at a serious relationship. He avoided any social setting where he might meet someone, preferring to spend his time with Wyatt and his family, or his other married friends.

Tessa was different.

There was something about her that had awakened a deep need inside him. A longing to have someone to share his life with. He'd never felt like he was missing out on anything, until now. He wanted a wife, kids, a family.

"Feeling better?"

Parker looked up to see Wyatt standing over him. His partner looked refreshed in a clean blue suit that held not a hint of smoke, unlike Parker's own. Wyatt had gone home to be with his family after being released from the hospital several hours ago, while Parker had stayed in case there was any change in Tessa's condition. He had thought of going home and grabbing a couple of hours sleep, but he knew what he would dream. Plus, if the man who'd tried to kill Tessa learnt she was still alive and managed to track her down, he hadn't wanted her left alone and unprotected.

"Yep. You?"

"Kisses from my beautiful wife and my cute kids, and two hours sleep? I feel like a million bucks." Wyatt handed him a cup of coffee and dropped into the seat beside him. "You get any sleep?"

Rubbing tired eyes, Parker tried not to be jealous that Wyatt had a family to sustain him, while he had nothing and no one. Pulling off the lid he stared at the steaming liquid. "This is black," he looked up surprised.

"Thought you could use it," Wyatt shrugged.

Swallowing several mouthfuls of the burning coffee. "Right now I'd trade sleep for clothes that didn't reek of smoke."

"Then I am your fairy godfather," Wyatt held out a bag. "I dropped by your place on my way back here."

"You are a life saver," he smiled, rifling through the bag that contained a clean shirt, pair of pants, sweater and a scarf.

"Go change, then we'll interview Tessa."

"Interview Tessa?" In the excitement of the fire and his daydreams of a bright and happy future, Parker had forgotten the reason that they had been at Tessa's place in the first place. "I don't know if she's up for that yet." Or that I am he thought.

Shooting him an incredulous look. "Parker, it's the 28th, he'll be killing another woman tonight, he's probably stalking her as we speak. We need to convince Tessa to tell us the truth and tell us who the girls are in the photo."

"We don't even know that we have the right link," he insisted, desperate to protect Tessa.

Raising an eyebrow, Wyatt didn't like to lose his temper, his usual way of expressing displeasure or annoyance was to subtly raise one eyebrow. "Parker, are you forgetting that she lied to us? To you? She sat as close to you as I am now, looked you right in the eye and told you that she didn't know those girls. Those *dead* girls."

"No I haven't forgotten. She was scared, and probably in shock and denial. But someone tried to kill her, Wyatt, now it's real to her. I'm sure she'll tell us whatever she knows." Snatching the bag of clothes from Wyatt's hand he stalked off to change, his good mood evaporated.

Changing quickly into the black pants, crisp white shirt and sweater, the same shade of caramel as his eyes, that Wyatt had packed, finishing up he met Wyatt at the door to Tessa's hospital room.

"You want me to go in alone?" Wyatt offered.

Glaring at him, Parker said nothing just opened the door quietly, expecting to see Tessa asleep in the bed. The doctors had stitched the wound to her head and determined that she did not have a concussion. Her breathing had improved to the point where they had taken her off the ventilator, although they were continuing with oxygen therapy, and her doctors wanted to keep her in the hospital under observation for another couple of days to monitor her lungs.

Instead of resting, Tessa was standing next to the bed rifling through a bag that one of the female detectives had sent over with some clothes for her to wear when she was discharged.

Hearing the door open her head snapped up. "Do you know where my dogs are?" she asked them without preamble. Her face was deathly pale, her small body looked even thinner than the day they'd met, the deep red gash on her forehead stood out in stark contrast to her white skin. Still, despite the headache that must be pounding inside her head, she stood alert and at attention.

When neither of them answered she tapped her foot in frustration. "My dogs?" she repeated her voice still croaky and hoarse from all the smoke she had inhaled.

Recovering, "They're fine. Whoever attacked you locked them in the main house," Parker assured her. Resisting the urge to pull her into his arms, stroke her hair and whisper to her that everything would be okay.

"I think you're supposed to be in bed," Wyatt told her.

Narrowing her eyes, she shot him a look that clearly said that she thought he was an idiot, and resumed pulling clothes from the bag.

Nudging him, Wyatt gestured at Tessa, Parker shrugged and Wyatt rolled his eyes and crossed over to her. "You lied to us, Tessa."

Ignoring him, she laid out clothes on the bed and began to pull her blonde curls into a ponytail.

"I'm going to ask you again. Do you know the women in the photos we showed you the other day?"

"No."

Frustrated Parker stalked over to her, Wyatt stepped out of his way. Placing his hands on her shoulders and forcing her to look at him. Up close he saw that her eyelashes were not white like the rest of her hair but a deep, dark black. "Tessa, we know that they went to your school, tell us who they are," he implored.

Her cool blue eyes bored into him as though she could see deep down inside him and into his very soul. "I don't know what you are talking about," pulling away, she went back to fixing her hair.

Throwing up his hands in frustration, "Tessa!" He walked to the window and ran his fingers through his thick black hair, struggling for calm.

"We could arrest you for obstruction," Wyatt said, hoping a threat might motivate her to talk.

"Go ahead, I'm right here," she shot back, undaunted.

Changing track, "Did you see who attacked you?" Wyatt asked.

"No."

"Do you have any idea who it could be?"

"No," louder

"Do you know who abducted Janice?"

"No," louder still.

"Do you know who killed Tiffany, Bianca and Dorothy?"

"No," she screamed, finally stopping what she was doing to glare at them.

"Tell us what you do remember then," Wyatt kept his voice calm, but Parker could see the almost imperceptible tremble in his jaw.

"I got back from the store. I went upstairs to change. Someone hit me from behind. I passed out, and the next thing I remember is waking up tied to the chair, the room full of smoke. I must have passed out again because when I opened my eyes next you two were there. That's it. That's all I know."

Incredulous Parker went to her. "Tessa, you're lying and we are just trying to help you," he entreated.

Her blue eye practically shooting arrows at him. "I didn't ask for your help and I don't need it."

Thrusting the photo at her. "Who are they, Tessa?" he asked his own irritation rising at her stubbornness.

Taking the photo with a trembling hand, she held it gingerly, staring at it as though it were precious gold. A ghost of something passed fleetingly across her face as she looked at it, but it was gone as quickly as it had appeared.

"He's going to kill them all, Tessa," he said softly. "Tell me who they are so I can save them."

Her fingers gently traced the faces on the photo. "I can't," she whispered so quietly he wasn't sure she'd even said anything.

"Let me help you," he reached a hand to her cheek and gently stroked it. A flicker of fear and longing flashed briefly through her eyes. "Tell me who they are so we can save them."

Her face turned stony again and she pulled abruptly away from him. "I don't know anything about your serial killer," she threw the photo at him.

His patience evaporating Parker barely resisted the urge to grab Tessa and shake her until the answers he needed tumbled out. "You are being unreasonable. If you know who they are, if you know who *he* is then just tell us. He tried to kill you, when he finds out that you're still alive he'll come back. We can protect you . . ."

"This isn't just about me," she yelled at him.

"So you do know what's going on," his frustration quickly mounting.

"Just leave it be, it's none of your business."

"I'm trying to help you." Aware their argument sounded more like a lover's quarrel than a police interrogation.

"I didn't ask you to," her voice catching she started to cough.

Staring into her eyes, it felt like he was drowning. Looking into her eyes was like looking into the ocean. Deep, bottomless and seemingly empty, but you knew that something was always swimming, unseen, just below the surface. Finally breaking contact, her eyes were as hypnotic as waves in the sea. "You are impossible," running his hands over his face.

"Look, Detective Bell," she spat out his name vehemently. "Sometimes in life there are questions that we just don't need to have the answers to. This is one of these times. Just leave it alone. It is not your problem. It's mine. Please, just leave me alone," the last a mere weary murmur, her strength failing she swayed unsteadily.

Grabbing her before she could topple to the floor, Parker lowered her carefully into a chair and knelt in front of her. "Try to take some deep breaths," he told her. She did, and coughed some more before lowering her head to her hands. Letting her rest for a moment then hooking a finger under her chin he nudged softly until she lifted her eyes to look at him. "He's going to kill you, Tessa," he said gently.

"Then so be it," she replied evenly.

Pushing tiredly to her feet, she grabbed a pair of jeans and a rose and lavender striped sweater from the bed and headed to the small bathroom. "I'm going to get dressed and then I'm going home," she announced without looking back.

"Your house is a crime scene, Tessa," Wyatt reminded her.

"I'll stay in the main house," she said in a voice that brokered no argument. He would have missed the shudder that rippled almost undetectably through her as she mentioned the mansion had he not been looking for it. She obviously hated that place with a vengeance.

"We'll drive you," Parker told her, hoping he could talk some sense into her on the way to her destroyed cottage.

"Fine," she replied tightly. "I'll meet you in the parking lot in ten minutes." With that, she entered the bathroom and closed the door, he heard the lock turn.

"Well that was a disaster."

Glowering at Wyatt he stalked from the room.

* * * * *

12:09 P.M.

Gliding down the highway, careful to remain just below the speed limit, Tessa was on the way to meet her friends.

To put an end to this once and for all.

She'd quickly located the car they'd left for her in the hospital car park without a hitch. After she'd been treated and some of her strength had returned, she had made a phone call organizing a meeting for today.

Her lungs still burned, but at least she could take a shallow breath without dissolving into fits of wracking coughs. Her head was still pounding, but thankfully the world had stopped spinning. She had left the hospital without being discharged, after dressing quickly in the bathroom, via another door in order to avoid the detectives.

Tessa hoped they weren't too mad at her, they seemed like good people, but right now she didn't have the time or energy to string them along, she had things to take care of. This had gone on long enough, there was no way she was going to let him hurt another person. Once she had seen her friends she was going to find him, leaving the others to deal with the police. Confident that no one would spill their secret, they all knew the stakes.

Thinking back to her conversation with Parker, Detective Bell, she realized how close she herself had come to telling him everything. The gentle way he had stroked her cheek, his intense, caring, caramel eyes that seemed to see right inside of her. He had been strong and solid, and he had risked his life to save her. The need to lean on him had been overwhelming and she had almost given in to temptation and told him the whole story.

When his strong arms had gone around her, stopping her from crumpling to the ground, for a split second she had felt safe for the first time in her life. Tessa had wanted to give him not just the answers to his questions but herself. She had seen the longing in his eyes when he had held her. He wanted her. She wanted him, she'd admit it, but she also knew that she could never have him.

As a child Tessa had learnt the hard way never to trust anyone. If life had taught her anything, it was that you relied upon yourself and yourself alone. That didn't stop her from wanting someone though, she was so tired of being alone. However, she knew that she would only ruin a relationship. She ruined everything that she touched.

Sighing tiredly, she was starting to think that leaving the hospital so soon had been a bad idea. Turning off the main road, she travelled a little way down a bumping lane that would take her to their meeting point. It was their special place. A quiet place in the middle of the woods where no one could find them. A place they had gone when they needed to be alone. Climbing from the car, she closed her eyes and leant against it for a moment until her head stopped spinning.

Although it was only midday it was dark and gloomy out, the clouds were still thick and grey, snowflakes still wafting slowly towards the ever-growing carpet that blanketed the ground. Reaching the spot she saw that she was the last to arrive, she stood in the shadows for a moment flashing back to the long ago afternoons they had spent here. They were all there, all that were left anyway, Melanie, Lauren, Carrie, Michelle and Gina, sitting around the picnic table that they had made themselves.

Spotting her, they hurried over. "Tessa, you look terrible," Carrie took her arm and helped her over to the table.

"I told you that you shouldn't have left the hospital," Michelle, an ER doctor, took her wrist and began to check her pulse.

"I'm fine," she told them, pushing away Michelle's well-meaning hands.

Michelle was not to be put off. "No, you're not. Do you have a concussion?" she asked as she peered into Tessa's eyes.

Shaking her head. "No."

"Smoke inhalation from the fire?" Michelle continued.

"Yes."

"How bad? Were you intubated?"

"Yes," she reluctantly admitted, they didn't have time to discuss her medical condition.

"Tessa," Michelle exclaimed. "You should still be in the hospital on oxygen."

"I'll be fine, but the police know that we all went to Harlwood. They have a photo of us, the one from the equestrian competition when we were twelve, but they don't have your names. It's only by some fluke that they got mine. Apparently he made some list for the police with clues on it instead of our names."

"So they have no idea who we are?" Lauren confirmed.

"Not yet. But they went to the school, so it's only a matter of time before Mrs. McKreeney sends the police your information."

"Do they know what happened?" Gina asked timidly.

Giving them all an encouraging smile, "No, and there's no way they can find out. If none of us tell them, and we all agreed that we wouldn't, then there's no one else who knows." She paused and looked around at each of their faces, the faces of the only people she had ever been able to count on. "We all agreed that we would keep this secret no matter what, that we would take it with us to our graves, but if anyone wants to back out then now is the time to do it."

Looking at each of the serious faces staring back at her, they all shook their heads. "We're in this to the end," Lauren said answering for all of them.

Nodding in relief, she smiled at them, there was no weak link in their group. "Okay then. There's one more thing . . ." she took a deep breath to calm her racing heart. "I'm going after him."

"Tessa, no," Melanie cried out.

"You should be in the hospital not chasing after a madman," Michelle told her.

Shivering, suddenly cold. "My mind is made up. If I go to him I can get him to leave the rest of you . . ."

"We agreed to death . . ." Carrie interrupted.

"I know we did, but there's no reason for all of us to die. This is not just about us, we agreed we'd do whatever we had to in order to protect them." They all fell silent as they thought about the reason they were all prepared to die for this secret, and knew that she was right.

Frowning Melanie broke the silence, "Someone's coming," she announced consulting her cell phone which was linked to the surveillance set-up surrounding the small clearing.

"What?" Lauren exclaimed. "No one knows about this place."

Patting her pockets Tessa pulled out a GPS chip. "Detective Bell and Detective Wyatt, they planted this on me," shaking her head, she held it up for them to see. "If I wasn't so out of it I would have figured it out," she shrugged apologetically. "Oh well they would have found you guys eventually. Gina you're next on his list, be prepared. Melanie when the time is right I'll need a distraction."

They sat in silence as they waited for Detective Bell and Detective Wyatt. Tessa almost laughed as the police tried to approach them inconspicuously. There was no way to sneak up on a group of geniuses that had spent their lives being paranoid and secretive. Deciding to put them out of their misery, she pushed wearily to her feet and stood in the middle of the clearing, "we know you're there, Detectives."

A moment later Detective Bell and Detective Wyatt and four or five other police officers appeared from the trees. "That was a dirty trick," she offered them a weak smile. "These are my friends, Melanie, Gina . . ." her mind seemed to stop working, "Lauren . . ."

The world started to spiral, her vision tunneled, and the ground felt like it was rocking violently beneath her feet. Legs giving out, she expected to hit the hard, rough ground and was surprised when instead her landing was soft and warm. Someone called her name but she was too tired to answer. Hands touched her, voices swirled around about, someone lifted her . . . carried her . . . then nothing.

* * * * *

2:24 P.M.

So angry he thought he would explode.

Tessa was ruining everything.

Somehow the police had found out about her, and she had led them straight to the others. Now they were all sitting inside a police station. He wasn't worried that they would give up their secret, but about how he was going to get to them.

He had been following Gina de Van when she had driven to the hospital dropped off her car and then been picked up by Lauren Angel. He'd followed them, at a distance, out into the country where they had stopped near a small clearing. It hadn't taken him long to figure out that this was their special place, the place they had gone to get away from him.

Knowing the girls as he did he'd guessed immediately that they would have set up surveillance around the site, so he had hung back, waiting to see where they would go next. When the police had arrived it had taken all of his self-control not to grab his gun and shoot everyone on the spot.

Now sitting outside the station some of his anger had dissipated. It wasn't as bad as it seemed. The girls would refuse to say anything, the police would eventually let them go and he would finish what he started.

* * * * *

6:41 P.M.

"They are all insane," Parker was fuming.

It had been an infuriating couple of hours interviewing Tessa's friends. They had given their names, but had refused to answer any questions about their past or the killer.

After passing out in his arms, Tessa had come to in the back of Wyatt's car. Her doctor friend had checked her out and recommended, insisted, that she go straight back to the hospital.

But Tessa had steadfastly refused, glaring at them all from eyes glazed with an undercurrent of pain.

Her betrayal had been like a knife through his heart. He had known it was a bad idea to let himself fall for another victim in a case and yet he had stupidly pushed rationality aside and let himself be seduced by her beauty and mystique. After waiting in the hospital's parking lot for nearly half an hour, they had gone up to her room to find it deserted. Luckily Wyatt had slipped a GPS into the pockets of her jacket, they had activated it and followed her out into the country.

His heart had momentarily melted, his defenses coming down, when she had collapsed. Holding her small, limp body in his arms had weakened his resolve. But her stubborn refusal upon regaining consciousness to say anything even remotely helpful had quickly reignited his anger.

"I think we should show her the video," Wyatt announced from his desk opposite Parker's own. While his partner's desk was a messy stack of papers and old coffee cups, his own was perfectly ordered, the papers in neat stacks, and the rubbish all piled in the bin.

"Of Dorothy being killed?"

"I know what you're going to say. She's been through a lot, someone tried to kill her, we shouldn't upset . . ." Wyatt began defending himself.

"No, I think it's a great idea. It might actually get her talking." Ignoring his conscience that was telling him he was only trying to hurt Tessa like she had hurt him.

Grabbing the copy of the video that sat on the top of the neat stack of papers pertaining to the case, he marched off towards the interview room where Tessa was waiting.

Arms folded on the table, her head resting on them, she looked tiredly up at them as they entered. Her face was ashen, her eyes slightly unfocused as she gazed at them with tired indifference. His resolve weakening again so he forged quickly onwards before he had a chance to back out.

"We've got something here that we think you should see," he told her, deliberately avoiding looking at her as he slipped the disk into the player. Tessa said nothing just shrugged disinterestedly, nodded her head wearily and waited.

Sitting on the table, making sure he kept his back to her, the three sat in silence as he pressed play and the TV sprung to life.

Chancing a cautious look at Tessa as Dorothy appeared on the screen. She was sitting rigidly in her chair, her eyes devoid of any emotion, staring unblinkingly, at her friend. Her face a cool, expressionless mask, as Dorothy spoke her final words and had the life choked from her.

Her apparent coldness was the icing on the cake of the anger that had been bubbling beneath the surface, held down by sheer force of will, for the last few months. Ever since he had been forced to put a bullet through the heart of fourteen-year-old Gina O'Hara.

He'd had enough.

Hurling the remote across the room and through the TV screen. Wyatt jumped as the glass shattered into a thousand pieces. Tessa sat as though she was carved from marble, empty eyes staring straight ahead.

"What is the matter with you?" he screamed, his voice reverberating off the walls of the small room making it seem even louder.

She did not move or even flinch. It was like she hadn't even heard him. Getting in her face he continued to rant, her passive face staring back at him. Now that he had blown the lid off his rage, he could not re-bottle it. "You are really something. She is supposed to be your friend. You just watched her die. Strangled by a psychopath. How can you just sit there? What? You can't even shed a single tear for her?"

"Parker," Wyatt shot him a warning look but he was beyond caring.

"You are cold. How you can watch this and not feel anything? Why on earth are you protecting him? He your lover or . . .?"

"That's enough," Wyatt pushed him out of the way and knelt in front of Tessa, waving a hand in front of her unblinking eyes. She didn't respond. She was trembling, so he shrugged out of his jacket and draped it across her shoulders, giving her a gentle shake. "Tessa?"

Parker watched unmoved. Drained and empty from his outburst.

"Get her doctor friend in here," Wyatt yelled at him, a hand on Tessa's wrist, the other stroking her cheek. She looked almost catatonic.

Before guilt could start to prick his conscience Parker left the room without looking back. "Wyatt needs help in there," he called out as he kept walking.

"Parker," J.J. yelled.

Ignoring him, he kept going.

"Parker!" J.J. yelled again, more insistently.

Almost there, he assured himself, as he entered the lifts, the door sliding closed, and he was alone.

* * * * *

8:13 P.M.

Slipping quietly from the police station, Gina de Van knew that she was walking to her death.

Since being brought to the station from their place in the woods, she had not had a chance to talk to any of the others. The police had kept them separated, presumably because they thought it would help to break them. The last several hours had been spent sitting in a cramped room being interrogated by a Detective Victoria Baker and Detective Thomas Keller.

They had asked her the same questions over and over again.

Who was the killer? Why was he trying to kill them? Was this secret really worth dying for? No comment, no comment, yes.

During her hours in the police station it had grown dark outside. The snow was still fluttering silently to the ground, the moon shone brightly through the clouds.

Passing an alley, she was not surprised when a hand was clamped over her mouth, another pinning her arms to her side.

"Guess who?" mocked a familiar voice in her ear.

She was pulled backwards into the shadows. He spun her around and pushed her against a cold brick wall, and she saw the face that haunted not just her nightmares but every waking minute of her life.

Gina was ready to die.

Keeping one hand pressed against her chest he pulled a syringe from his pocket and plunged it into her shoulder. The effect was almost immediate. She felt woozy, her limbs suddenly heavy, he lowered her to the ground and propped her up against the wall.

"Anyone give anything away in there?" he asked, leaning so close she could feel his breath against her face.

"You know better than that," she told him, her voice sounding far away to her own ears.

Giving her his familiar smug smile. "Tell me where they are and I'll let you go."

She gave a weak laugh. "We both know you have no intention of letting any of us go alive, and even if you did I've had enough. What you did to us ruined my life."

He shrugged, and pulled a small video camera out of a backpack. "We're gonna make a little farewell film. This is what I want you to say," he showed her a board with her lines written out on it.

Moving away from her, he held up the camera and pressed play. She stared back sullenly at him, she had no intention of playing his ridiculous game. If he wanted to kill her, fine, but she would have no part of this. He frowned at her and waved his cardboard script, she smiled sweetly at him but said nothing.

Rage flaring in his eyes he pulled on a ski mask, set the camera on a trashcan and came towards her. Setting the board on her lap so that the camera could capture it, he then readied another syringe. Before injecting her he leant in close to her ear, "She'll pay for this," he murmured.

Something glinted in the moonlight.

Then a dull burning sensation ripped through her wrists and the world faded to black.

* * * * *

8:29 P.M.

Stalking up the ramp from the station's underground parking garage Parker frowned as he saw that it was still snowing. Once again, the snow did nothing to calm his frazzled nerves, the sticky wet flakes irritating him as they stuck to everything in sight. He tried to remember where he had left his car, Wyatt had driven him to Dorothy's murder scene two days ago and he hadn't been home since.

Shrugging he decided to walk, maybe it would help him work out some of his anger, sitting in the dark cold garage for the last hour certainly hadn't helped. Crossing the alley beside the station, he was almost knocked over as a white van came screeching out then rocketed off down the street. Muttering under his breath he was about to continue when he realized something wasn't right. Nothing opened onto the alley, it was a dead end, there shouldn't be any cars coming from it.

Running down the alley he almost tripped over the unconscious body of Gina de Van. She was lying propped up against the wall, eyes closed, face white, an ever-growing pool of blood spreading slowly around her.

Her wrists had been slashed.

Flashing back in time. Six months ago. His stressed and exhausted mind jumping frantically from half formed thought to half formed thought.

He had gone alone, to check on her, on Gina, Gina O'Hara, to see how she was doing. She was only fourteen, pregnant and alone. Her mother died when she was eight, her own boyfriend had killed her father. She had seen him do it. She'd been so scared, so vulnerable, she had needed someone, and she'd reached out to him. He too was alone in life. His sister gone, his adoptive parents deceased, his biological mother in prison.

She had not heard him arrive, had not known he was watching as she held the gun over her newborn daughter. He remembered her eyes, the biggest, brownest eyes he had ever seen. When she saw him, realization dawning not only in her eyes but in his own as well. She had been chillingly and completely in control. Grabbing the baby and clutching it to her chest as a human shield. Speaking in a calm, cool voice as she bragged about her crimes, admitting everything. Her gun never wavering as she held it aimed directly at his head.

Reasoning with her had proved fruitless. He had talked with her, begged with her, pleaded with her. None of which had any affect. At the last, she had released the safety, pointed the gun at the baby's tiny head and told him that it was all his fault. That he had failed her just like everyone else in her life.

The roar of the gun had ripped through the still night.

He had been surprised as he watched the red spot blossoming on her chest. Gina fell to the ground still clutching her baby. He'd run to her, performed first aid even though it was clear she was already dead. Then he had just sat, holding the crying baby in his arms, and wept. That was how Wyatt and the others had found him when they had arrived.

There had been no other choice he knew that. On the job he had shot to kill before but that had been different. That had been fully grown men, evil men who had killed and tortured. Not a baby-faced child with freckles and pigtails. She had been just a little girl. So young.

In his dreams she fell as she had that night. Her eyes locked onto his. He had been unable to look away. Watching surprise flash through her eyes and then nothing.

She had betrayed him, used him, he knew that. But he had betrayed her too. He had been so caught up in himself, of the feeling of having someone to care for, that he had not seen what had been right in front of his eyes the whole time. He had not seen her for what she really was. If he had maybe he could have gotten her the help that she needed. Maybe she would still be alive.

Coming back to the present, he dropped down beside Gina de Van's limp body, yanked his cell phone from his pants pocket and called for help. Shrugging out of his sweater, he pulled his shirt over his head, not bothering with the buttons. Ripping the shirt he grabbed one of Gina's hands and wrapped part of his shirt tightly around her wounded wrist, then reached for the other to do the same.

"Gina?" he kept a hand wrapped tightly around each of her bloody wrists. "Gina, can you hear me? My name's Parker, I'm a police officer. You're safe now, he's gone."

There was no response.

"Come on, Gina, stay with me. An ambulance is on its way, okay. We'll get you to the hospital and you'll be fine. Just stay with me," he begged.

Footsteps sounded and someone called his name, help was on its way, but he knew that it was too late. Gina de Van was going to die. Just like Gina O'Hara had died. Just like Tiffany Poppy, Bianca Kingston, and Dorothy Dallas had died. Just like Lauren Angel, Carrie Marble, Michelle Joseph, Melanie Gardner and Janice Peters would soon.

Just like Tessa would.

It seemed that death was surrounding him from every side and there was nothing he could do to stop it.

Then, "Parker," a voice whispered weakly from beneath him as Wyatt appeared and dropped down at his side, clamping his hand around one of Gina's slashed wrists.

Gina's eyes were slowly opening, staring blankly up at him. "Gina? Can you hear me?"

Slowly she nodded, her breath coming in gasps.

Looking at Wyatt for confirmation, then back to Gina, "An ambulance is on its way, just hold on okay."

Nodding again.

"Gina, who is he? Tell me his name, please. So we can save the others."

Her eyes cleared as she focused on him. Her mouth moved but he couldn't hear her. Leaning down so his ear brushed her lips, "Can't . . . sorry," she wheezed.

Before he could protest, sirens sounded in the distance, coming quickly closer. "Go wait for them, show them where we are," he ordered, taking Gina's other wrist from Wyatt's hand. "Gina, please," her strength fading she was losing consciousness. "Gina, stay with me honey, come on," her breathing becoming more even as she passed out. "No. No," he couldn't lose another person. "Gina, come on, come on."

Hands on his shoulders pulled him up as the paramedics squatted at Gina's side. Reluctantly letting go of Gina's wrists so the medics could bandage them. "She gonna make it?"

Bundling her onto a stretcher. "She's lost a lot of blood, blood pressure's dropping," the paramedic shrugged. "Fifty, fifty."

Following them down the alley towards the ambulance. "I'm going with her," he announced. Helping them load Gina into the back of the ambulance and climbing in behind it.

* * * * *

9:12 P.M.

Breathing deeply he surveyed the room. It was a mess. Just like his carefully laid plans. And it was all Tessa's fault. She had ruined everything. Just like she had ten years ago.

Anger simmering the entire ride back from the station it had exploded when he had reached the house. He had trashed most of the downstairs rooms, throwing things through windows, breaking furniture, punching holes in doors and walls, until finally he was too exhausted to continue.

He had waited so long for his revenge, planned it all so carefully, and Tessa had no right to try to take it from him. After what had happened all those years ago, he had bounced around the country moving from meaningless job to meaningless job. He had tried to recreate things everywhere he had gone but nothing had compared to what he had had here.

Staring at the chaos around him, he forced himself to regain control of his emotions. He was sure that Gina would not survive. He had been so flustered when he heard the footsteps approaching that he had left behind the script. The script that he had labored so thoughtfully over that Gina had refused to read. What a waste. It had been an absolute stroke of genius to stage her death as a suicide.

The police would soon be on to him. They had the girls, they had the link it wouldn't take them long to figure out who it was that they were looking for. Taking a long, slow, deep breath, he counted to ten to calm himself, and figured out a new plan. If he ditched Lauren, Carrie, Michelle and Melanie, he could still get Tessa. And, he gleefully reminded himself, he still had Janice.

Feeling more at peace, he smiled and headed for the stairs.

* * * * *

10:02 P.M.

Standing as a doctor walked down the hall towards him. Parker tried to read the doctor's blank face to see if the news was good or bad.

"Detective?" the middle aged woman asked upon reaching him.

"Yeah."

"You were the one that came in with Gina de Van?" she confirmed.

"Did she make it?"

Sympathy flicking in her eyes. "I'm sorry she died a few moments ago. She lost too much blood there was nothing more we could do."

Despair washing over him even though this was the news he had been expecting. "But she was awake and talking to me," he protested weakly.

"I'm sorry," the doctor repeated.

Nodding, Parker turned without another word and headed for the hospital's small dingy bathroom.

Inside he splashed cold water over his clammy skin, enjoying the icy feel of the water on his face. Looking at himself in the dirty mirror he saw that he looked drained, he was pale, dark circles under his eyes, the stress of the last few months had taken its toll on him.

Rushing to one of the toilets he threw up.

* * * * *

11:27 P.M.

Lying alone in the dark Janice knew what was coming.

When she'd heard him trashing the place she knew that things had not gone well. She wasn't sure whom he was up to on his list. It was hard to keep track of things lying here tied to the bed. He came every now and then to give her something to eat and drink, the rest of the time she reflected on things, her life and stuff.

She had figured out where they were. The place he had chosen had to be the house where Tessa and her friend Eleanor had been taken when they were abducted.

The place where Eleanor had been killed.

No one knew exactly what had happened to Tessa that weekend. She had never told a single living soul, not even one of her best friends. But Janice knew that whatever had happened to her, whatever she had seen had changed her forever. She had never been the same after that.

If Janice was right about where they were, and if she was right about what he intended to do to Tessa, and she was sure that she was, then he had chosen the most horrific setting possible. He had also made sure that he had chosen a setting where nobody would think to look for them. Nobody knew where Tessa had been taken. She was not even sure how he had figured it out, but somehow he had.

Footsteps clomped slowly up the stairs towards her room and she readied herself for what was to come. The key turned in the lock and the door swung slowly open, he flipped on the light, making her eyes squint reflexively closed. She heard him move towards the bed. Forcing her eyes open against the glare, she saw him looming over her and felt fifteen all over again.

"I know where we are," Janice told him.

Smiling savagely. "Perfect setting don't you think?"

"You are going to burn in hell," she spat at him.

He said nothing, just pulled back the covers, revealing the clothes he had dressed her in earlier. An exact replica of her Harlwood Academy School uniform.

"It'll be just like old times," he whispered in her ear as he climbed on top of her.

NOVEMBER 29TH

Another night spent in a hospital.

It had been almost three hours since the doctor had told him that Gina had died. After throwing up in the bathroom Parker had cleaned himself up and headed for the door intending to call himself a cab and head home for a couple of hours sleep. But had found himself unable to leave. He'd been sitting here in the waiting room completely oblivious to the hustle and bustle of the hospital's emergency room.

Recalling the many times he had been through ER's while he was living in foster care. He had spent three years in the last, and worst, foster home that he and Mattie had lived in. His foster parent's only biological son had taken great pleasure in tormenting the smaller children who came and went. The property had been out in the country, quiet and secluded, no one around to hear them scream.

The boy, Malcolm, had been tall and thin, with long, stringy black hair that hung to his shoulder, and small, evil, soulless, black eyes. Malcolm burnt the bottom of the children's feet with cigarettes and snapped little bones like they were nothing more than sticks. Parker himself had had both his arms broken by the boy.

Malcolm's favorite way to torture his young foster siblings was to lock them in a closet strapped into a straightjacket he had picked up somewhere along the way. Fighting back panic and the urge to struggle uselessly against the straightjacket, crying out only made things worse, Malcolm would return and do something even more terrible.

Chest tightening as his mind flashed back to the terrified little boy he had been back then, the complete darkness in the closet so dense it was like you could feel it. To this day he couldn't wear a jacket, or stand confined places, the familiar feelings of being trapped and helpless would come flooding back.

When Malcolm was done torturing them he left would leave them in one of the beds in the giant room that was shared by all the children living there at the time, sometimes up to twenty. His foster parents had known what was going on, what their son was doing, but had done nothing to stop it. When they had discovered one of the bloody, broken children, they had simply driven them to one of the nearby hospitals with a weak excuse as to how the injuries had occurred. Then delivered them straight back into the waiting arms of their malicious, psychopathic son.

"I'm really sorry, Parker," a voice said from above him.

He started, blinking to clear his blurred vision, and saw Wyatt hovering anxiously over him. He said nothing just stared at his friend, he was not in the mood to talk.

Wyatt handed him a bag. "Your fairy godfather is back."

Looking in the bag he found another clean outfit and gave a reluctant smile. "Thanks."

Wyatt sat beside him. "You look terrible," he said mildly.

Nodding, Parker knew that he must. His shirt and sweater had been drenched in blood and he had been too weary to find anything else to wear, so he sat bare-chested, his face and body still streaked with Gina's blood.

"You tell them?" he asked referring to Tessa and her friends.

"Yeah."

"How'd they react?"

Shrugging, "They weren't surprised, and they're still not saying anything."

Sighing and rubbing tired eyes, he hadn't slept in days. He never slept regularly, it came with being a cop, but everything that had happened in the last six months had really started to wear on him. "He wanted to stage it to make it look like a suicide."

"Yeah I know, we read the script, but something happened to ruin it, he never filmed her. Maybe she wouldn't go for it. What exactly did you see?"

"Not much. Just a white van, it was too dark to see inside and I didn't get a plate." Their one chance to get something concrete on this guy and he'd blown it. He'd been too distracted by his own irritation over Tessa to pay attention.

"The van came out of nowhere, you weren't expecting it. Give yourself a break. Hey, I got some good news for you."

Parker looked over at him skeptically. "What?"

"Marty found a print on the cardboard, I don't think he was planning on leaving that behind. I think you spooked him. Anyway why don't you clean up and change, then I'll drop you off at your place so you can catch a few hours sleep."

"You going back to the station?"

"Yeah, thought I'd have another crack at the girls. Maybe they'll be more talkative now that Gina's death has sunk in."

Raising a disbelieving eyebrow.

"It's worth a shot," Wyatt told him. "Better than doing nothing anyway."

"I'll go with you," he pushed wearily to his feet.

Wyatt stood too. "Parker, I think maybe you need . . ."

"I'm fine," he interrupted.

"If you think you're up for it maybe you could take another shot at Tessa, I think she wants to open up to you." Seeing his hesitant face Wyatt continued softly, "She's not Gina. She's not going to betray you. I know you've been feeling really lonely lately, I think she'd be good for you. Once we find the serial killer who wants her dead of course. You're my best friend, I want you to be happy, if you think she can do that, Parker, then go for it. I don't want to see you miss out on your chance at happiness because you're scared."

He wasn't ready to go there yet. "Give me a minute," he said and left to find a quiet spot to change.

* * * * *

2:48 A.M.

Sitting alone in the dark Tessa readied herself for what was to come. She was exhausted, her head still ached, her lungs still burned, but she was ready. In a way she wished that she had done it all those years ago.

When she had seen Dorothy tied to the car, blood streaking her face, it had taken everything in her not to bolt for the door. Her eyes had been fixed on Dorothy's face and she'd hardly even seen what *he* was doing.

Detective Wyatt had been worried about her, he'd called for Michelle to come and check her out. He had wanted to take her straight back to the hospital but she had refused. She needed to stay here so that when the time was right she could disappear, she needed help from her friends to do that. Besides after what she'd done last time they would have put a cop on her door if she'd gone to the hospital.

Instead, they had brought her here, to a room filled with bunks, she assumed it was where the officers slept if they were working a case and didn't have time to go home. After setting her up in here several hours ago, they had left her alone to rest. They had not even come to tell her that Gina had been killed. Gina had wanted to die, she'd never said it but Tessa could tell, she had had enough. She couldn't cope with what he had done, with what they had done, anymore.

Her thoughts straying to Detective Bell. To the way that he had looked at her when he'd made her watch that video. To the things that he had said to her. He had called her cold, asked how she could watch without shedding a tear. It had taken every ounce of her strength not to completely break down. Detective Bell had asked why she was protecting him, but nothing could be further from the truth. She wasn't protecting him, she wished he were dead. She was protecting her friends. When he had suggested that this monster was her lover she had almost been physically sick.

How could he think those things about her? She thought that he was different. The way that he had looked at her had made her feel like she was the only person in the world. She had allowed herself to develop feelings for him, something she never ever did, she'd permitted it because he was damaged, just like her. She knew it from the moment that she saw him climb from the car in front of her house.

She wanted him, but she could never have him, and now she wasn't even sure if he wanted her anyway.

Growing up in her house had taught her nothing about how to be part of a family. Her mother suffered from depression and was emotionally abusive, her father abandoned them when she was ten, and her big brother had left home two years later. She used to dream about having a real family, with a mom and dad who loved each other, and lots of brothers and sisters. But that was not her reality, and she knew nothing about being part of a real family. Even if she did, after everything that she had done she didn't deserve one.

Thoughts wandering again to Detective Bell's cold, hard, angry eyes staring at her she felt the dam inside her ready to burst. It was all too much, everything that had happened years ago, the murders, the fire, the lies, the secrets and everything that was still to come.

Drawing her knees up to her chest, she wrapped her arms tightly around them, buried her head and let herself cry. Great heaving sobs that wracked her aching chest, she almost welcomed the searing physical pain that matched her emotional pain so perfectly.

Unaware of Detective Bell's presence until he sat on the bed beside her and pulled her against him, his arms firmly encircling her. Surprised, at first she tried to pull away, she could not afford to let herself lean on anyone at this point. But he wouldn't let her go, holding her tightly and softly pushing her head down against his chest.

Relenting she allowed herself to rest against him, her hands grabbing fistfuls of his sweater as she cried, clinging to him as though he were her lifeline.

He cradled her head with one hand, the other stroking her back soothingly. "It's okay," he said gruffly. "Shh, it's okay."

Holding her until her sobs slowly ceased, she stayed snuggled safely against him, unwilling to leave the security of his arms.

Eventually he gently pulled back, not letting her go instead holding her at arms length. "Let me help you," he implored, wiping away a stray tear from her cheek.

"I can't. I want to but I can't." Whenever she was around him the urge to tell him everything was overwhelming, she had never felt that way before.

"You're shaking," he took one of the blankets from the bed and draped it around her shoulders, rubbing her arms to warm her.

Wavering, Tessa knew that if she stayed near him, letting him touch her, comfort her, then she was going to give in and reveal all. Physical proximity invariably brought about emotional closeness, and that was something she just couldn't afford right now.

Walking to the window, she stood watching the snow, and thinking about the people out there going about their lives, happy and content, and wished desperately that she was one of them. "I'm sorry, Detective Bell," she whispered, and she truly was. Any pretence that she did not know who the killer was gone, he knew she knew, and she was not going to insult his intelligence by pretending otherwise. "I won't let him hurt anyone else."

"Parker," he corrected and came to stand behind her, radiating warmth and safety. "You mean that you're going to sacrifice yourself to save the others."

Neither confirming nor denying it. Parker took her by the shoulders and gently turned her around to face him. Refusing to meet his eye, he put a finger under her chin and nudged until she reluctantly looked up at him. He was so tall, so strong, his caramel eyes looked at her so tenderly that it made her knees go weak.

"I . . ." he stared down at her, his eyes turbulent, and for a moment she was sure that he was going to say that he had feelings for her. He'd been so gentle and so sweet and he'd looked at her with such deep longing.

Waiting on tender hooks for him to continue, "I want to help you," he said finally. "Talk to me, we'll work something out, I promise. You don't have to do this."

Disappointment washing over her, until that moment Tessa hadn't realized how desperately she had wanted to hear him tell her that he cared about her, that he wanted her, that she wasn't alone.

Tears welling up in her eyes again, threatening to cascade down her cheeks. "You don't want to help me, to get involved with me. Trust me. I ruin everything I touch." Heart breaking she tried to pull away from him. She wasn't sure what had stopped him from telling her that he liked her, but it cut deeply, she was a fool for allowing herself to fall for him.

He wouldn't let her go. "Tessa, what happened all those years ago to make you think that way," he asked, keeping his voice gentle.

"You mean when I was a teenager, the night I ended up in the hospital?" she asked knowing full well which event from her past he was referring to.

He raised an eyebrow, knowing that she knew what he was talking about. She sighed reluctantly, "You mean with Ellie." She felt her heart tighten as she said her friend's name. She had never told anyone what had happened. What she had done and what she had not done that long ago night.

Tears falling unnoticed down her cheeks until Parker reached over and wiped them away, tucking a stray curl behind her ear. "I can't," she whispered. Against her better judgment, she wearily laid her forehead against his chest. Hesitating for a moment, then his arms encircled her and pulled her close.

Holding her again while she cried. His heart beating comfortingly under her ear, his chin resting on the top of her head, she felt safe, content even. He didn't push her to share about her past, but for once she longed to explain to him everything that had happened to Ellie, to herself, to all of them.

Eventually he pulled away, "I'm going to tell you something that I've never told another living person." The eyes that bored into her were almost as haunted as her own.

Leading her back to the bed, he pulled her down so that she sat in his lap, and taking a deep shuddering breath, he began. "Six months ago I killed a girl. She was only fourteen. Her name was Gina. When we met her she was huddled in the back of her boyfriend's truck, he had just killed her father. Her mother had died when she was young, she had no one, and so she reached out to me. I tried to help her but I ended up shooting her."

"Parker, I'm sorry," looking up at him she saw that he was staring off into the distance trapped in a dark memory he couldn't shake. She knew the feeling.

"I had to shoot her, she was holding her newborn baby in her arms, she threatened to kill it," he continued in a far-away voice, and she knew that he was reliving every moment of his worst nightmare. "It was my fault, I tried to help her. No," he corrected himself, "I was trying to help myself. I grew up in foster care."

Pausing to regain control of his emotions, Tessa remembered the many times as a child that she had wished for someone to come and take her away from her family. Even foster care had seemed like a preferable option.

"I was adopted by a wonderful family when I was ten, but before that," she felt him shudder against her. "We, my sister and

I, we lived in some horrible homes, the last one was the worst. When we moved in with the Bell's, I did okay after a while, I made friends, started focusing on school, I was happy. My sister was a different story, she couldn't get over what had happened to her while we were in foster care. She was raped."

She felt her own body shudder involuntarily at the mention of rape. Nauseous, she sucked in a shaky breath. Parker noticed and pulled back so that he could see her properly. "You okay?" he asked, peering worriedly at her and reaching for her wrist to take her pulse. "You know you should still be in the hospital."

"I'm fine," she whispered, her voice trembling. "Keep going," she knew that it was important for him to tell what he needed to tell.

"I didn't protect my sister. She was all I had and I failed her. I didn't do anything until it was too late. I didn't want to fail Gina, when I looked at her, I saw my sister. That was a mistake. Matilda was innocent Gina was not. She killed her father, and she was going to kill her baby, and me. Mattie . . . she didn't mean to do what . . ."

Horrified understanding dawning. "Your sister killed someone."

"It was an accident," he said defensively, misinterpreting her exclamation.

Struggling to breathe, her body rigid, the room seemed to be closing in on her. "Tessa?" She heard Parker's voice but it was muffled, like they were underwater. "Tessa, sweetheart, breathe," he shook her gently but firmly. "Tessa, look at me." She blinked and his anxious face came slowly into focus. "You okay?"

Nodding unsteadily, unwanted memories that had been carefully and deeply buried had sprung to the surface.

Unconvinced, "You look like you've seen a ghost. I'm going to get your friend Michelle, she's the doctor right?"

Forcing herself to breathe evenly. "No, it's okay, I'm fine."

"No. You're not," he reached out his thumb and gently traced the gash on her temple. "You look terrible," he murmured softly.

Everything was moving too fast. She wanted him, but she couldn't have him. She'd thought that he wanted her but now she wasn't so sure, he was sending her mixed signals. What she was planning to do was not something that she could take back. She would never be free to have a relationship with him, and yet . . . no.

Standing she moved quickly away from him, she couldn't think clearly when she was near him. He followed her, grabbing her arms and spinning her around to look at him. She tried to avoid his gaze but his eyes were like magnets drawing her own eyes to his against her will.

They stood in silence gazing deeply into one another eyes, he stooped slowly and she was sure that he was going to kiss her when . . .

The door opened. "Parker, we need you."

"I'll be right there," he said, straightening quickly. The door closed again and the moment had passed. "Come on, you need to rest." So did he, she thought, he looked like he hadn't slept in days.

Gently pulling her across the room, Parker pushed her softly down onto one of the beds, covering her carefully with a blanket. "Sleep now, we'll talk later." He went to stand but stopped and looked back down at her. "Promise me you won't do anything until we talk," his eyes bored into her.

Remembering the look in his eyes when he had talked about the notes blaming the police for the deaths of her friends. The guilt and pain. Thinking of everything that he had been through with Gina and his sister. She couldn't lie to him, betray him, so she simply said nothing.

Finally he sighed, knowing that she was not going to promise anything, then bent and brushed a soft kiss to her forehead.

She watched him go and wished that somehow, anyhow, she could stay and have him. Have a family and a life with him. But she had made her choice a long time ago and now she had to live with the consequences, even if it cost her a chance at everything that she had ever wanted.

Rolling onto her side, Tessa pulled the blanket up to her chin and, as she had almost every night when she was a child, cried herself to sleep.

* * * * *

4:19 A.M.

"Alright, lets lay out what we know so far. See if we can't piece together some sort of history, maybe figure out who this guy is," J.J. announced.

After Wyatt had interrupted his near kiss with Tessa, Parker had reluctantly followed him to the small conference room where the others were already seated and waiting for him.

"I think it's safe to say that those girls are not going to tell us anything, so we're on our own," J.J. continued.

"And the press now know about the note, the list, someone leaked it and they are having a field day with it," Wyatt reminded him.

They all sighed in frustration. They tolerated the media and used them from time to time but more often than not the media were about as annoying as a swarm of flies at a summer barbeque.

Victoria Baker and Thomas Keller had been brought in to help with the case that had now racked up four deaths and still seemed to be going nowhere. "Let's just start with the forensics," J.J. instructed. "Wyatt, you take notes," he gestured at the whiteboard that took up most of one wall of the cramped room and threw him a marker.

"So far the forensics are almost non-existent," Marty told them, his bird-like face pained. Parker had never seen him look so depressed, he usually took even the worst of cases in his stride, and never became personally involved. "We have a strand of hair from Bianca Kingston's murder scene and a fingerprint from Gina de Van's murder scene, but unless we have something to compare them to they're virtually useless."

"No hits on IAFIS or CODIS?" J.J. demanded, referring to the FBI's Integrated Automated Fingerprint Identification System, and Combined DNA Index System, that were used to identify possible suspects.

"Nothing. We can still use them as evidence against this guy, if we ever catch him, but they're not going to help us find him."

"So that's another dead end," J.J. was running his hand through his thick brown hair so frequently it would be no surprise if he was bald by the end of this case. He was under pressure from the mayor and the public to find the serial killer and get him off the streets. The press were, as always, making things worse by playing up the serial killer angle, suggesting that the victims were random, that anyone could be on the killer's list, and that the whole city was at risk.

"We get anything from Tessa's house?"

"Not much," Marty shook his head. "They doused the outside of the house with an accelerant, and then set it alight. They wanted the house to burn slowly, with lots of smoke, making her terror last as long as possible."

Parker shuddered at the thought of someone out there who hated Tessa so much that they could do this to her.

"Zak, please tell me you have something more helpful," J.J. shot the medical examiner a hard stare.

"Victim number one, Tiffany Poppy. I found black fibers in her mouth and nose, indicating that she was suffocated, probably just to cause a loss of consciousness. There were traces of etomidate in her system, so I'm guessing he drugged her, and then raped her before amputating her arms and legs. Cause of death was exsanguination. Victim number two, Bianca Kingston. She was also drugged with etomidate, raped and then put in the water tank . . ."

"She was unconscious when he put her in?" Wyatt interjected.

"No, I'm sorry. The drugs in her system were almost gone so she was definitely awake and aware when he put her in there. Water in her lungs, so cause of death is asphyxia due to drowning. Victim number three, Dorothy Dallas. She was not drugged, the blow to the head probably stunned her enough for him to tie her up. Cause of death was asphyxia due to manual strangulation, consistent with what was shown on the video," Zak gave an involuntary shudder as he presumably flashed back to watching it.

"What's etomidate?" Thomas asked.

"It's a short acting, IV anesthetic agent used for general anesthesia, usually for short procedures such as reduction of dislocated joints. In a typical dosage it would knock someone out for approximately five to ten minutes, and would take about thirty to sixty seconds to induce unconsciousness. He knew what he was doing it's not easy to overdose someone with this drug, the difference between an effective dose and a lethal dose is massive."

"Is any of this going to help us find him," J.J. snapped, he was in no mood for a medical lesson.

"Maybe. The drug would probably only be available in a hospital . . ."

Tapping his pen against the table, J.J. cut Zak off, "Good. We'll contact all hospitals in the area see if anyone reported any etomidate stolen."

"Any defensive wounds on the victims?" Victoria asked.

"Not really . . ."

"Not really?"

"If you'd calm down and . . ." Zak frowned at J.J.

"Calm, down? I've got a serial . . ."

"Let me finish," Zak spoke over the top of him, he was never intimidated by J.J.'s frustrated outbursts. "The head wound on Dorothy could be interpreted as a defensive wound, she fought back, and it made him angry, he hit her. But he grabbed and overpowered each of victims very quickly. I found some black fibers under the fingernails of Tiffany, probably from when she was clawing at his hand to try and breathe while he was suffocating her."

"Any lead on the fibers?" Wyatt asked.

Parker struggled to listen as Marty took over the explanation and droned on and on about fibers. His mind wandered back to his earlier encounter with Tessa. He had left the hospital still angry with her, and arriving back at work, he had intended to give her a rough going over in the hope of forcing her to tell him who the killer was. However, when he had walked in the room and heard her heart wrenching sobs his anger had fled instantly.

Remembering the way she'd felt in his arms, small and vulnerable, she'd fit perfectly beneath his chin, holding her had felt so right. She had resisted him at first, tried to pull away, but then she'd relented and allowed him to comfort her. He didn't know why he had refrained from telling her exactly how he felt about her. He'd wanted to, holding her in his arms he had known that he was going to do whatever it took to have Tessa.

When he'd looked into her eyes he'd seen a desperate longing, for him, for safety and peace. She wanted him, he knew she did, and yet, for some reason he had pulled back from telling her what was in his heart. Tessa had wanted to tell him everything, he was sure of that, but she was scared. Distrustful. He knew that unless he could find this guy Tessa was going to sacrifice herself to save her friends and protect her secret. Nothing was going to stop him from finding this killer, arresting . . .

"Parker? Parker," J.J.'s voice interrupted his thoughts.

"What?"

Tapping his watch in annoyance. "Give us a rundown of the girls' history."

Focusing his mind he started to recite, "All the girls, except Carrie Marble, started at Harlwood Academy in pre-K, Carrie joined the school a couple of years later in the second grade. The school sent out the records earlier today, we've confirmed that each of the women is who they say they are. They were all identified early on as being gifted and were placed in a special class. They attended some lessons with the rest of their peers but they also took advanced math, science and English literature classes.

"At this stage it seems like the other girls were very quiet, shy, bullied by their peers. Tessa . . ." he felt his cheeks heat as he mentioned her name, and cleared his throat, embarrassed. "Tessa was best friends with an Eleanor Matthews, she was in the regular class, the two had been friends since pre-K. Tessa was outgoing, enthusiastic, lacking in academic motivation, and regularly got in trouble for her many 'experiments'. In the sixth grade Tessa and Eleanor were abducted one Friday afternoon in September, not long after school started back. Tessa was found late Sunday night, covered in blood and wandering down the side of the road miles from her school. Eleanor was never seen again.

"After she was taken Tessa changed completely, she became quiet and withdrawn, joined the advanced class and started hanging around with the other girls from the class. She became very focused on her studies. In the tenth grade Tessa is in some sort of accident, gets sick and spends three months in the hospital. According to one of the girls in her class, the rumor going around the school was that her friends injured Tessa. Then later that year one of the girls from the advanced class, Chelsea Ward, and her boyfriend commit suicide by driving their car off a cliff, that was in November . . ."

"What date? What date in November?" Victoria cut in.

Consulting the police report from the incident. "How did we miss this," Parker exclaimed seeing where Victoria was going.

"What?" J.J. frowned.

"November 20th, Janice Peters was abducted November 20th. That cannot be a coincidence."

"Okay, so the girls were in the tenth grade when this started, this has to involve someone from the school. I'm guessing it's linked to whatever really happened to Tessa that landed her in the hospital just months before one of her friends commits suicide," J.J. was smiling now, pleased they finally had some direction.

Wyatt turned from the board where he was busily writing down everything they were saying. "We have a complete list of students in the same grade, someone had to know something."

To Victoria and Keller, "We need a list of all the teachers that worked at the school and had any contact with any one of our eleven girls." When he was excited J.J. spoke at ten times the speed of a normal person. "Get a list from the school, and do whatever necessary to track down those teachers. Beth what are you thinking?"

"About the killer or the girls?"

"Both."

Nodding, "I'll start with the girls. Their intelligence made them social misfits with their peers, so they avoided interactions with anyone outside their circle. That made them very close, they relied on one another, they trust one another. I would say that none of them were close with their families, probably raised by nannies. They became their own little family. Whatever secret it is that they're hiding they are not going to tell you."

"If they don't tell us he's going to kill them," Marty cut in.

"They are aware of this. And I believe that they are all fully prepared to go to their graves keeping this secret. Four of them already have," she reminded them.

"Tessa wants to tell me but she's scared," Parker added, remembering the way she had stared up at him.

Beth raised a knowing eyebrow but didn't comment on it. "She might want to tell you but she's not going to. You centered the girl's history around Tessa, do you think that she's at the centre of this?"

Instantly defensive. "Do you?"

She gave him her best psychiatrist smile. "Yes I do. I think that somehow this is all related specifically to Tessa Micah. She was the leader of the group she kept them all together. Tessa is a smart girl, very intuitive, but also emotionally damaged."

"Do you think there's a link between what happened to her when she was eleven and what happened later on, to all of this?" Parker asked.

Pondering that for a moment before answering, "No. I think that what happened later is a separate issue, and I think that is related to what is happening now. Did Tessa ever tell anyone what happened to her when she was abducted?"

"No. She never told anyone anything, not the police, not the doctors who treated her at the hospital, not her family, not the child psychiatrist her grandparents sent her to, not even her friends. No one knows what happened that weekend," Parker's heart broke for the terrified little girl Tessa must have been, alone with no one to trust, he was sure that whatever she had seen haunted her to this day.

Giving him a sympathetic smile. "Tessa keeps a lot inside," Beth warned. "That kind of pressure gets to anyone eventually."

"Any insight into what their secret is?" Wyatt asked.

"I think that they were sexually abused, probably by a teacher or staff member at the school. They would have been perfect targets for a pedophile. Young, vulnerable, shunned by their peers, lacking self-confidence, it would have been easy to manipulate them into keeping quiet. None of them have had a serious relationship, they aren't married, no boyfriends or fiancée's. They all still avoid social relationships with friends, they're quiet, they don't share much about themselves."

"That could be the reason that Chelsea Ward committed suicide," J.J. said thoughtfully.

"What about her boyfriend? How does that fit in?" Zak asked puzzled.

Beth shrugged, "I don't know. Maybe Chelsea wasn't part of the abuse, maybe she was and she wanted a boyfriend anyway."

"And Tiffany was married," Wyatt reminded her.

"It's not a rule. Many people who are sexually abused as children or adolescents, or adults, have relationships. I was just making an observation," Beth said defensively.

"Very interesting," J.J. was tapping his pen impatiently on the table top, ready to move on. "What about our killer?"

"This is definitely personal. If we stick with the pedophile theory for the moment, I think that something happened to scare him off. He left, he's spent the last ten years moving from place to place, trying to re-create what he had here. He was never able to do that, blamed the girls, and came back to reclaim what he had."

"What do you think scared him off?" Thomas questioned.

"Maybe whatever happened that landed Tessa in the hospital."

"Are we agreeing with the rumor that her friends did something to her?" Victoria wanted to know.

"I can't see them hurting one another. If they were abused, and I'm almost positive that they were, then they were all each other had. Without each other they had nothing."

"What about the notes and video's, I still don't get why he's doing that," J.J. was still hung up on this.

"I think he's doing them to throw you off track, to distract you from focusing on him. His notes keep you focused on the victims. He is relieving himself of any guilt over their deaths by laying it all on you," Beth paused to shoot him a sympathetic glance, she knew that this was a sensitive area for him. "He gave you the list, you didn't find them, so it's your fault, not his, that they're dead."

"Great," J.J. said sarcastically. "Okay, people, let's take another shot with Tessa and the others, tell them what we think happened . . . what?" he asked Beth who was shaking her head.

"I don't think it's a good idea to confront them yet. If they were abused and you confront them it could make them shut down altogether," she cautioned.

"How is that different from what they're doing at the moment?

They're already not saying anything," J.J. countered.

"I think you should have a go at some of the other girls from the school, see what you can get, someone might know something. Tessa and her friends are smart girls, perhaps coming at them with facts might make a difference."

"Fine. Victoria and Thomas, you take the teachers, Parker and Wyatt, you have a go at some of the students from the school. The girls still here?"

Wyatt nodded. "Yeah, we told them we were keeping them here in protective custody."

"We can't do that without their consent," J.J. reminded.

"Yeah but they don't know that," Wyatt shot back with a grin.

"Okay then, Beth, I want you to try talking to the girls, see if you can pick up on some body language or something. Lets try to make some progress this time."

They were being dismissed.

* * * * *

6:34 A.M.

She'd tried to make him angry while he was raping her.

Angry enough to kill her right there and then.

But it was like he hadn't really been there. He was there in body but not in mind. He had been in the past. He'd been thinking about Tessa. Imagining that she was her.

Janice was ready to die. She was sick of this horrible pink room. Her wrists and ankles were rubbed raw from the ropes that kept her tied to the bed. Her muscles were stiff and sore from days of lying in the same position.

The place was quiet. Deadly quiet. She knew that he was still here. Somewhere in this huge house of death. He was here, biding his time before he went to find and torture and kill another of her friends. When the dark came again he would leave. Leave her here alone.

Tears of exhausted frustration began to slide down her cheeks. She was tired, so tried. Tired of her life, tired of this house, tired of being alone and scared, just plain tired.

She was ready to die.

* * * * *

5:31 P.M.

Standing watching her sleep, Parker felt an overwhelming tenderness wash over him. Sitting beside Tessa on the bed, he reached out a hand and gently stroked her forehead. Smiling down at her, he realized that she gave him a peace, a focus, which he had not felt before. He wanted to wake her up and tell her everything that he was feeling, but she needed to sleep. He was glad she was finally getting some rest, she was exhausted, physically, mentally and emotionally.

While she'd been sleeping, he and Wyatt had been tracking down as many of Tessa's classmates as they could. They had been able to locate ten who still lived nearby and had agreed to come and see them. A list of appointments had been made for the following day.

Tessa began to whimper in her sleep, trapped in a nightmare of her own. "Shh," he whispered soothingly, brushing his knuckles across her cheekbone. "It's okay, it's okay."

"Parker," Beth was standing in the doorway. "I thought you might want to talk."

Nodding he pressed a soft kiss to Tessa's cheek, tucked the blanket around her and followed Elisabeth from the room.

Meeting her in J.J.'s office. "The boss gone for the night?"

She nodded then delved right in. During his time working with her he had learnt that she always preferred to go straight to the heart of the matter. "Are you sure that getting involved with

Tessa, a victim in a murder investigation, is a good idea?"

"Are you saying it's not?"

"What do you think?"

Used to her method of answering a question with a question he sometimes like to use it right back at her. "You mean because of what happened with Gina?"

Arching an eyebrow at him. "Yes, because of what happened with Gina. You felt that she betrayed you. Just like your mother betrayed you by choosing her love of drugs over her love for you. And like your foster parents betrayed you, bringing you back time and time again to be abused by their son. Do you still feel that way?"

Considering for a moment. "I still feel that way, but I no longer feel controlled by those feelings."

After he had shot Gina O'Hara, J.J. had insisted that he speak to a shrink to work through his feelings. At first, he had been cynical, like most officers involved in a shooting, but Elisabeth had been patient. She had never pushed him to talk to her, spending their sessions sitting at her desk working while he sat there in self-righteous anger. Eventually he had given in and began to talk her, opening up not just about his feelings over the shooting but also about his past. He had been surprised by Elisabeth's insights.

Giving him a warm smile. "That's good progress, Parker, congratulations."

Pride blossomed through him at her praise, making him feel like a second grader trying to please his teacher. "I'm ready to be happy now," he said simply.

"And you think Tessa will make you happy?"

"Yes."

"Have you told her how you feel?"

Guilty, "I was going to but I wimped out."

"Why do you think that is?"

"I ... I don't know," he answered truthfully.

"Is it because you think she doesn't feel the same way?"

"No, I'm sure that she does. I guess . . . I guess I just wasn't one hundred percent certain that I was ready."

"But you are now?"

"Yeah, I am."

"Do you think Tessa will tell you who the killer is?"

"She wants to."

"That's not what I asked," she smiled.

"If I'm honest then no I don't think she's going to tell me."

"Does that bother you?"

"I understand her reasons, she thinks that keeping her secret is the only way to protect her friends. I understand her I just don't agree with her."

"So you don't see her silence as a betrayal?" Beth asked leaning forward sending her long, dark hair tumbling over her shoulders.

"I'm more worried at the moment about what her secret is going to do to her than what's it's going to do to me."

"You think she's going to hurt herself?"

"I think she's going to sacrifice herself. She told me that she wouldn't let him hurt anyone else. I think . . . I think . . ." he could hardly bare to say the words aloud in case it made them come true.

"You think she's going to go straight to him, try to kill him herself?"

Nodding. The thought scared him more than anything else. He knew the pain, the feeling that part of you had died, when you took the life of another human being. He couldn't bear the thought of Tessa having to go through that. "Or she's going to let him kill her." He didn't know which was worse.

"How are you going to stop her?"

"I'm going to find him before she can. As long as she's here in the station I can keep her safe. And maybe you could talk to her."

"I'll talk to her," Beth nodded. "Parker," her serious black eyes boring into him. "Even if you find the killer that's not going to be the end of this. Everything she's been through is going to have had an impact on her. Do you think you can handle that?"

"Of course I can," he snapped back immediately.

"This is not something you can take on lightly. You have some serious thinking to do. Tessa's going to need a lot of help, of support, probably counseling, she's going to need someone she can count on indefinitely. If you can't be that person then it's not fair to Tessa or yourself to start anything with her."

NOVEMBER 30TH

11:32 A.M.

"The next one's ready to go," Wyatt stuck his head in the door, then disappeared again.

This would be number six, Parker moaned to himself.

Standing and stretching his tired muscles, he had spent the night here at the station. Not just because he couldn't be bothered catching a cab back to his place, but because he had wanted to stay near Tessa. He'd crashed in the bed next to hers.

For once he had slept a deep and dreamless sleep. Tessa on the other hand had not been so lucky. She had woken him several times during the night, whimpering and moaning in her sleep, once she'd awakened screaming. He had held her in his arms, rubbing her back to calm her and whispering soothingly in her ear, until eventually she had started to relax. She wouldn't tell him what had been haunting her dreams, and after the last nightmare had refused to go back to sleep.

The door opened again and Wyatt entered with a plain looking woman in her mid-twenties. "This is Claudia Lance."

Claudia's skin was too tanned, her face too made up, her skirt too short, her hair dyed an unpleasant shade of blonde that did not suit her in the least. Parker had seen more young women who looked and dressed in the same manner, than he liked to count turn up here at the station. Dead or raped.

Young women, hardly more than little girls, just like Claudia were so busy trying to be the centre of attention that they paid little heed to just who's attention they were actually attracting.

"Have a seat," Wyatt was saying to Claudia, pulling out a chair for her. "Can I get you anything to drink?"

"No, thank you," she had an unpleasantly high and squeaky voice.

"Thanks for coming and seeing us on such short notice," Parker began, giving the same speech he had already used five times today. He and Wyatt had been taking turns leading the interviews it was back to his turn.

"No problem," she shot them a sickly sweet smile, her eyes straying to his left hand to ascertain whether or not he was married. Seeing no ring she moved slightly in her chair managing to reveal even more of her long tanned legs.

"We wanted to ask you some questions about some of the girls who went to your school."

"Harlwood Academy," she said for apparently no other reason than to hear the sound of her own voice.

"You're aware of what has been going on in the news?"

False concern on her face. "Yes it's just absolutely awful."

"You know that we believe the lives of five others of your classmates might be in danger?" The list and the other potential victims had been all over the previous night's late night news. Reporters had been camped outside the station ever since Gina's murder, desperate to catch a glimpse of the other women involved in the case that had made international news.

"Oh yes, it really is just awful," Claudia made her voice go up and down as she spoke.

"Do you remember the girls in the advanced class?"

"Tessa and her friends?" Jealously flickered in her small brown eyes.

"What can you tell us about them?" Parker did not expect her to tell them anything of importance. So far they had heard the same information that they already knew from each of the other five women they had interviewed.

All the women had remembered Tessa. Some had remembered a couple of the other girls. They'd all had the same story. The girls in the advanced class were quiet, shy, not popular and yet never bullied or picked on. They focused heavily on their studies, went on regular weekend study camps. They never dated, never attended parties or other school social functions.

"I was never really friends with them, so I didn't know them very well. They were always doing schoolwork, they never came to any parties. The teachers all loved them, especially Tessa," she spat out Tessa's name viciously.

"You didn't like Tessa?"

"Everyone thought she was so perfect," her eyes blazing.

"She went through a lot," Parker told her reproachfully.

Glaring at him. "You mean because of what happened with Eleanor. She probably faked the whole thing . . ."

"She faked the death of her friend when she was eleven?" Parker interrupted.

"Fine," Claudia sighed reluctantly. "That's an exaggeration. But Tessa wasn't perfect, okay?" Anger fading from her eyes, edgy apprehension taking its place. "One day I heard them talking, they were saying that I would never be one of them, at the time I thought they were just talking about being their friend. But later . . ." Claudia was biting her lip nervously.

"What is it, Claudia?"

"I'm pretty smart too, not as smart as Tessa," again jealousy lurked in her eyes. "One semester I was in the advanced class."

Excitement started to bubble. "When was this?"

She thought for a moment, "Eighth grade."

All pretence at snobbery and flirting gone she now looked just plain scared. "What happened, Claudia?" he asked softly.

A faraway look on her face as she remembered. "They had already been in his class the previous semester, it was the second half of the year." Her voice had dropped and she spoke softly, "He was a new teacher, he took the advanced class a couple of lessons each day."

Thinking of Beth's theory that Tessa and her friends had been abused by a teacher. "Did he hurt you, Claudia?" Parker pressed gently.

She shook her head vehemently. "No, he never laid a hand on me."

"But," he prompted.

"But I think he might have done something to them, to the others."

"Did they ever say anything?"

"No, they never said anything to me."

"Did you ever see him hurt them?" It was like getting blood from a stone.

"No, I never saw him touch them."

Starting to lose his patience. "Then what, Claudia? There must be some reason that you think he did something to those girls."

She stood and crossed the room to stare out the tiny, grimy window. They gave her a moment then Parker went and stood behind her. "He could be a killer, Claudia. We need to know what he did to them so that we can find him, and stop him from hurting anyone else. If we don't find him then he's going to kill Janice Peters, and then come after the others."

Wringing her hands Claudia slowly turned to look at him, tears standing in her eyes. "I read something," she whispered so quietly he had to strain to hear her.

"What did you read?"

Twitching nervously. "It was something Chelsea had written,"

"The girl who committed suicide?" guiding Claudia back to her chair.

Head bobbing up and down like a pogo stick. "This would have been about two years before that. I thought it was her diary but she said it was just a story, for her English class."

"What did it say?"

"It was about a girl who was depressed and suicidal because she was abused by her teacher . . ." her voice now a quiet monotone.

"If he did anything to you it wasn't your fault, you know that don't you? You were a student he was a teacher, he took advantage of you," Parker told her carefully.

"He didn't touch me," eyes defensive, then guilt and shame battling in them. "One time I thought I saw him watching me change for gym. I had an orthodontist appointment that day, I was late, I was alone in the changing room, he said it was an accident, he didn't know I was in there. Maybe if I had said something . . ." chin quivering as she fought back tears. "Maybe none of this would have happened."

"It's not your fault, Claudia," putting a comforting hand on her knee. "You can't know that things would have gone differently if you'd said anything."

"Did you tell anyone what you'd read, what had happened?" Wyatt asked.

Sniffing, "No, I told you Chelsea said it was just a story, and he never really did anything to me."

"How did you feel about him? Was he popular with the other girls?"

"Some of the other girls had a crush on him. He was kinda cute I guess. He was young, in his early thirties I think. He had reddish brown hair and hazel eyes, and really tanned skin, he was tall and fit, but he was creepy."

"What do you mean?"

"He was always watching us, hanging around, he was weird. I never liked him and neither did Tessa and her friends." Her stricken eyes stared at them, "I should have said something shouldn't I? Then maybe they'd still be alive . . ."

"You can't think that way, Claudia, it was not your fault. If you'd said something back then it might not have changed anything. There is something you can do now though, you can tell us his name so that we can find him and stop him."

She continued to cry, muttering over and over again, "It's all my fault."

"What was his name, Claudia?" he pressed gently, giving her a small shake.

"Mr. Riley," she managed to choke out through her sobs. "Dylan Riley."

* * * * *

11:55 A.M.

"They're interviewing Claudia Lance," Carrie announced returning from the bathroom and closing the door carefully behind her. Pacing around the room, like she always did when she was tense. "Claudia knows things, she was in our class for a while. Chelsea said she read her diary one time."

"Relax, Carrie," Tessa soothed. "Even if she knows . . ." still unable to say it after all these years, "What she thinks she knows, she still doesn't know everything. And she definitely doesn't know why we're keeping this secret. Besides, I think they already figured out what happened to us."

Biting her nails, "If they know his name then they can find him," Michelle muttered fearfully.

Shaking her head confidently. "They won't find him," Tessa assured them. "He'll be using an alias."

Pouring herself a cup of coffee, she knew that she was ready to do what needed to be done. Parker's boss had set them up in a small interview room, with drinks, pastries and a stack of magazines. The detectives had been surprised when she and her friends had agreed to their request to remain in the security of the stationhouse. She was sure that after what happened with Gina he was not going to attempt an attack on the others, but it made her feel better to know that they were someplace safe.

"Detective Bell likes you, Tessa," Melanie announced, changing the subject.

The others smiled teasingly. "He definitely has a crush on you," Carrie grinned.

"He didn't say that he likes me," Tessa told them, a glimmer of disappointment flashing quickly in her eyes. Thinking back to last night she remembered how sweet Parker had been. All night her sleep had been plagued with nightmares, but he had been there when she'd awakened screaming. Holding her in his strong arms once again while she cried, and when she'd said she wasn't going back to sleep he had sat up with her, despite his own exhaustion. He'd been sweet and understanding, but he had still hung back from telling her how he felt about her.

Despite how wonderful he'd been she felt uncomfortable about letting him see her vulnerable, it was something that she avoided at all costs. Maintaining her composure was something that had become vital to her own survival, relying on no one but herself so that she could never be let down.

"He does though," Michelle assured her.

"You like him too," Lauren stated.

Reluctantly she nodded. "It doesn't matter though nothing can ever happen."

"That's not true, Tessa, if you like him then go for it," Lauren pushed.

"I can't."

Frowning, Carrie said, "You mean you won't."

"You deserve to be happy, Tessa, we all do," Melanie said, coming to sit beside her.

Tessa didn't believe that was true, she didn't believe that she would ever deserve to be happy after all the things that she had done.

Understanding her silence Michelle spoke softly, gently, "Tessa, whatever happened with Eleanor, it was not your fault, you *do* deserve to be happy. We all want that for you."

Indicating the others. "That's why we don't think you should go after him, Tess," Melanie told her.

"We went over this already, we agreed . . ."

"You didn't really give us a choice," Michelle reminded her.

"There is no other choice," she said stubbornly. "Everything that happened was my fault, so it's my responsibility to make things right."

Wrapping her arms around her Lauren gave her a sad smile. "Oh, Tessa, that's not true. It was never true. You were not responsible for what happened, I wish you'd believe that."

Coming to kneel in front of her Carrie continued, "We think that it would be better if we went after him together."

"No," Tessa shook her head forcefully. "We stick to the original plan . . ." breaking off as the door opened, they all turned to see who was there.

A slim woman in her forties with beautiful olive skin, long brown hair and dark, dark eyes was smiling back at them. A long red scar crossed her cheek, starting just under her right eye and weaving all the way down to her chin.

"I'm Elisabeth, Parker wanted me to talk to you, Tessa."

This must be the psychiatrist that Parker had told her about. Resisting the urge to frown, she'd told Parker that she was not going to talk to any shrink.

"We'll go," Melanie offered as she and the others moved towards the door.

"That's okay we can go somewhere else," Elisabeth told them pleasantly.

"No, no that's fine," Michelle smiled back and closed the door behind her.

Elisabeth took off the powder blue jacket of her pantsuit and took a seat opposite Tessa. "Did Parker tell you some of the things that we've talked about?"

"You helped him after the shooting," deliberately burying her irritation. Tessa did not like psychiatrists, they pretended to care, to listen, but in the end they wouldn't lift a finger to help.

"He's really worried about you."

Tessa wasn't used to having people worry about her. The idea of Parker worrying about her sent shivers down her spine, and with them another wave of regret over how what she was going to do would affect him. "I don't want to hurt him."

Elisabeth nodded. "I know. But you will."

Tears pricked at the back of her eyes, she kept them back by sheer force of will, and practice.

"Did he tell you about his past?" Elisabeth continued. "He grew up in foster care, it was a really rough time for him and his sister. Especially for his sister."

"He told me," she kept her composure perfectly.

"He carries around a lot of guilt, sometimes it eats him up inside."

Unable to think of anything to say Tessa simply said nothing.

"He really likes you, Tessa."

"He didn't say that," she pointed out. Again feeling a surge of disappointment that Parker had been unable to tell her what he was feeling, what she needed to hear.

"But you know that he does."

"I guess so." If she was honest his actions had made his feelings abundantly clear, and yet she still wanted, needed, to hear him say it.

"You care about him?" Elisabeth pushed gently.

"Yes."

"And you want to tell him?"

"Yes."

Elisabeth said nothing for a moment, just studied her with a shrink's inquisitive eyes. Tessa kept her own eyes and face carefully impenetrable. "Do you trust him?" Elisabeth finally asked.

Searching for an answer she finally shrugged. "I don't trust anybody."

"Your trust has been betrayed before."

A statement not a question so she offered no answer.

Leaning forward Elisabeth took Tessa's cold hands in her warm ones and gave them an encouraging squeeze. "Tessa, were you sexually abused?"

Snatching her hands back, she shot the psychiatrist a frosty stare. "I don't know what you're talking about," she said haughtily.

Not put off by her defiance. "Tessa, I just want to help you," Elisabeth implored. "So does Parker, and so does everyone here. But I can't help you if you won't talk to me."

Pushing back her chair. "Look, I don't mean to be rude but I didn't ask for your help and I don't need it. I told Parker that I didn't want to talk to you and I still don't."

"Parker's scared that you're going to go after this guy alone and end up getting yourself killed."

Turning her back Tessa said nothing.

"You want him to kill you," Elisabeth persisted calmly. "You think that you deserve to die. That's not true, Tessa, you don't deserve to be killed for something that someone did to you."

Spinning around she spat out through clenched teeth, "What I think is that you should go now."

When Elisabeth made no move to leave Tessa stormed out herself, pushing through the door, heading straight for the bathroom. Ignoring the surprised looks of the other detectives and the concerned voices of her friends calling her name.

Entering the bathroom, she locked the door behind her and turned on the tap, splashing freezing water over her hot, clammy face. Looking at herself in the grimy mirror, she saw that she looked terrible. The huge black and blue bruise on her forehead stood out in stark contrast to her deathly pale face. Her bloodshot eyes stared back at her miserably.

Elisabeth was wrong, so were her friends. They didn't know what they were talking about. They didn't know what she had done. She deserved everything she got.

* * * * *

12:48 P.M.

"Thanks, Claudia, you were really helpful," Parker smiled at her as he walked with her to the elevator. They'd spent another hour with Claudia going over everything she remembered about Dylan Riley.

Catching Elisabeth's eye he gave her a discreet nod. He hoped that she'd been able to get through to Tessa, who had been adamantly against the idea of talking to a shrink. Hopefully she wasn't too mad at him for sending Elisabeth to talk to her anyway. He decided he didn't care if she was mad. Angry he could deal with, dead he couldn't.

"I'm sorry I wasn't more helpful," Claudia was saying, dabbing at her red, puffy eyes to try and wipe away the mascara smudges.

"You did great," he stopped as they both frowned in confusion as a screeching siren sounded throughout the building.

"Fire evacuation," Wyatt said running over to him as everyone began to pour towards the stairs.

Joining the hoards, they slowly weaved their way through the quickly emptying building, spilling out though the front doors. Outside the midday sun was breaking through the clouds. The snow had ceased and the temperature had risen a couple of degrees. The street and the sidewalk were flooded with police officers as everyone stood in groups exclaiming animatedly at the unusual turn of events.

Fire trucks came roaring down the street, sirens wailing, as throngs of people moved to the sides making a path to the building's doors. Scanning the windows for any sign of fire or smoke he found none.

Chatting with Wyatt and some of the other detectives, as they waited for the building to be cleared, so they could get back to the ever-mounting pile of cases awaiting them. Spotting J.J. standing by the door with a couple of the other lieutenants and a few fire fighters.

Pointing at them, "Wyatt, lets go see what's happening." Finally making progress on their case Parker was anxious to get back to it and track down Dylan Riley.

Fighting their way through the crowds. "J.J. what's going on, can we go back in there yet?" Parker asked when they finally reached them.

Turning to look at him, a serious look on his hairy face. "There was no fire."

"Someone set the smoke detector off by accident?" Wyatt asked.

"No, someone rigged it to go off," J.J.'s voice booming loudly above the noise of the multitude.

"Someone rigged it to go off?" repeated Wyatt frowning in confusion.

Heart dropping Parker felt a shiver of fear and horrified understanding. He began to scan the mass of people fanned out in front of him, desperately searching for any sign of Tessa. Struggling to draw a breath, he couldn't see her anywhere. His heart was beating so hard he thought it would break through his chest at any second.

"She's gone," he forced out through his constricting throat.

"Who?" the fire fighter asked puzzled.

"It was a diversion. Tessa's friends. So she could get away. She's gone to find him," his voice sounding faraway to his own ears as he bit back the panic that threatened to engulf him.

Placing a comforting hand on his shoulder. "We'll find her, Parker," Wyatt soothed. "Try not to get carried away."

"We're too late. He's going to kill her," his vision blurring, for a second he thought he was going to pass out, and almost welcomed the blissful ignorance that would come with unconsciousness. "He's going to kill her."

* * * * *

1:26 P.M.

Paying the cab driver, Tessa hurried up the front path to Michelle's bright yellow front door. Michelle was not a gardener. Her front yard was nothing more than long, overgrown grass and a single tree stripped of all but a couple of stray red leaves which clung forlornly to the branches. The grey, bare tree reminded Tessa of herself. Empty, alone, and with everything that she'd ever had taken from her.

Locating the spare key, hidden inside the porch light, she let herself inside. Having memorized the layout to each of her friend's houses, she was able to find her way around even though she had never been inside the house before. Michelle's taste in decorating was modern, the walls painted vivid oranges, greens, purples and blues. Her furniture was stark whites and metals, the bare floorboards covered in brightly colored rugs.

Like her own home, and the homes of all her friends, there were not many personal items on display. There were no happy family snaps hanging from the walls, or set on tables. In fact, there was nothing to indicate that Michelle spent much time here at all.

Going straight to the bathroom Tessa took a quick shower, enjoying the steaming hot water that gently massaged her tired muscles. Leaving her hair to drip dry, she went to the bedroom, rifling through the huge walk in wardrobe to find something suitable to wear. Eventually settling on a pair of jeans, a pink sweatshirt, pink sneakers and a thick fleece lined jacket.

Back downstairs she thought about having something to eat but her nauseous stomach protested so she simply drank some water. Taking the car keys from a drawer in the kitchen she headed to the garage and into Michelle's old car.

Fastening her seatbelt, she turned the engine on and then simply sat.

She'd been deliberately avoiding thinking about Parker and

everything that she was about to do. She knew he'd be mad when he found out about the fire evacuation diversion, but she hadn't had a choice. There was no way he had been going to let her out of that police station alone, and what she had to do had to be done whether she like it or not. She hoped he'd forget about her, that he'd find someone who deserved his trust. She hoped that he'd be happy, something he could never be with her.

* * * * *

2:02 P.M.

"How'd you do it?" Parker demanded, glaring stonily at the four blank faces staring back at him. Struggling to stay calm, he was ready to start shaking some sense into these girls, to force them to tell him where Tessa had gone.

Lauren, Melanie, Carrie and Michelle said nothing.

"Look we know it was you so you might as well just tell us," he snapped.

Still they said nothing.

About to say something he would probably later regret, when Wyatt jumped in before he had a chance, "We talked to some of the girls who went to your school." Giving them an understanding smile, "Some of them thought that you might have all been abused by a teacher."

The girls continued to stare at them, not a flicker of emotion crossing any of their faces.

"They thought the teacher who hurt you was Dylan Riley."

Not a hint of recognition in their eyes. They were good, not quite as good as Tessa, but good nonetheless.

Panic was coursing through every vein in his body. Tessa was going after a killer and she had more than a little advantage. They had nothing more than some unfounded suspicions and denials from the only people who knew the truth. Unless he found her she was going to die, and he had never even told her how he felt about her.

"Tessa is going to die," unleashing his anger before it consumed him. "He's already tried to kill her once, if we hadn't got there when we did she would have died in that fire. How can you call yourself her friends and just sit there doing nothing to stop it?"

"Tessa knows what she's doing," Melanie told them evenly.

"You were sexually assaulted by a teacher, we know that, why are you still trying to keep this a secret?"

Four pairs of eyes stared unflinchingly back at him.

"We know that something happened to land Tessa in the hospital. The other girls from your school thought that you did something to her."

"We are aware of that," Lauren shot back frostily, if looks could kill.

"Does that have anything to do with what's happening?"

Nothing.

"This is ridiculous," throwing his hands up in the air. "You're all . . ." he broke off as the door behind him opened, and the girl's faces dropped, they looked as though they'd seen a ghost.

Speaking over the top of one another.

Melanie, "You can't be here."

Carrie, "We wouldn't have said anything."

Michelle, "Tessa would have taken care of everything."

Lauren, "What are you thinking?"

Brow creasing in confusion, looking from the four surprised faces in front of him to the young woman standing in the doorway. "Who's this?" he asked the young officer escorting her.

"I don't know sir, she wouldn't give her name. Just said that she had vital information about the 'Poison Pen' serial killer. Said she'd only talk to the detectives in charge of the case," the officer explained, referencing the nickname the press had devised for their killer.

The girl at the door remained where she was. She had smooth black skin, tightly curled black hair and big grey eyes, her face creased with worry.

"And you are?" Parker asked.

Opening her mouth to answer the others cut her off, "Don't!" they shouted simultaneously, leaping to their feet.

"I take it you know her," Wyatt commented wryly.

Frowning reproachfully at the other four girls. "Thank you," she said to her escort, who apparently took this as a sign to leave. Then turning to him and Wyatt, the newcomer looked them straight in the eye. "My name is Chelsea Ward."

The girls sighed in irritation. "You shouldn't have done that, Chelsea," Michelle told her.

"Aren't you the girl who committed suicide by driving her car off a cliff?" Unsure if he was more surprised about the apparent resurrection of a girl who had been dead for ten years, or that her friends seemed to already know this.

They ignored him. "It's about time I should have done it. I never should have let things go this far," Chelsea shot back.

"Did you fake your own death?"

Shaking her head. "We wouldn't have told them, they never would have figured it out," Carrie muttered.

"Does someone want to let us in on this discussion," he tried again.

"I'm telling them everything. It's the only way to put a stop to this. It's what we should have done from the beginning," Chelsea continued as though he were not even in the room.

"Chelsea, no," Melanie eyeballed her. "Tessa went after him, she'll take care of it."

"Hey!" Parker threw his chair against the wall to get their attention. Five exasperated faces frowned back at him. "You want to tell us what's going on?"

"No," Lauren, Carrie, Michelle and Melanie said emphatically,

"Yes," Chelsea said at the same time. "I'm telling them," she shot her friends a glare, daring them to disagree.

Defeated they shrugged and reluctantly resumed their seats.

"Yes that was me," Chelsea answered his earlier question. "Only I wasn't in that car when it went over the cliff."

"What about your boyfriend, Jasper Conner?"

"He's right outside."

"Why did you do it? Why did you fake your own deaths?" trying to form a picture in his mind of what was going on and coming up blank.

"How much do they know?" Chelsea addressed the question to her friends.

Four identical stony faces stared back at her in stubborn silence.

Crossing the room, Chelsea pulled a chair over so that she sat directly in front of them, tears in her eyes. "We can't turn on each other now. Not after everything we went through together. Janice is gone. Tiffany, Bianca, Dorothy and Gina are dead. Tessa has gone after him," her composure cracking. "He's still running our lives after all these years. Not anymore. I'm putting a stop to it. I never should have let you do it, but I was scared," tears falling freely now but her voice was still strong, "can't you understand that?"

Wiping a tear from Chelsea's cheek. "Yeah we understand," Carrie told her, face softening, as she gave her friend a hug.

"Are we in this together?" Chelsea asked, uncertainty hovering in her grey eyes.

Exchanging unreadable glances the others turned back to her and nodded their agreement. "We're in this together," Lauren confirmed.

Watching them hug one another, Parker reluctantly gave them a moment to reconnect. Anxious to press forward, Tessa's time was quickly running out, but he knew that they would be more cooperative in solidarity than divided.

"Your friends have refused to confirm anything," Wyatt told

Chelsea, passing them all a box of tissues.

Giving her friends a grateful smile. "They did it for me. Everything they've done has been for me. Tell me what you think you know."

Chelsea moved her chair so she was sitting by her friends, as he and Wyatt moved to sit opposite them. Waiting until they cleaned themselves up and regained some control over their emotions before beginning.

"You were sexually abused by a teacher from Harlwood Academy?" he began gently.

Shame flickering in each of their eyes. "Yes," Chelsea was the unspoken designated leader.

"The teacher who abused you was a Dylan Riley?"

"Yes."

"When did it begin?"

"Eighth grade."

"When did it stop?"

"Tenth grade, up until . . ." she trailed off and looked a silent question to her friends.

"They know that Tessa was in an accident but they don't know any of the details," Michelle answered.

"Up until the night that Tessa ended up in the hospital," Chelsea finished.

"What does this have to do with what's happening now?" Parker still couldn't see the connection. There was more to this story than they were telling.

Chelsea looked to her friends for permission, they reluctantly nodded their consent.

"We've come this far we may as well tell them everything," Carrie said, defeated.

Readying herself with a deep breath. "Okay, detectives, you wanted the truth well here it is . . ."

Ten Years Ago

February 5ᵗʰ

"What camp is it supposed to be this time?" fifteen-year-old Gina asked, tossing her long brown ponytail over her shoulder.

"Math," Lauren supplied, pulling her jacket more tightly around her shoulders. "You'd think someone would notice that we never take books on these camps. It's a study camp."

"No one notices because no one cares," Chelsea shot back cynically.

They continued on in silence through the thick woods that surrounded the usual place for these impromptu 'camps'. It was a beautiful winter's night. The giant moon hung low in an inky black sky, stars twinkled merrily around it. Snow was still thick on the ground, and the whole world glittered in the silvery moonlight.

Breaking the silence, "I think we should do something," Tessa announced, breathing heavily.

"Tess, you know what he said he'd do if we told," Melanie's petrified eyes bored into Tessa's.

Meeting her gaze. "I know what he said, but we can't go on like this. Besides if we . . ." she broke off, seized by a fit of coughing.

"You okay, Tess?" Michelle asked, concerned.

"Just a cold," Tessa choked out between coughs.

Laying a hand on Tessa's forehead. "You're burning up," Lauren exclaimed. "You shouldn't've come."

Shooting her a look that said that was clearly not an option.

"He won't be happy that you're sick, Tessa," Dorothy chimed in.

Conversation fading as the log cabin came into view. It was a beautiful looking place, especially draped in thick, white snow. Candlelight spilling out of the large windows on either side of the thick wooden door, the dormer windows that peeked out of the roof, were dark. From the outside it looked like something out of an old fashioned Christmas card. Inside it was a place of nightmares.

The car in the driveway confirmed that he was already there. The girls steps slowed subconsciously the nearer they got. After being dropped off at the school, where their parents and teachers thought they were boarding a bus to be taken to their camp destination, the girls had instead hiked for over an hour through the woods to the small hidden cabin.

Coming to a complete stop, just feet from the front door, they postponed the inevitable for as long as possible.

"We should go in," Tiffany spoke up, but neither she nor any of the others made any attempt to move.

"Tessa, you're shaking, are you cold?" Janice asked worriedly.

"I told you I'm fine," Tessa wheezed.

"Fever, chills, shortness of breath, cough, you are definitely not fine," Michelle shot back.

"You left out headaches, chest pains, muscle aches and nausea," Tessa told her glumly.

"Tessa," Michelle, an amateur doctor, chastised. "That sounds like pneumonia."

"I'll be . . ."

"Fine," the others finished for her.

Shrugging Tessa moved forward, the others trailing along behind her. Opening the door, they were met by the familiar sight of the cabin's warm living room. The room was sparsely furnished with a large wooden table and six matching chairs in a corner near the small kitchenette. A couple of rocking chairs and a couch were grouped around the fireplace, and a rickety timber staircase led to the upstairs bedroom.

A fire roared and crackled in the fireplace, there was no electricity in the cabin the only light came from the candles that were set on the tables and benches. As they entered, a man turned to look at them, a wide smile spreading across his face.

"Ah, girls, you've finally arrived," Dylan Riley came towards them.

Slowly they came further inside, shrugging out of coats and scarves, they stood nervously around.

"Close the door, girls, it's cold out there," Dylan ordered.

Carrie obediently closed the door and Dylan passed her a combination lock. As she snapped it closed the girls hearts sunk as their only means of escape was sealed off.

"Dinner first or shall we get started right away?" he asked them *indicating the neatly set dinner table and the food cooking away on the gas fuelled stove.*

No one said anything.

Tessa swayed unsteadily, Dorothy and Tiffany quickly grabbed hold of her before she could fall over.

Dylan frowned at them. "What's wrong, Tessa?"

"She's sick," Michelle told him, as Tessa answered, "Nothing."

Looking from one to the other, Tessa shot Michelle a look then said to Dylan, "Really, I'll be fine."

"Okay then. I think dinner first and then desert," he winked at the girls, who shuddered with revulsion.

Pairing up the girls took their seats at the table, two to a chair, around the table, two sets of identical china were set in front of each of the seats. As usual, Tessa shared a seat with Dylan Riley.

Dishing up the meal, one of his favorites, Dylan was the only one who talked as they ate. The girls sat in silence, eating and exchanging worried looks with one another as they kept an eye on Tessa, who looked progressively worse throughout the meal.

Clearing away the dishes he left them in the sink. "I think these can wait," Dylan said, hungry anticipation all over his face.

Reaching for Tessa he pulled her to her feet, letting go of her as she doubled over, wracked by another coughing fit. Michelle knelt at her side, her eyes growing wide in horror as Tessa moved her hand away from her mouth. "Tessa!"

"What is it?" Lauren asked worriedly.

"She's coughing up blood," Michelle told them, lifting Tessa's blood splattered hand for the others to see.

"I'm fine," Tessa persisted weakly, her ashen face shining with sweat, her eyes glassy and unfocused. "I think I'm gonna be sick," she mumbled.

"Get her outside if she's going to throw up," Dylan snapped, grabbing Tessa's arm and yanking her towards the door. Quickly undoing the combination lock and throwing the door open, pushing Tessa roughly outside. She stumbled and sank to her knees, retching.

Pushing sluggishly to her feet she came back inside. "I'm fine," she repeated like a broken record.

"She's not fine, I think she might have pneumonia," Michelle interjected.

Sneering at her, "And when did you get your MD, Doctor Michelle?" Turning on Tessa, "You're ruining everything," he slapped her across the face, sending her tumbling to the ground. "Well if you're sick I'll just have to choose another 'friend' for the night."

"No, use me," Tessa pushed valiantly back to her feet, Dylan's bright red handprint standing out in stark contrast to her deathly pallor.

"You're sick," he spat out as he looked around at the others.

"No, please," she moved unsteadily towards him.

Preoccupied by his choice he didn't notice the knife in her hand until it was too late. Plunging it into his shoulder, her aim off because she was sick. Tessa pulled it out and was preparing to stab him again, when he snapped to attention. His huge hand encircling her thin wrist. "Drop it," he yelled.

"No," she shrieked back thrashing wildly under his grip.

Keeping hold of her wrist, he put his other hand on her elbow and moved them in opposite directions. Snapping her arm as though it were nothing but a twig. Screaming in agony, Tessa dropped to the floor as he released her, lying where she fell as she cradled her broken arm.

Frozen in stunned silence the others didn't know what to do.

Dylan shouted in fury, picking up one of the kitchen chairs he hurled it across the room, where it went flying through one of the windows. The glass shattering as cold air came whipping through the cabin.

Calming himself with several deep breaths, he regained some control over his anger. Barely aware of the blood flowing down his arm and soaking his shirt, as he smiled wickedly down at Tessa. "You will pay for that."

Looking at the others he pointed at each of them in turn as he sang, "eenie, meenie, miney, mo, catch a tiger by the toe, if he hollers let him go, eenie, meenie, miney, mo. Chelsea, dear, looks like you're the winner."

"No, leave her alone," Tessa whimpered softly from the floor.

Squatting beside her he yelled at the others, "Upstairs now. You can be a watcher today, Tessa," he whispered in her ear. Then lifted her into his arms, ignoring her moans of pain, and carried her up the stairs.

* * * * *

No one moved until they heard his car door slam, the engine stutter unhappily to life and the car take off down the deserted road. Carrie and Lauren went quickly to the bed, wrapping their arms around a sobbing Chelsea. Michelle crossed the room and dropped down in front of Tessa, whose head was cradled in Gina's lap.

"*Tessa?*" *she said lightly tapping her friend's cheek.*

Face pale, cheeks flushed, Tessa's eyes opened slowly, glittering brightly with fever. "*I need you to stay with me, okay, Tess?*" *Michelle told her as the others gathered around. When she got no answer,* "*Okay, Tess?*"

"*Okay,*" *Tessa replied weakly.*

Carefully maneuvering Tessa's arm to examine it. "*Sorry*" *she murmured when Tessa winced in pain. When Dylan had snapped the bone he had done it with enough force to cause a compound fracture, where the bone came all the way through the skin.*

"*How bad is it?*" *Janice asked.*

"*Bad,*" *gently lowering Tessa's arm.* "*The bone came through the skin, so it's an open wound, that means a high chance of infection. Infection means she could lose her arm, or she could . . .*" *Michelle trailed off unable to say the word.*

"*We need to get her to the hospital,*" *Melanie bit at her nails nervously.* "*But we have no phone, no car and no way of getting her there.*"

"*We need to get help somehow,*" *Tiffany fretted.*

"*The school is the closest place to here, but we'd need to take her with us,*" *Dorothy thought aloud.*

"*We can't take her with us, it's freezing out there,*" *Lauren protested.*

"*Well we can't leave her here. If anyone sees this place they're going to figure out what's been going on,*" *Dorothy fired back.*

"*Tess, you hanging in there?*" *Michelle asked.*

"*Yes,*" *she whispered back softly.*

"*How are we going to get her there?*" *Gina questioned.*

The girls thought for a moment. "*The table,*" *Chelsea announced.* "*If we turn it upside down we can lie Tessa on it and use the legs to pull the table along. It should slide along the snow like a sled."*

"That's perfect," Carried beamed.

"Okay then," Michelle started doling out orders, "Before we move her I need to stabilize her arm. I'm gonna need some things to make a splint. I'll need two pieces of something rigid and some strips of material to wrap it up. We need to find as many blankets as we can to cover her, it's cold out there, and she's in shock."

Hurrying off to find the things they needed and to ready their makeshift sled. Returning quickly with two smooth pieces of wood from the broken chair and some strips of material they'd ripped from the bed sheet.

"Sorry, Tess, this is going to hurt," Michelle cautioned.

Taking the hand of Tessa's good arm. "Here, squeeze my hand," Gina told her.

"Ready?"

Pressing her eyes firmly closed Tessa nodded unsteadily, "Ready."

Applying the splint as quickly as she could. "Done."

Tessa let out a shaky breath, as the others came back upstairs.

"We're ready down there but how are we going to get Tessa down the stairs?" Carrie asked.

"I can walk," Tessa put in immediately.

"I don't know," Michelle said warily. "You were already pretty wobbly on your feet, and now with this."

Coughing, "We don't have time to waste," Tessa told her adamantly.

Nodding her consent, "Okay, but we go slowly and you tell us if you need a break."

Painstakingly they half assisted, half carried Tessa down the stairs and lowered her onto the table, covering her with several blankets to keep her warm. "Tessa, you need to stay awake," Michelle warned.

Maneuvering the table through the door they started on their trek back to the school. A trip that took them an hour on a good day. Clouds had crept back, blocking out almost any light that the moon gave out. A strong wind had blown up, buffeting them as they wound their way through the thick forest.

"Hey I just thought of something," Chelsea said as the girls switched

places and another four took their turn at pulling the table. "What are we going to say happened to her?"

"We didn't think of that," *Bianca moaned.*

"Of course we didn't. We're used to Tessa coming up with all our plans," *Carrie shot back.*

"Well we better think of something, because we certainly can't tell them the truth. That the teacher who rapes us snapped her arm because she tried to kill him," *Melanie panicked.*

"I've got it. We'll tell them that the camp was cancelled, so we went back to the school to call our parents, and Tessa fell down the stairs," *Janice told them triumphantly.*

"That should work," *Dorothy nodded.*

"Okay then that's our story and we stick to it no matter what," *Michelle looked around to make sure they were all in agreement. Nine heads nodded their confirmation.* "Tessa, you with us?"

"I'm with you," *came the weak reply from the bundle of blankets.*

"Hey what's one more secret?" *Tiffany said with a wry smile.*

Laughing mirthlessly they continued on in silence.

* * * * *

April 28th

"Tessa!"

At the sound of her name she turned towards the door of her hospital room, a grin breaking out on her face as she saw her friends. She had been in the hospital for almost three months, being treated for pneumonia and numerous infections. Her arm had almost healed and she was due to be released in a week. Her grandparents had so far forbidden her friends to come and visit while she had been in the hospital and she was dying to see them.

"We brought you flowers," *Michelle announced setting them down on a shelf that was already overflowing with a colorful array of bouquets.*

"And this," *Gina pulled a huge, fluffy teddy bear from a bag and passed him to Tessa.*

"He's beautiful," Tessa smiled back.

They waited while the nurse finished checking Tessa's blood pressure, making a note on her chart. *"You are doing much better, Miss Micah. I'll leave you in the very capable hands of your friends."*

When the door was safely closed behind the nurse Carrie kept watch through the window while the others clustered around Tessa's bed, their smiles gone.

"What is it? What's wrong?" Tessa asked immediately.

Tears spilling from her grey eyes, Chelsea whispered, *"I'm pregnant."*

Understanding dawning immediately. *"Dylan,"* she stated.

Chelsea nodded.

"Who knows?"

"No one," Lauren told her, putting a comforting arm around Chelsea's shoulders.

Pausing to think for a moment, *"we can't tell anyone about this,"* Tessa told them, taking charge of the situation as the others had known she would. *"People would think that the baby is Jasper's . . ."*

"But we haven't . . ." Chelsea interrupted.

"That doesn't matter," Tessa told her. *"That's what they'll think. But Dylan will know. And if he finds out you're pregnant with his child he'll want the baby, we cannot let that happen. At any cost."*

Looking to see if the others agreed, they all knew what would happen to that child if Dylan ever got his hands on it.

"We tell Jasper," Tessa announced. *"We tell him everything."*

"Everything?" Melanie repeated nervously.

"Everything," Tessa nodded.

"What if we can't trust him? What if he tells? What if he blames us?" Dorothy was panicking.

"It's okay," Tessa soothed. *"If I wasn't sure that we could trust him then I wouldn't have suggested it. Has Dylan done anything while I was in here?"*

"No," Tiffany shook her head for emphasis. *"He's backed off. I think he's scared someone will connect him to what happened. He's taking some heat for 'cancelling' the camp and 'letting' us go back to the school on our own."*

"People bought the story?"

Exchanging glances. "Well . . ." Lauren started.

"Well what?" Tessa prompted.

"There's a rumor going around that we hurt you," Melanie said softly.

"Let me guess it was started by Claudia?"

Gina nodded.

"Who cares what they think as long as we keep our mouths shut no one can prove anything."

"You have a plan?" Janice confirmed.

"I have a plan. But once we start down this road we won't ever be able to take it back. So if someone wants to back out then now is the time," she warned them.

Holding out her hand one by one the others placed their hands on top of hers. "Okay then here it goes."

* * * * *

November 20th

"Are you absolutely sure we're doing the right thing?" Chelsea asked for the hundredth time.

"I don't see another option, do you?" Tessa asked.

Shaking her head. "No. I'm just nervous I guess," Chelsea apologized.

"I know," Tessa smiled and gave her friend a reassuring hug.

"Maybe we should have met somewhere else," Chelsea was looking nervously around as if expecting someone to jump out of the woods at any moment.

"I can't think of a better place to put this all behind us than right here," Tessa replied pointing to the cabin.

"What if he comes here today?" Chelsea insisted.

"He won't," Tessa told her confidently. "I took care of it."

"What did you do?"

"Nothing for you to worry about, I just made sure that he was . . . otherwise occupied today," Tessa answered vaguely. "You have the papers?"

she asked changing the subject.

"I got 'em," Jasper replied pointing to a bag.

"Okay, you two ready to do this?"

"We're ready," Chelsea's voice trembled.

"It's going to be okay, Chels, I promise," Tessa told her, tears pricking at her own eyes.

"I'm going to go get him," Chelsea gave her a quick hug and hurried inside.

Jasper and Tessa stood in silence for a moment, the wind howling around them, then Jasper spoke, "I'm really glad you trusted me, Tess."

Tessa smiled at him. "I knew you wouldn't let me down. I knew you wouldn't let Chelsea down."

"Thank you, for everything."

"You're welcome."

Taking her shoulders in his hands Jasper turned her to face him, bending down so that they were eye to eye. "It wasn't your fault, Tessa. I wish that you'd believe that."

She said nothing, but felt a tear escape and slide down her cheek.

"What can I say to convince you?"

Giving him a sad smile. "Nothing. But what you can do for me is look after them, make sure they're safe."

Pulling her against his chest. "Done," he said into her hair.

"It's time," Chelsea said from behind them.

"Let me say goodbye one last time," Tessa whispered, taking the tiny baby from his mother's arms. Cradling him gently, she kissed his soft little cheek and stroked his tiny baby hand as it clutched her finger. Tears flowing down her cheeks now, the wind making them feel like small drops of ice.

Chelsea's arms went around her. "We're doing the right thing, Tess," she said, their roles momentarily reversed.

"I know. If Dylan found out about Tanner he would stop at nothing to get him. This way even if he somehow found out he'll think that you're all dead," giving the baby a last kiss she gave him back to Chelsea. "You sure you've got everything, birth certificates, driver's licenses, bank account details?"

Laughing softly. "Yes, mom," Chelsea said as she put the baby in his car seat.

"Oh and don't forget to take the baby seat, not just the baby, out before you push the car over the cliff," Tessa called out.

Chelsea said nothing, just raised an eyebrow and gave her one last hug before climbing into the car with Jasper, the other girls came outside to wave them off.

"Once a year on this day, we call each other. And in an emergency," Tessa reminded them all.

As the car took off, a loud crash of thunder broke the stillness as the heavens opened and rain came pounding down. A flash of lightening brightened the sky to give them a last look at their departing friends.

"To the grave," Tessa whispered to her friends. "We take this secret to our graves, Chelsea, Jasper and Tanner's lives depend on it."

"To the grave," her friends repeated. Arms wrapped around one another as they stood in the pouring rain and watching their friends head off to a new, better and safer life . . .

"And so we drove off, stopped the car on the edge of a cliff, got out, got Tanner out and pushed the car off the cliff," Chelsea finished.

For a moment Parker could think of nothing to say. This was insane. This story sounded like something straight out of a soap opera. Eventually asking the only question that really mattered, "Do you know where she is? Do you know where Dylan Riley is?"

Five heads shook in the negative.

The clock was ticking

"What about the cabin?" Surely that must be the place Dylan would choose to stage his revenge.

Rolling her eyes at him. "What you think we didn't check that out already?" Lauren asked.

"You faked your own deaths," he still couldn't believe they had really done it. "How?"

"It wasn't that hard. Tessa organized all the papers we needed, set us up with some money and a place to live. Look, we did what we did because we had no choice, it was the only way we could keep Tanner safe, to keep him away from Dylan," Chelsea said softly.

"So you were keeping the secret so that nobody would find out that you and Jasper were really alive, because if they did they would find out about Tanner and then Dylan would know that he had a son," Parker summarized for his own benefit.

Chelsea nodded.

"How did you hide your pregnancy?"

"Same as most teenage girls who wind up pregnant, baggy clothes and stuff. We were lucky, other then the eleven of us we didn't really have any friends, and my parents were never very interested in me, so they weren't a problem. Michelle and the others, except Tessa, delivered him."

Frowning in confusion. "Tessa didn't help?"

"Tessa can't stand the sight of blood. Since Eleanor was . . . you know, and Tessa was covered in her blood. If she sees someone with blood on them, she goes almost catatonic, she gets really pale and she starts to shake. And if she gets blood on herself, she becomes hysterical, she can't breathe and she cries. You have to get the blood off her right away or she completely loses it," Lauren explained.

Remembering how Tessa had reacted when she'd seen the video of Dorothy's death. At the time, he had thought she was just heartless and unfeeling, but Dorothy had had a head wound, a bloody head wound, and he now understood that was all Tessa had seen.

"Does it have to be a lot of blood?" he asked.

Michelle shook her head. "I've seen her freak out over a paper cut."

"What did you do with the baby after he was born?" Wyatt questioned.

"We hid him until it was time to leave," Chelsea told him.

"Why did you hang around until after he was born? Why not go straight away?"

Chelsea shrugged. "I don't know. I guess that everyone wanted to be there when the baby was born."

"I have a question about Tessa," the girls looked at him expectantly. "If she was so smart why was she in a normal school, did she skip any classes?"

"She wouldn't," Melanie answered simply.

"She was miles ahead of us, of the teachers," Michelle added. "But Tessa doesn't let anyone tell her what to do."

"Was she bored in her classes?"

"Tessa didn't study she just read, she has a photographic memory so she remembers everything she's ever read. She spends hours reading, anything and everything," Carrie explained.

"How did the abuse start?" Wyatt asked bringing the conversation back to the topic at hand.

Lauren took over the story telling, "He started at the school as our teacher in the eight grade. The first lesson he told us he was taking us on a field trip. He took us to the cabin, and he . . . he raped us."

"That first time he, you know, with all of us, but after that he usually only did it with Tessa. He made us watch, he called us the 'watchers'," Carrie added.

"He usually only raped Tessa?" Parker echoed, his heart tightening.

"She was his favorite. He was obsessed with her," Michelle told them, looking at the others who nodded, "she had some private classes with him, because she was like advanced, advanced."

"What did he do to her in their private classes?" Fear washing over him as he thought about the horrible things Dylan Riley might have done to Tessa when he had her alone.

"She wouldn't tell us," Chelsea answered.

"Where did he do it?"

"Only ever at the cabin," Melanie replied.

"At your 'camps'? How often did you have them?"

"Yeah only ever at the camps, and we had them like, what, once a month?" Lauren looked to her friends for confirmation.

"You said that he told you he'd kill you if you told anyone what he was doing."

"He told us that if anyone told then he'd make that girl choose one of us for him to kill," Chelsea shuddered. "We still should have said something."

"You were kids, he took advantage of you, he manipulated you," Parker reassured them. "So that night Tessa tried to kill him?" he was amazed at her bravery.

"Yeah," guilt in Melanie's eyes, mirrored in the eyes of her friends. "I'm not sure that she knew what she was doing though. She was delirious, I think she just subconsciously enacted what we were all wanting to do. Tessa always blamed herself for everything that happened that night. She thought Chelsea getting pregnant was her fault, if she hadn't been sick, he never would have raped Chelsea that night and this would never have happened."

"That's crazy," Parker exclaimed, he hated the thought of Tessa blaming herself for something that to everyone else she was so clearly not responsible for. He got the impression this was something she did often.

"That's Tessa," Carrie shrugged helplessly. "It wasn't her fault, it was our fault. It just all happened so quickly. If we had backed her up, maybe we would have killed him and then all of this . . ." she waved her hand around, "Maybe it wouldn't have happened."

"You can't think like that," Parker told her. Thinking of the number of people that blamed themselves for this series of events, when the one person who really was to blame probably thought he was innocent.

"Tessa almost died. She was sick, she had pneumonia, and he attacked her. Snapped her arm like it was a twig, it got infected," Michelle reminded them, they were not going to be persuaded.

"If Tessa hates the sight of blood why did she stab him?" Wyatt asked confused.

Jumping to her defense. "We told you," Lauren frowned at him. "Tessa had a fever, she was delirious, she didn't know what she was doing."

"What happened while Tessa was in the hospital?" Parker was still shaken by the thought of how close she had come to death.

"We panicked," Carrie said flatly. "Tessa was our leader, she was the one who held us all together. Without her we kind of fell apart. We hid Chelsea's pregnancy but other than that we just waited for Tessa to tell us what to do."

"What would you have done if Tessa had of died?" Wyatt asked.

They looked at one another but none of them seemed to be able to come up with an answer. At last Chelsea said, "I really don't know what we would have done."

"She was a brilliant actress, without her I don't think we would have been able to pull it all off," Melanie added.

"And you really saw no other way out?" Wyatt pressed.

"Dylan would have taken Tanner. He would have destroyed him, turned him into a monster just like himself," Chelsea defended their decision.

"What about an abortion?" Wyatt continued.

"That wasn't an option," Chelsea replied in a voice that indicated the topic was closed.

"What did Tessa mean when she said that she kept Dylan 'otherwise occupied' that day," Wyatt questioned, changing track.

"I don't know, she wouldn't tell us what she did," Michelle shrugged.

"You said Dylan was obsessed with Tessa, why do you think that?" The knowledge that the lunatic who Tessa was on her way to confront was obsessed with her only added to his terror.

"Everything he did was about Tessa. He was stalking her. He had rooms full of photos of her. He tried to control everything that she did. He didn't care about the rest of us," Michelle clarified.

"Tessa knows this and yet she went straight to him?"

"She feels responsible for Tanner. For all of us," Melanie explained.

"Responsible enough that she's willing to risk letting him kill her so that she can keep him away from the rest of you?"

Looking at one another. "You still don't get it," Carrie told him.

"Get what?" Feeling like he had somehow missed the entire point of their story.

"He doesn't want Tessa dead," Chelsea told him.

"I don't understand," but he was very afraid that he did.

"He wants her alive and all to himself," Michelle added.

Blood pounded in his ears, his throat closed, he couldn't breathe, forcing words out, "Tessa knows this?"

"It's why she went," Melanie said sadly. "Somehow he found out about Tanner, that's why he did all of this, he thought it would make Chelsea come back. Tessa won't let him hurt Tanner."

Forcing himself to calm down, he was no good to Tessa if he was too terrified to do his job.

Chelsea frowned at him in confusion, then asked her friends, "Does he like Tessa?"

Lauren nodded. "Yeah, only he was too chicken to tell her how he felt about her. She was really upset about it."

His heart stopped. "Would she have stayed if I'd told her?"

Unsure if he wanted to hear the answer, the seconds seemed like hours.

"No," Carrie finally said. "She would have gone anyway. She would have done anything to protect Tanner."

"I should have told her how I felt," Parker murmured more to himself than anyone in the room. "I should have stayed by her side and refused to let her out of my sight."

"She knew how you felt. That's why we did the fire evacuation thing," Michelle admitted sheepishly. "Sorry about that."

He couldn't care less about the evacuation now. "She knew how I felt?" he confirmed, feeling like a weight had been lifted from his shoulders.

"Yeah she knew," Melanie smiled at him reassuringly. "It made her really happy, happier than any of us have ever seen her."

"She felt the same way?"

"Of course she did, she was just too scared to say it out loud. Tessa doesn't trust anyone, least of all herself. She thinks she ruins everything she touches," Lauren told him.

"She told me that." Relief that Tessa felt the same way about him only added to his determination to find her.

"Then that's proof of how much she likes you, she never opens up about herself. Not to anyone," Carrie smiled encouragingly.

"Tessa knew where she was going though?" Wyatt asked.

"Yeah, she said she knew where he was," Lauren replied.

"If Dylan is obsessed with her then he would choose a place that was significant to Tessa's past," Parker was thinking aloud.

Remembering the shadow he'd thought he'd seen moving in one of the windows of Tessa's mansion just before they'd smelt the smoke and discovered the fire. At the time he'd thought it was nothing more than his imagination, but now . . . "What about Tessa's place? It's in a deserted location. And she said she hasn't been inside the main house since she inherited it from her parents. That could be a good place to stash Janice and wait for Tessa."

Shaking her head. "He wouldn't go there. And Tessa didn't inherit that place from her parents, it was from her grandparents. Her parents are still alive," Chelsea explained.

"If the estate belonged to her grandparents why did they leave it to their grandchild and not their kid?"

The girls looked at one another. "Tessa wouldn't like us telling you about her family," Lauren cautioned.

"Right now all I care about is anything that can help me find her. Tessa angry I can deal with, Tessa dead . . . or worse, I can't," he snapped.

"Fine," Michelle sighed. "Tessa's mother is in a psychiatric hospital and her father lives overseas with his new wife and kids."

Waiting for details, none were forthcoming. "I'm going to need more than that girls," he prodded.

Sighing again, Michelle elaborated. "Tessa's mother suffered from depression. She was really hard on Tessa when she was little. Cold and distant. She never spent any time with Tess, just sat alone in her room drinking and painting, she never even knew when Tessa went missing. When Tessa was ten her father, he travelled a lot for work, left them because he was 'in love' with this woman he met in Paris. Her mom became worse, started mixing pills and alcohol, so they moved in with Tessa's grandparents, her father's parents. About two years after that her mom tried to kill Tessa and Daniel . . ."

"Who's Daniel?" Parker interjected.

"Tessa's brother," Lauren supplied.

". . . in the middle of the night," Michelle continued her narrative. "She was drunk and she thought that God told her to kill her kids. So she woke Tessa up, made her take some pills then took her to the bathroom, filled up the bath and tried to drown her. Daniel heard them and came in, he knocked his mother unconscious and pulled Tessa out of the bath. She wasn't breathing. Daniel did CPR and saved her life. Their mom pleaded guilty to attempted murder and made a deal to go to a psychiatric hospital for treatment."

"This happened where Tessa lives now?" Parker couldn't imagine the terror the little girl would have felt as her mother held her head under water.

"Yeah, the main house," Carrie confirmed.

"No wonder Tessa hates that place. After everything she's

been through it's a wonder she can get up in the morning," he was utterly amazed by her resilience.

"Tessa puts on a brave face but inside she's . . ." Lauren began but trailed off, unsure how to end the sentence.

"She's really messed up," Michelle supplied. "Don't hurt her, Detective Bell," she warned seriously. "She's been through enough."

"Where is Daniel? Would Tessa go to him for help?" Wyatt changed the subject.

"She doesn't know where Daniel is, no one does. When their mom tried to kill them, Tessa was twelve and Daniel was eighteen. After it happened he just took off, Tessa was devastated," Melanie told them.

"So he wasn't around during the time you were assaulted by Dylan Riley?" Wyatt checked.

"No," Lauren shook her head.

"Would she have known how to contact him? Maybe opened up to him?"

"He always sent her a card on her birthday but other than that as far as we know she didn't know how to get in contact with him," Carrie explained.

"What about her dad? Does she talk to him?"

Shaking her head vehemently. "No way," Melanie said. "She hates him. He didn't even come to see her after Eleanor was killed, or after her mom tried to kill her and her brother left."

"He did try to get in contact with her a few years later. What like ninth grade?" Carrie looked to her friends for confirmation. The others nodded. "But Tessa would have nothing to do with him," Carrie continued.

"Was she close to her grandparents?" Parker hoped that she had been, that she had not been totally alone.

"I guess, they were kinda close," Michelle nodded. "But they were pretty self-obsessed, and her grandmother was sick for a while, cancer."

"Now I don't want to make anyone mad, but," Wyatt started cautiously as all eyes turned to look warily at him. "I think that we would be remiss if we didn't consider the possibility that Tessa is somehow involved with Dylan Riley."

Speaking over the top of one another in anger.

"Are you insane?" Parker shouted at him.

"How dare you say that about Tessa," Chelsea pushed to her feet, outraged.

"Tessa hated him, she would never be involved with him," Michelle snapped.

"Calm down, calm down," Wyatt soothed. "I'm not saying she is just raising the possibility. Tessa spent a lot of time alone with him, and she seems to know exactly what he's going to do . . ."

"Tessa's really good at reading people," Lauren said defensively.

"I understand that. If she is involved I'm thinking Stockholm Syndrome . . ."

"Where hostages identify with their captors and feel sympathetic towards them?" Melanie asked.

"But Tessa was never a hostage," Michelle pointed out.

"But she did spend time alone with him and we don't know what he did or said to her during those times," Wyatt reminded them.

"Tessa would never, ever, be in any way involved with Dylan," Chelsea said adamantly.

"I agree," Parker echoed immediately, he did not have any doubt about Tessa's loyalties.

"Me too," Lauren nodded, as did the others.

"Okay, okay," Wyatt said holding up his hands in surrender. "I give up." But Parker caught the look on his partner's face, Wyatt was going to store the thought away until it could be disproved by someone who wasn't emotionally invested in Tessa.

Sighing in frustration. "This is all very interesting but it doesn't help us find Tessa and Dylan. Are you sure that you don't know where he is?" Parker asked Tessa's friends. They exchanged glances and shook their heads, but he had seen a flicker of something in their eyes. Something that gave him hope. "You do know where they are."

Once again, they glanced at one another. "We don't know for sure, it's just an idea," Carrie warned.

"It's better than nothing," he pointed out.

"Dylan would only have chosen a place that was significant to Tessa's past, and there's only place, one event, we can think of that would be suitable to him," Melanie met his eye.

Comprehension flooded through him. "The place where Ellie was killed."

Surprised faces looked back at him and Parker had the feeling that he had somehow said the wrong thing. "What?"

"It's just that no one but Tessa ever called her Ellie, everyone else called her Eleanor," Melanie gave a sad smile.

"What about you guys, you never called her Ellie?"

"We were never really friends with Eleanor, she was always Tessa's friend. Back then Tess didn't really hang out with us, we were in the same class but it was always just her and Eleanor. They'd been friends since the very first day of pre-K. They were crazy those two," Melanie laughed.

"One time," Carrie joined in laughing, "Tessa decided that she wanted to try and make her own fireworks. She and Eleanor set fire to the lab and almost burned down the school."

"What about the time that she decided to make her own hot air balloon. She and Eleanor were about fifty feet in the air when the balloon started to come apart," Chelsea reminisced.

"Eleanor was the perfect match for Tessa, she was fun and bright and adventurous, she brought out Tessa's fun side. After Eleanor died Tessa just shut down, she was never the same after that," Lauren twisted her hair around her finger.

"Did Tessa ever tell you what happened that weekend?"

"No. She never told anyone. After the police found her

217

covered in blood and wandering alone by the side of the road, she didn't speak for months. Whatever happened to her out there changed her forever, she was only eleven," Chelsea whispered softly.

"Did you ask her about it?"

"Of course," Melanie nodded.

"But she wouldn't tell you anything? So you don't know *anything*?" Parker pressed.

"We know what we think happened," Michelle replied.

"What do you think happened?"

"I'm guessing the same thing *you* think happened," Melanie answered. "They were raped, Eleanor was murdered, and Tessa somehow managed to escape."

"So you think that Dylan is hiding out at the place where Eleanor was killed?" Forcing himself not to think about the possibility of eleven-year-old Tessa being raped right now or he'd lose it and this was the break he had been hoping for.

"Yes, but we don't know where that is," Carrie warned.

"Dylan Riley managed to find out where it happened," Wyatt pointed out. "Would she have told him?"

"No. If she didn't tell us then she didn't tell anybody. He probably followed her, we told you he was stalking her. She goes there, wherever there is, every year on the anniversary of Eleanor's death," Melanie supplied.

"Does what happened with Eleanor have anything to do with what's happening now?" Wyatt asked.

"I don't think so. If Dylan was the one who killed Eleanor then Tessa would have done anything to make him pay," Lauren said, the others nodding their agreement.

There was one thing that was still bothering him but Parker wasn't sure if he wanted to know the answer. "Did Tessa go there to kill him?"

"Of course not," Lauren shot back outraged.

"She's tried before," Wyatt reminded them gently.

Annoyed, "We already told you that she was sick, she didn't know what she was doing," Carrie spoke with exaggerated patience as though speaking with a small child.

"You're sure?" Parker pushed. He knew from experience that taking a life, no matter how justified, changed everything. It had ruined his sister's life and it had almost ruined his own.

"Tessa wouldn't do that," Chelsea insisted.

Satisfied, he changed the topic, "Tell us about Dylan Riley."

The girls said nothing.

"We heard that he was pretty cute . . ."

Melanie cut him off, "He was disgusting."

"But if this hadn't happened?" he pushed carefully, painfully aware of everything the man had done to them.

Sighing, "I guess he was kind of good looking for a pig," Carrie admitted reluctantly. "Lots of the other girls had a crush on him."

"He was really smart, not as smart as Tessa though, that always bugged him," Michelle smiled smugly.

"Organized, compulsive, a brilliant actor, he had everybody fooled. The other teachers all loved him, the other girls all wanted to be in our class to have him as a teacher." Chelsea shook her head. "All we wanted was to be as far away from him as possible."

"And he was a monster," Lauren added.

"How do you mean?"

Looking to the others for permission, when they nodded Lauren continued, "He killed Tiffany by," she shuddered, "By cutting off her arms and legs. When Tiffany was seven her brother was in an accident, they were sledding, he fell, his leg got cut off. Bianca he drowned her, when she was three she fell into her family's pool and nearly drowned. You seeing the pattern?"

"He killed them with their greatest fear." Beyond terrified at the thought of Tessa in the hands of this man.

Lauren continued, "Dorothy's father was left brain dead after a car accident, she was in the backseat at the time. And Gina's aunt committed suicide by . . ."

"Slashing her wrists," Parker finished.

Nodding, "And Gina was the one to find her, she was eight."

"How did he know so much about you?" Wyatt asked.

Melanie shrugged, "Who knows."

"And Tessa," Parker continued the theory through. "Tessa's greatest fear is not death by a certain method but being alone."

The girls nodded in confirmation.

Mind wandering to his own worst fear; failure. Not the fear of failing tests, or even failure in life, but the fear of failing those who were counting on him. In the past he'd let down so many of the people who had depended on him, and each time it was like a part of him had died. Dylan Riley was not going to make his worst fear come true. He was not going to fail Tessa.

Focusing his mind back on the present, glancing at the clock on the wall he decided it was time to wrap things up. At long last they had a lead, not to mention a lot of background on Tessa, it was time to get moving and track down where she had gone. "Okay girls, you've been really, really, helpful. If you don't mind we'd like you to remain somewhere safe until we have Dylan Riley in custody."

"We'll stay at my place," Michelle answered for all of them. "It's big enough for all of us."

"We'll have an officer stay with you at all times," Wyatt told them.

They all stood, Chelsea paused, "You'll find Tessa," it was a statement not a question. "Don't let him hurt her, she deserves to be happy."

"One more thing," Michelle said sheepishly. "When she left here she was going to my house. She was going to take my car, but she probably ditched it early on and took another one."

"We'll need the plates of all your cars," Wyatt told them, they all nodded in acquiescence.

Lingering at the door. "Is there something else?" Parker asked them.

"Tessa wanted us to give this to you," Carrie held out an envelope.

The hand he held out to take it was visibly shaking. Wyatt wordlessly followed the girls out the door to give him some privacy.

Alone he sat staring at the pale pink envelope in his hands. It smelled like Tessa's perfume. Opening it slowly he pulled out a single piece of paper, the same shade as the envelope, it was folded in half. Taking a deep breath to steady his pounding heart he unfolded the paper.

Dear Parker,

I wanted to write this note to apologize for hurting you. I'm sorry. I never wanted to hurt you but this is something that I have to do. I hope you can understand that. By the time you read this I'm sure you'll have heard all about my past from Chelsea and the others. Tanner is my responsibility and I have to do whatever it takes to keep him safe. Don't come looking for me. I don't blame you for doubting me but I promise you that I am not now and never was involved with Dylan Riley. I hope you can be happy Parker, don't let your fear hold you back. You deserve to be happy. I'm sorry that things had to end this way. I wish things could have turned out differently. I wish that . . .

Please forget about me

Tessa

A tear splashed onto the pink paper, making the ink smudge. Folding it back up he slid it back inside its envelope. He was going to find Tessa and he was going to tell her exactly how he felt about her.

* * * * *

7:41 P.M.

All she could think about as she drove was Parker.

By now he would know more about her past than anyone other than her friends.

Tessa had known that Chelsea would eventually turn up. She'd told her to stay away but she knew that Chelsea wouldn't be able to help herself.

Pushing the button to activate the window, she held her face up to the cold air, letting it wash over her. It had grown dark while she'd been driving. The moon was rising sleepily through the sky, the stars slowly coming out.

She'd chosen a white car from the rental agency. She'd pondered over both a black and a white car but eventually settled on white, with the reasoning that it tended to blend into the background more than a black car would. Neither too old or new in order not to draw undue attention to herself. Tessa always paid attention to detail.

It made her uncomfortable to think of Parker knowing so much about her. She had known that the others would tell him everything that Dylan Riley had done to them. Especially everything that had happened the night Tanner was conceived. She supposed Parker needed to know about that but there was no reason for them to tell him about her mother.

That night was just one of the things that plagued her dreams.

She had been awakened from a deep sleep. By the time she had realized what was happening her mother had already forced several pills down her throat. Groggy, she'd been unable to stop her mother from dragging her down the hallway, it had been like she was trapped in her own body. She'd watched helplessly as her mother had filled the bath with water. Her limbs had been heavy as she'd desperately tried to fight against her mother as she held her head under the water.

The terror that had washed over her as the water had entered her lungs was forever etched into her mind. After that she remembered nothing until she heard Daniel's voice calling to her as though from miles away. She'd opened sticky eyes to find his worried face hovering over her as she lay on the bathroom floor. The police and paramedics had shown up soon after, they'd taken her straight to the hospital, and by the time she'd returned home the following day Daniel was gone.

Anger flared up inside her as she thought about her brother. As kids they'd never been too close, he'd been six years older than her, and thought she was nothing but a child. But when their parents were having one of their nightly screaming matches she would take her pillow and her teddy bear and sleep on the floor in his room. She had been, and still was, devastated that he had left her without a word. Daniel was her big brother, he was supposed to take care of her, look out for her, instead he'd left right when she needed him the most.

As far as Tessa was concerned she had no family. Her father, Patrick, had not come to see her after Ellie was killed. He hadn't wanted to miss the birth of his and his new wife, Bridgette's, first child. He had not come to see her after her mother had tried to kill her, Emilie was no longer his concern he told her over the phone.

When he'd finally come to see her, four years after he'd left, he had wanted her to go with him to France to get to know Bridgette and her little half brother and sister, Patrick Junior and Serena. She had refused to see or speak to him.

Her mother had been no better a parent. When she wasn't drunk she had been busy ignoring Tessa altogether or shouting and screaming at her. After her father had left her mother got worse, and they'd moved in with her grandparents. Emilie had refused to leave the house and had started mixing pills with her alcohol. Her parents had never known how to deal with her, or even cared enough to try.

When her mother had been admitted to the psychiatric hospital Tessa had hoped that Emilie might finally get the help that she needed. But it was not to be. The psychiatrist treating her mother did nothing more than keep her heavily medicated and in an incomprehensible daze. As far as Tessa was concerned psychiatrists were lazy and useless. The psychiatrists who her grandparents had sent her to after Ellie had died and her mother had tried to kill her were just as incompetent.

Shivering, the cold air was starting to give her a headache. Keeping one hand on the wheel, she dug out a bottle of aspirin from her bag. Usually she hated to use medications, but when she got there she was going to need her wits about her. Putting the window back up as she dry swallowed a couple of the pills. If she was going to get Janice out of the house alive then she couldn't afford to be distracted.

From the moment she'd found out about Janice being abducted she'd known the place that he had chosen. There had only ever been one place he would choose. She remembered the day he had followed her there. To the place where Ellie had been killed. She went there every year on the anniversary of Ellie's death. He had thought he was so clever hanging back and staying out of sight, but she had sensed his presence immediately. He was nowhere near as clever as he thought he was.

Shaking her head as she thought of everything that must be going through Janice's head as she lay in that place waiting to die. She should have gone after Janice right away. It was a mistake not to. One of many that littered her past.

She had known from the beginning that being friends with the girls in her class would lead to nothing but heartbreak for everyone involved. She should have learnt after Ellie was killed. It was like she was cursed, she brought misery to anyone close to her.

If her friends had figured out where she was going then the police would soon be on her tail. That wasn't a problem, she wouldn't need much time. The police had never connected the house near to where she was found to Ellie's death. But Parker had an advantage that the police officers at the time had not had, he knew that Janice had to be held somewhere secluded. If he tracked down where she had been discovered then it wouldn't take long to find the house.

She hoped that Parker had read her note. She hoped that he would understand why she was doing this. She hoped that he would leave her to do what she needed to without interfering. She hoped that he would move on and finally allow himself to be happy.

She hoped that, for his own good, he would forget all about her.

* * * * *

10:28 P.M.

Hardly able to contain his glee.

Tessa would be on her way here by now. He'd been busily planning the whole evening. First they'd have dinner, just like they used too. Then they'd head upstairs so that they could get . . . reacquainted. They'd spend the night together in the room he'd prepared especially for her. Then in the morning he'd kill Janice and head off to start a wonderful life with Tessa. Wonderful for him at least he grinned.

Tessa would try to bargain for Janice's safe release, but he would allow her only one trade. Her life for Janice or her life for Tanner. He knew what she would choose. For some reason that he couldn't fathom Tessa felt responsible for Tanner, she thought that if she hadn't been sick that night then he would never have been conceived.

As he waited for Tessa to arrive, he thought back to the first time he had seen her. He had been working as a counselor at the children's hospital where Tessa's psychiatrist worked. That job had been where it all began. He'd had the opportunity to meet many vulnerable, susceptible young girls, most of them had been abused, physically, sexually or emotionally, usually by a relative. It had been an enjoyable job, but in the end he had gotten everything out of it that he could, and had decided that it was time to move on.

Tessa had been twelve, her grandparents had insisted that she see someone after her mother had tried to kill her. Even back then Tessa had been stubborn and self-assured. Her grandparents could make her see the psychiatrist but they couldn't make her talk to him. She had sat there in silence every day for five months, until at last the psychiatrist, a particularly obnoxious old man who had always been unpleasant to Dylan, had told her grandparents not to bother sending her in again.

After watching her, intrigued, for several months he had finally made a move and tried to talk to her. Making sure the whole things seemed casual and unplanned, he'd approached, introduced himself and offered her a candy bar from a vending machine. Her bluey green eyes had shot pure hatred at him from the second he had identified himself as a psychiatrist.

From that moment he had known that nothing would stop him from having her.

Sneaking her file from Dr Obnacious, or 'Dr Obnoxious' as Dylan always thought of him, he had read and memorized it. Then he'd begun following her until he was convinced that he had learnt everything possible thing there was to know about her.

Deciding that her school was the best way to keep in touch with her he had faked references and applied for a job there as the teacher of Tessa's class. He'd bluffed his way through his interview, and helped along by his high IQ, had easily beaten out the other candidates for the job.

Recognition had bloomed on her face the second she had seen him at her school. But for some reason that had never been clear to him, she had never told anyone that he was not really a teacher. She had never mentioned knowing him from the hospital, or that he was supposedly a counselor with a different name, in any of the times they had been alone together.

Following Tessa's 'accident' and Chelsea's suicide attempt he had been forced to leave, worried that one of the girls would break down and tell everything, but he had vowed to come back for Tessa.

He had known since the beginning that they were up to something. Ever since that weekend where he had been robbed and locked in his basement by a masked intruder, coincidently the same weekend that Chelsea committed suicide.

When he'd found out about Tanner he had been furious. The knowledge that they had conspired against him to keep him from his son had almost caused him to go on a killing spree there and then. It had taken everything in him to restrain himself, to bury his feelings and turn them into something constructive. To come up with a calm and rational plan of attack, and it had been well worth it.

For the last ten years he had been forced to move from place to place. Assuming one identity after another. Determined to figure out exactly what they had been trying to hide from him. Eventually resorting to bugging their houses, all except Tessa's, she was almost as paranoid as himself. Her house was like a fortress, wired to the hilt to keep trespassers out. After almost a year he had finally overheard a conversation of interest, on the anniversary of Chelsea's 'death' they had called one another for their annual catch up.

Once he'd learnt about Tanner he had been determined to get back his son whatever the cost. Now it paled in comparison to having Tessa. She was the one thing that he'd always wanted but had always remained tantalizingly out of reach. He was going to have Tessa all to himself for the rest of their lives. He might not have Tanner but he and Tessa would have a family of their own.

He was in control now, and he was about to get everything that he had ever wanted.

DECEMBER 1ST

12:19 A.M.

"Where's the file? It should be here by now," Parker was pacing backwards and forwards across his lieutenant's office.

"It's the middle of the night," J.J. gestured at the black window.

"I should have told her," he continued as though J.J. hadn't spoken. "I shouldn't have let her out of my sight."

"She had her friends fake a fire evacuation so she could get out, there was nothing you could have done to stop her. She already had her mind made up," his partner pointed out. "She wanted to do this."

"We get anything on the friend's cars?" J.J. asked.

"All accounted for. We found Michelle's at a car rental place. We confirmed Tessa rented a car and got the plates, we put out an APB but she's had a massive head start," Wyatt filled him in.

"About her friends, faking someone's death . . ."

"Technically they just let everyone else assume that Chelsea and Jasper had committed suicide," Parker defended.

Glaring J.J. continued, "Chelsea and Jasper left a fake suicide note, they had false driver's licenses . . ."

Interrupting again, "Actually they legally changed their names." After talking to the girls, he and Wyatt had looked into the steps that had been taken for Chelsea and Jasper to successfully fake their deaths and start a new life.

Annoyed, "they were underage so they couldn't do that legally," J.J. retorted. "We'll need to talk to them about it later."

Shrugging, "Chelsea will deny anyone else was involved," Parker told him.

"I thought she told you otherwise," looking from him to Wyatt.

Shooting his partner a warning look, "I don't remember that."

"We'll need to talk to them later," J.J. repeated through clenched teeth.

Three heads turned as the door opened and Victoria and Thomas entered. "What did you find?" Parker pounced on them immediately.

"We've got bad news," Thomas started.

Parker steeled himself.

"There's no record of Dylan Riley before the year he started at Harlwood Academy."

Heart sinking as another lead faded into nothingness. "That's not his real name," he murmured.

"Dylan Riley never existed before he got that job and he left without notice the week after Chelsea Ward 'committed suicide'. It's like he just fell off the face of the earth. Sorry, Parker," Thomas shot him a sympathetic glance that was mirrored in each of the other faces that peered worriedly over at him.

Apparently, the news that he was personally involved with Tessa had spread, but he was beyond caring about that now, all that mattered was getting her back safe and sound. The clock was ticking and all he could think about was finding Tessa before she disappeared forever with Dylan Riley, or whoever he really was.

"We're not going to find him through his name. We have no idea who he really is, no idea who he was before Dylan Riley and no way of knowing his current identity. It's been ten years he could have gone through a dozen names in that time. There is no way we are going to find this guy through his name," Victoria repeated.

"We need the file. That's what I've been saying. The girls said that he would be hiding out near where Eleanor was killed . . ."

Interrupting, Wyatt corrected, "No, they said that was what they thought."

Glaring at him, "They seemed pretty sure about it. Besides it's not like we have any other leads."

"What exactly are you suggesting we do? Find out where Tessa was found then get in our car and drive around out there and hope that we just happen upon the place where Dylan Riley's hiding out?"

"Yes. That is exactly what I'm suggesting."

Wyatt threw his hands up in the air in frustration. "Parker, that is a ridiculous waste of time."

"Well Tessa's life is at stake, do you want me to just sit back and do nothing?" The thin veil that had been holding back his emotions bursting wide open, sending his anger spurting out.

"Just because this is about your girlfriend . . ."

"She's not my girl . . ."

"Stop it you two," J.J. thundered glowering at them as though they were a pair of bickering five-year-olds. "You're both tired, and this case has been nothing if not draining, but we're almost there and we need to stay focused. Take a seat," he ordered.

Reluctantly Parker sat, feeling like as long as he was on the move he was making at least some progress. When they were both seated J.J. continued, "Okay so the friends think that this guy is hiding out near where Tessa's friend was killed?"

"They said he was obsessed with Tessa and he would only go somewhere related to her past," he summarized tersely.

"And there's no where else they think he would go?"

"No, they seemed pretty sure that he'd be there," Parker gave his partner a look, daring him to disagree.

Wyatt said nothing.

"But they have no idea where this happened, where the girl was killed?"

"That's why we need the file. It will say where Tessa was found. She was eleven, she couldn't have gone far on her own."

"She wasn't like most eleven-year-olds. She's a genius remember," Wyatt cut in.

Frowning at him, "She was a scared little girl. She wasn't thinking like a genius she was thinking like a terrified child who'd just witnessed a murder." To J.J., "She was so traumatized that she didn't speak for months after she was found," he defended his position.

"We can't check with her family?"

"Dad lives overseas, she hasn't had anything to do with him in years, didn't even come to see her after all of this happened. Brother disappeared years ago and no one knows where he went. Grandparents died a few years ago. And her mom is in a psychiatric hospital."

Raising an eyebrow. "Maybe we should go talk to the mom, she might know something."

"I don't think so. Apparently she was pretty uninvolved in Tessa's life. She didn't even know that Tessa was missing that weekend."

"What about the cop who found her?"

"He's dead, killed by a drug dealer," Parker answered shortly. According to Tessa's friends, she had grown quite close to the officer, and had been devastated when he had been killed. Another person for her to add to the list of those she had trusted and had left her.

Nodding slowly, "Okay. When we find out where Tessa was found after her friend's murder, you can go out there, drive around, and see what you can find. At this point it can't hurt," J.J. gave his permission.

Quenching the desire to spring to his feet and cheer he managed a composed, "Thanks, J.J.."

Wyatt sighed but said nothing.

"But in the meantime I think we go talk to the mom. Thomas, Victoria, you two go see what you can get out of her. And we'll give the dad a call, maybe we'll get lucky and he actually knows something, or he might have heard from the brother. It's worth a shot," J.J. said noting Parker's disbelieving face.

Opening his mouth to protest he stopped as the door opened, a young curly-haired officer standing there, a file in his hand. "Sorry to interrupt, sir, but this file arrived, about the murder of an Eleanor Matthews." The young officer started as Parker sprang to his feet, ripping the file from his hand.

"Parker, you don't find her tonight and you're off this case," J.J. announced before he could dart out the door. "You're involved with Tessa, I won't have that messing things up when this gets to court. You want to be her hero, find her tonight."

The warning was pointless, if he didn't find Tessa tonight, they'd never find her. "Let's go," he called over his shoulder to Wyatt as he grabbed the car keys from his partner's desk and sprinted down the stairs.

* * * * *

1:06 A.M.

Parking the car she had rented a short distance from the house Tessa decided to walk the rest of the way. She did not want Dylan to know she had arrived until she was ready, she still had to rescue Janice. She wanted her friend safely out of the way before she announced herself. No one else was going to die for her mistakes.

It was pitch black outside, clouds had once again rolled slowly across the great, open sky, and snow was fluttering and twirling down to the ground as though dancing to a song only it could hear. Tessa had wanted to approach in the dead of night so she had driven around and around in circles before finally making her way here.

Walking towards the house she thought of all that lay ahead. She'd known that it would always come to this. She should have just accepted it and gone off with him like he had originally demanded. It would have spared her friends a world of pain.

But she had been weak, and scared, and self-centered. She

hadn't wanted to be alone. To be trapped with him forever. Because of her four people were now dead. Not to mention the numerous lives that had been irrevocably destroyed.

No more. She was putting a stop to it now. She would give him what he wanted and he would leave the others alone. Sighing, maybe it was for the best. At least she wouldn't be able to ruin anyone else's life.

Stopping as the house came into view. The huge, imposing Tudor style mansion sat atop a small hill. Surrounded by nothing but acres of long, waving grasses. Once kept neatly trimmed, when the house had been abandoned the grounds had grown wild, and the house was slowly becoming increasingly dilapidated.

Tessa hated this place. Hated the memories that it invariably brought back.

Every time she came here she thought of Ellie. Sweet, trusting Ellie.

As children the two girls had been inseparable. Ellie had been the sister that Tessa had never had but always dreamed of. The two had even looked like sisters, Ellie's hair had been a darker blonde, and not quite as curly, Ellie's eye's had been a paler blue and her face had been covered in freckles instead of the light dusting that covered Tessa's own face.

Thinking back to the mischief that they had gotten themselves into. A laugh mingled with a sob escaping from her throat as she thought of the silly things they had done. The time they had turned the gym into a snow filled winter wonderland. The time they had frozen the school's pool so that they could go ice-skating in the middle of the summer. The time they'd decided to build their own log cabin, they'd thought it would be more fun to cut down the trees themselves. Unfortunately, one of the trees had crashed down on the headmistress's brand new car.

Every silly thing they had ever done had been her idea.

Including everything that happened that weekend.

Ellie hadn't wanted to go, she'd been scared, but Tessa had

insisted that everything would be fine. She'd always been too impulsive. She never thought through the consequences of her actions, just went blindly off doing whatever seemed fun at the time. It had been a mistake that had cost Ellie her life.

Squeezing her eyes shut as she remembered Ellie's lifeless body lying on the ground right here at this house. Blank, empty eyes staring back at her. Pressing hands to her ears as she heard Ellie's screams in her head as clearly as though her friend was standing right in front of her.

Ellie's face, pale and terrified, tears streaming down her cheeks, pleading silently at her for help. She'd wanted to help but she hadn't known what to do. The man had been too big, too quick. His eyes cold as he took the life of a child as though it had been nothing.

She had sat in the cold for what seemed like hours, next to Ellie's lifeless body, as it slowly grew dark. Until she'd heard voices coming towards them, then she had run, and run, and run, until her chest burned and her legs felt like they were about to fall off. Then she'd dropped to the ground, curled up in a ball and wept.

Eventually the sky had been completely black, the stars winking on one by one, and she'd slowly started for home, wandering along the side of the road. She had not even noticed the police car's headlights coming towards her.

The face of the police officer that found her was forever burned into her memory. Seeing that she was covered in blood, he'd asked if she was hurt, she hadn't known how to answer him so she'd simply said nothing. He'd checked her over then wrapped her up in his coat and carried her to his car, driving her straight to the hospital. He'd been sweet and gentle with her, talking away about his own little girls, his soothing voice slowly calming her racing heart.

Guilt, and fear, had prevented her from saying anything to any of the doctors at the hospital. They had sent her to the psychiatric ward when she wouldn't speak. She spent several days there, alone and scared, with no visitors but the policeman who found her.

Eventually the doctors discovered who she was, and managed to track down her grandparents who'd been holidaying in Egypt. They'd come to collect her and brought her home, where a huge argument had ensued between them and her mother, who had been so drugged out of her mind that she had not even noticed her eleven-year-old daughter was missing.

The first time she'd been left alone, Tessa had swallowed her terror and snuck off to come back to the house to see if Ellie was still there. She was. Her body still lying where she had been killed.

Her sense of responsibility for everything that had happened was overwhelming and she had withdrawn from the world. Refusing to say anything for months, to her family, her friends, or to any of the shrinks that her grandparents had insisted she see.

Eventually she had realized that she could never make up for what she'd done to Ellie if she didn't get out there into the world. So she'd gone back to school, applying herself with a vigor she'd never possessed before. Then she'd gone to college, once again making the most of every opportunity that came along. After graduating she'd decided that the best way she could honor the memory of the friend she had gotten killed was by bringing joy to other children. So, she had decided to write children's books. Every book that she wrote was for Ellie. To keep her memory alive.

But it seemed like reaching back out into the world had been a mistake too. And had only led to her causing more pain to her new friends.

Taking a deep breath, she walked slowly towards the house. She had failed Ellie. And Tiffany, Bianca, Dorothy and Gina.

There was no way she would fail the others, no matter what it cost her.

* * * * *

1:51 A.M.

It was dark again.

Janice liked the dark, it was so peaceful.

She had no idea how long she had been here now.

The days and nights melded into one long continuous blur.

It had been hours since she had last eaten.

She thought she was hungry but it was hard to tell.

Her mind felt like it was full of cotton wool.

Making it hard for her to think.

To focus.

She had figured out why the room she was in looked familiar.

It was Tessa's room.

Not her room now, her old room.

From when she was a child.

In her old house.

Before she moved in with her grandparents.

She'd only been there a few times but she was sure it was the same as the room she was in now.

He was still here.

She couldn't hear him but she could sense him.

He hadn't been up to see her in a long time.

Watching the stars slowly come out like millions of tiny lights being turned on in a huge black house.

It was what she spent most of her time doing, watching as the sky slowly brightened as the sun rose.

Then watching it sink slowly, a huge orange ball.

Her back was sore from days of lying here on the bed.

Arms and legs numb from lack of use.

Wrists and ankles felt like they were rubbed raw from the ropes that kept her tied up.

She was so tired.

Footsteps sounded on the stairs.

But something was different.

They didn't sound like him.

Her heart jumped.

Someone had found her.

Someone was coming to rescue her.

The lock clattered at the door.

After a moment, the door swung open and the light was switched on.

Her pupils dilating immediately in protest to the sudden bright light.

Her eyes sprung reflexively closed.

Waiting for someone to come to her.

When no one came she tentatively tried opening her eyes.

A small figure stood frozen in the doorway.

She thought her eyes were playing tricks on her.

It couldn't be.

"Tessa?"

The person moved towards her.

Reaching the bed the girl nodded, "It's me."

Tessa stretched out a hand and gently stroked her forehead.

"Why did you come?"

"To save you," Tessa smiled.

She began to work on the knot at one of her wrists.

A moment later she had it undone, Janice tried to lift her arm but it felt like lead.

"Did he hurt you?" Tessa asked as she worked on the rope at her other wrist.

Knowing that Tessa was not asking about her physical wellbeing. "Yeah he did."

Her other wrist coming undone Janice slowly moved her heavy arms down to her side.

Tessa started on her ankles.

Soon they too were undone.

Tessa sat on the side of the bed but wouldn't look her in the eye.

"I'm sorry," she whispered.

"Tessa, look at me," Janice whispered back with as much insistence as she could muster. "Tessa."

Slowly her friend lifted her eyes.

They glistened with unshed tears.

"I'm sorry," she whispered again.

Typical Tessa, blaming herself for everything. "It wasn't your fault. We knew what we were getting ourselves into."

Tessa shrugged but said nothing.

Hope was surging through her, strengthening her.

Slowly Janice pushed herself up.

Head swimming she resolutely ignored it.

Almost falling backwards as her stiff arms folded, Tessa grabbed hold of her keeping her sitting.

"Does he know you're here?"

Tessa shook her head. "And he won't until you're long gone. Can you stand?"

Nodding determinedly.

Tessa helped pull her to her feet.

Swaying unsteadily, if it wasn't for Tessa's hands on her arms she would have toppled to the ground.

Steps slow and uneven they made their way to the door.

Tessa switched the light off then helped her lean against the wall.

"I'll lock the door again so he won't know you're gone."

A lock-picking expert Tessa closed the door and snapped the combination lock back on.

Progress was slow as they made their way down the hall towards the door.

"We're almost there," Tessa whispered.

Disbelief and joy were surging through her, spurring her on, she had thought she was ready to die but now that freedom was so close Janice realized how much she wanted to have a second chance at life.

A chance to do it right.

Frowning Tessa stopped suddenly at the top of the stairs.

"What is it?" Janice asked her, puzzled.

"Something's not right."

They both turned too late.

Dylan Riley was there.

Swinging his arm in Tessa's direction, he slammed a baseball bat into the back of her skull.

Eyes rolling back in her head, Tessa swayed and collapsed.

Stumbling, Janice pressed herself against the wall to keep from falling down the stairs.

Dylan bent down beside Tessa, quickly patting her down. To check for weapons Janice supposed.

While he was preoccupied, she started slowly backing away down the hall, while she still had a chance.

She had almost made it to the window at the end of the hall when Dylan looked up.

He smiled at her and slowly walked towards her.

Backing up against the wall, Janice pressed against it as he reached her.

For a moment neither of them moved, and for a second longer she allowed herself to think that she might still get out of this alive.

Without a word, he puts his hands on her shoulders.

She thought he was going to drag her back into her prison.

But he pushed her backwards.

Glass shattered around her as he shoved her through the window.

She was barely aware of the shards that pierced her skin.

It felt like she was falling in slow motion.

Her mind flying back to the day her baby brother had fallen from a tree, his broken body lying on the ground below her.

She saw Dylan's face grinning at her from the shattered

window.

Then nothing.

* * * * *

2:13 A.M.

Enjoying the cool night air that wafted in through the broken window as he stared down at Janice's dead body lying on the ground below him. Shards of glass lay scattered around her. Dylan could just make out her dead, empty eyes staring sightlessly back up at him.

A sense of peace settling over him.

Things were going just as he had hoped. Janice was dead and there was nothing left standing in the way of him and Tessa being together. No one knew where they were. And even if her friends decided to tell the truth, which he seriously doubted they would, they had no idea of the location of Eleanor's murder.

Leaving the window, Dylan went to Tessa and knelt beside her, pressing his fingers against her slender white throat. Relieved to feel her pulse throbbing beneath his hand. He had tried not to hit her too hard, she was obviously still suffering the after effects of the fire, he'd hit her just hard enough to temporarily knock her out.

Lifting her easily into his arms, he carried her down the stairs and through the house, out the back door and down to the abandoned stables. Placing her in the chair he'd left prepared, he grabbed some rope and tied her wrists and ankles to the chair's arms and legs.

Waiting for her to regain consciousness, he gazed at her angelic face. It had been ten years since he had last seen her but she had not aged at all. White blonde curls framing her face, smooth ivory skin sprinkled lightly with freckles, black lashes fanning out against her cheeks, she looked exactly the same as he remembered.

Wishing she would hurry up and wake up. He loved Tessa's eyes. They appeared blue one second, green the next, yellow specks in their centers if you looked closely. And they were always carefully expressionless.

That was one of the things he had taught her. How to mask her emotions, to cover them up and make them invisible to the outside world. Remembering those classes they had spent alone together, those were among the happiest times of his life.

Despite his best efforts with Tessa, she had somehow never learnt how to let go of her emotions. He had taught her many things, but the one thing he'd never managed to teach her was the ability to give up feelings altogether. It was her one failure.

Guilt, remorse, empathy, sympathy were all a waste of time as far as he was concerned. If life had taught him anything, it was that emotions did nothing more than interfere with the things that needed to be done. He had learnt this lesson very early on.

Hours upon hours had been invested in trying to train Tessa to let go of the confines of human emotion. He had managed to teach her how to hide her feelings, to mask her emotions with a blank face and empty eyes. But he had never been able to teach her how to truly let go of emotions as he had learnt to do.

Looking back up he saw that she was awake and staring at him with a deep intensity. For once her eyes were an open book. She did not bother to hide the disgust and pure hatred that were aimed directly at him.

Mildly annoyed that he had missed her regaining consciousness. She was always one step ahead of him. He both loved and hated that about her. She was the only person he had ever met that had been a challenge.

Smiling at her. "You're awake."

Glaring back at him in silence.

"Long time no see," he commented mildly.

"Not long enough," she muttered, her voice croaky.

"I still have the scar from our last encounter," he pulled down the neck of his black sweater to reveal the scar on his shoulder.

She shrugged. "My aim was off. I was sick that day."

Ignoring the comment, he reached over and pulled up the arm of her jacket and pink sweatshirt revealing the jagged scar across her arm. "I see you still have your scar too."

She said nothing just stared in silence for a moment at the scar on her arm. Lost in thought, as he was, of the last time they had seen one another. He remembered the fury that had burned through him more severely than the knife. It had never occurred to him that Tessa would try to kill him.

Remembering her lying on the floor, semi-conscious, her injured arm bleeding, groggy from the pain and, as he found out later, the pneumonia. Hurting Tessa that day had been a mistake. If he hadn't then maybe things would have turned out differently.

"I have a headache," she announced suddenly.

"Of course you do," he pointed to the gash on her temple.

"Well that one's not your fault," she admitted reluctantly. "But you hit me on the head with a baseball hat."

"I know how much you hate drugs. I thought you'd rather the baseball bat than a shot of sedatives," pleased at himself for how thoughtful he'd been. Thoughtfulness was not usually an emotion he had much time for, but he knew that it was one Tessa valued and he'd decided to make an effort.

"The police think you tried to kill me," she commented absently.

Noting her dilated pupils, he hoped he hadn't given her a concussion, he didn't want anything to get in the way of tonight's plans. Her words registering. "They thought I tried to kill you?" he repeated. "The fire?"

Nodding, "They think that was you."

"I would never try to kill you. And even if I did I certainly wouldn't do it with a fire," voice rising in anger. Not so much that he was suspected of attempted murder, he was after all a murderer, but that anyone would accuse him of anything but a perfectly planned and implemented kill.

"I know that," she told him calmly, not even a trace of fear in her eyes.

"Did you tell them it wasn't me?"

Shrugging distractedly. "I let them assume whatever they wanted. I learnt that from you."

Pleased, it was one of the things he'd successfully taught her years ago. An effective way of hiding the truth from someone was to let them assume they knew what was happening and simply go along with it. "Like you did with Chelsea's 'suicide'?"

"We never told anyone that Chelsea committed suicide, they jumped to that conclusion on their own," she responded tiredly.

"Chelsea left a note . . ."

"That simply said goodbye," Tessa interjected.

"Very clever," he laughed softly. "They assumed Chelsea and Jasper committed suicide and you let them." Tessa was a model student. "You know who tried to kill you?"

"They weren't trying to kill me just warn me," she answered.

There was no point in pushing her to say more. Tessa never shared anything about her past.

"You knew where I was," smiling satisfied.

Rolling her eyes she refused to respond.

Standing he started to pace aimlessly around the empty stables, traces of the previous residences still remained. A faint moldy smell wafted from the loft, where hay was still scattered, it mixed with the smell of old manure, to create a pungent aroma.

It was ironic that the place where Eleanor was killed was so closely linked to Tessa's favorite pastime. He'd never understood horse riding. Giving up control of one of a person's most basic freedoms, the ability to decide where one goes, to an animal. Tessa loved horse riding though, and like everything else she tried, she was brilliant at it.

"How do you always know what I'm thinking?" he himself was

brilliant at reading people, but to Tessa it came so easily. It had taken him years to perfect the ability of reading a person's body language, of the things they didn't say as well as the things they did. To be able to predict what a person would do based on their previous behavior. But Tessa seemed to possess an innate ability to do this, even before he'd met her.

"I read your mind and I know everything about you." She turned her head to look at him, "Michael Mitchell Morley."

Panicked disbelief coursing through him as he stalked back over to her, "how do you know my name?"

Barking out a laugh. "I'm smarter than you. That was always one of your weaknesses. Underestimating your opponent."

Fury crackling out of every pore. "How did you find out my name?" He was so horrified that someone knew his real name that her insults didn't even register.

Smiling sweetly. "I traced your background after I met you at the hospital. I was taught to never talk to strangers."

Lunging at her, he wrapped his hands around her throat, seeing red as he tightened them, squeezing as hard as he could. She wiggled beneath him, but her restraints prevented her from doing any damage.

Vision clearing he realized what he was doing. Releasing her, she dragged in several ragged breaths, mocking eyes staring back at him.

"I know all there is to know about you," she taunted breathlessly. "Born Michael Mitchell Morley to Mitchell and Candice Morley. Your mother left when you were four. After she left, taking her money with her, your dad became a drunk and a gold digger. He moved around the country from one rich woman to another, using them till they figured out his game. Want me to go on?"

Lost for words he fought the urge to choke her again, anything to make her stop talking.

"I know what you did to them," Tessa continued goading.

"No one does," he shot back, sure that there was no possible way she could have found out. No one knew what he had done.

"That's not true. I know," her angelic face beamed up at him as though they were talking about nothing more than a birthday party.

"You can't," he protested weakly.

Raising an eyebrow. "When you were seventeen your dad died of heart failure. I'm guessing you injected air into a vein with an empty syringe."

Fuming he said nothing just glared at her. It was not possible that she could know about this.

"After he died you took off. Disappeared."

She watched calmly taking in his obvious discomfort.

Continuing gleefully. "Then a couple of months later your mom mysteriously falls in front of a train. I don't think it was an accident."

Baffled, "How can you know that?" It wasn't possible. It just wasn't possible. He'd been so careful. Made sure that no one was around, that there had been no witnesses. He'd even gotten rid of the homeless man that had been lingering around the train tracks that night. He hadn't been sure how much, if anything, the man had seen but it was better to be safe than sorry.

"I know everything," she answered smugly.

Resuming his aimless pacing. "That is not possible," he snapped at her.

She just laughed.

Infuriated, "I know things about you too," he said childishly, as though they were eight year olds locked in a juvenile battle of wits.

"You know nothing about me except what you did to me," Tessa scowled.

"I know about your mother. How she tried to kill you," he wracked his brain trying to think of everything he had ever read about her, everything he learned following her.

"So what," she laughed. "You read that in my file. I know all about what you did to the girls there. You were supposed to be their counselor. You were supposed to help them, instead you took advantage of them. I found them all. They told me what you did to them. The same things you did to us."

"I . . . I know about Eleanor," he stammered helplessly looking over at her from across the stable.

"No you don't," she scoffed. "You know she died, and the only reason you know where is because you followed me. Wow how clever of you. You don't know anything about what happened here," her aquamarine eyes were practically shooting fire at him.

Feeling himself start to lose control, things were not going as he had planned. His father's voice ringing in his ears, telling him that he was a failure. That he was good for nothing. That he was the reason that his mother left. Because she knew how pathetic he was, that he would never amount to anything. That he was the reason that each of his stepmothers left.

After the deaths of his parents he had vowed that he would never again lose control. That he would maintain it at all costs. A life without control was not worth living. It was not to be tolerated. It was not. It was not. It was not.

He was starting to hyperventilate. Fear and failure. His two greatest enemies. As long as Tessa was around he was always going to be a failure. She was smarter. He hadn't wanted to admit it but he had no choice. He was never going to win against her.

His father's voice taunting him, 'failure. You're a failure son. A failure. You'll never be anything but.'

Shaking his head, trying to clear the voice.

It wasn't true. He wasn't a failure. He'd beaten his father and he'd beat Tessa. He didn't want to but he had to. He had no choice. He'd had such plans for the two to them. Together forever.

Maybe they could be, he thought to himself. Fingering the gun in his pocket.

Turning he saw Tessa standing right behind him.

* * * * *

3:33 A.M.

"Am I insane?" Parker asked his partner, breaking the heavy cloud of silence that hung over the car. After almost two hours of driving around near where Tessa had been found after Eleanor's death they were yet to find anything promising. Tall trees towered over the car on either side of the road, their thick branches meeting over the top and forming a spindly tunnel.

"Are you kidding?" Wyatt joked. "Of course you are, it wouldn't be half so much fun being your partner if you were sane."

"I'm serious," he glared half-heartedly.

Sighing, "You mean about Tessa?" Wyatt asked.

Nodding, he stared out the window, snow was starting to fall softly again. "I've only known her a couple of days. How can I feel so strongly about her that I . . ." he couldn't think of a way to end that sentence.

"How do you feel about her exactly? It's not just white knight, damsel in distress syndrome is it?"

"I almost wish it were," Parker murmured. After so many years avoiding any chance at a relationship he wasn't sure he could face the possibility of starting something with Tessa. And yet he knew he was going to anyway.

Wyatt raised an eyebrow and waited for him to continue.

"I . . . I think I'm in love with her," hearing the words out loud he groaned at his own stupidity. "Oh man, I am such an idiot."

"Why?' Wyatt pressed.

"What do you mean why? I've only known her a few days," he repeated.

"So?"

"So? A few days. How can I be in love with her after a few days?" he asked incredulously.

"Sometimes that's all it takes."

"You mean like love at first sight?" he felt like a junior high kid, he was so inexperienced.

"Kind of. I knew the first time I saw Casey that she was the woman I wanted to spend my life with."

"You met her as a sophomore, you really knew she was the one?"

"Yeah," Wyatt nodded thoughtfully as though he'd never really considered it before, "I really did."

"What about Jennifer Knightly?" he asked. Referring to the girl with whom Wyatt had cheated on Casey with when he was a senior. It had almost ended their relationship, but eventually they'd managed to work things through. Parker had helped things along. Wyatt was like a brother to him, and he and Casey were the perfect couple.

"I'm not saying things always go easy. People make mistakes. But when it's the one, then it's the one." Glancing over at him carefully, "Speaking of which, things are not going to go easy with Tessa. Are you sure you're ready?"

"Ready for what?"

"Tessa's been through a lot, Parker. A lot. More than any person should ever have to."

"I know that."

"Do you? Do you really? She was abducted when she was eleven, saw her friend killed and had who knows what done to her. Her mother tried to kill her. Her mom, her dad, her brother, all walked out on her. A maniac who now wants to keep her as a sex slave sexually abused her for years. And she went willing to him knowing all of this because of a misguided sense of guilt and responsibility for everything that's happened to her."

"You mean she's damaged?" he asked even though he already

knew the answer.

"In a way. Parker, she seems like a really sweet girl, but she's also really messed up."

"We can help her, save her."

"Are you sure she even wants to be saved?"

"I'm sure."

Wyatt shot him a look. "The letter?" he asked.

Parker nodded. "She said she wished that things had worked out differently. If we can find her before he takes off with her then we can help her. I can help her."

"It might be too late to help her," Wyatt warned.

"You and the Bell's helped me," he reminded.

"You were just a kid when they took you in. You had a childhood, you had parents who loved you, you had friends who supported you . . ."

"Tessa had . . . has supportive friends," he cut in.

Ignoring the interruption, "Parker, you had a stable life with the Bell's, but Tessa's never had that. She's never had anyone to trust, anyone who was really there for her."

"Well now she has me."

"Are you sure you want her? That you have genuine feelings for her? Because if you get her to trust you and then you change your mind, that could break her."

Hesitating slightly, Wyatt picked up on it instantly. "She's not Gina. She's not your mom. She won't betray you."

"I'm sure," Parker said and felt deep within himself that he was indeed ready for a serious relationship.

"Then I'm here for you, me and Casey, whatever you need."

Smiling at his friend, then staring out the window, heart tightening again. None of this mattered if they couldn't find her. They could already be too late. She'd been gone for over twelve hours.

Frowning suddenly as they passed a small lane. "Hey slow down."

Wyatt slowed the car to a crawl. "What is it? You see something?"

Rolling down his window to see better. "Tyre tracks, recent," he said excitement bubbling. "Down there," he pointed.

Turning the car. "It could be nothing," Wyatt warned.

"And it could be Tessa."

* * * * *

3:49 A.M.

Distracting Dylan a.k.a Michael by taunting him about his past, about how she was smarter than he could ever hope to be, had given Tessa time to saw through the ropes that bound her wrists and ankles.

She'd seen the madness building in his eyes as she talked to him, pushed him. The change from the overflowing abundance of cocky control when she had first awakened to the pure insanity that lurked there now. She'd studied him in silence for several minutes before he'd realized that she was conscious.

His control had slowly fled as she had reminded him of his past. Of his mother's abandonment. His father's alcoholism. Of the murders that he'd committed. She'd taken a gamble on the exact method he'd used on his father but she could tell from the shock that flew across his face that she'd been right. She had not even needed to mention the murder of the homeless man.

Michael had been hearing his father's voice in his head, telling him he was a failure. Reading people had always been a gift that had come so easily to her, one of many, and it had not taken her long to figure out what made Michael Mitchell Morley tick.

The hours that they had spent together, while horribly unpleasant, had also been very educational. She hated to admit it, but Michael had taught her to conceal her emotions, had helped her hone her skills of reading body language and the non-verbal communication that people used with those they knew well. They had also given her the opportunity to study Michael. She had spent hours of her free time researching him until she learnt all there was to know about him.

With Michael it was always all about control. And fear. The things that had motivated him since childhood. His fractured youth had driven him to keep a desperate grip on control. His genius was both a blessing and a curse, for it enabled him to use his madness in a deceitfully cunning way. It was also the key to his downfall. Take away his control and he had nothing.

It hadn't surprised her that he had brought her to the stables. For it was right here in this very room that Ellie had been killed. Although there was no way for Michael to have known this she was sure that he had found Ellie's body buried in a shallow grave right outside this building.

If he had found this place by following her here then he would have done a thorough job of searching it for clues. It wouldn't have taken him long to find the body. It had been her biggest fear all those years ago. That the police would find this place and then unearth the tiny body buried here. If they had found it then they would have found out the truth of what had really happened here that fateful weekend.

While cutting herself free she had cut her wrists and fingertips several times, making her hands slippery with blood. Tessa hated blood with a passion, ever since Ellie had been killed. Taking the terror that flooded through her, and the pain from her head and her hands and burying them carefully. She would feel them later but right now she needed to focus.

Pushing wearily to her feet. The stress of the last couple of weeks plus the beating her body had taken in the fire had almost depleted her reserves of strength. Forcing herself onwards, she had just one more thing to accomplish.

Approaching Michael slowly, she waited behind him until he turned and saw her.

Pure madness in his eyes now he jumped when he saw her standing there and not tied to the chair where he had left her.

"Hello, Michael," she said softly, locking her eyes onto his.

"Tessa," he began nervously, eyes darting from the chair and back to her. "How did . . .? You can't . . ."

Showing him the razor blade she had hidden in the sleeve of her sweatshirt.

"Michael," she began but he cut her off.

"It's Dylan. My name is Dylan," his voice high with hysteria.

Shaking her head calmly. "No it's not, it's Michael. Michael Mitchell Morley," she needed to keep him on edge.

Pressing his hands to his ears and squeezing his eyes closed as though that could somehow make her disappear. "No, no, no, Michael is dead. He died a long time ago."

"No he didn't," she pressed. "He's standing right here. Dylan Riley doesn't exist, you made him up. When I first met you, you were calling yourself Randall Baker," she reminded him patiently.

Shaking his head from side to side so quickly his face became almost a blur. "No, no," he screeched, opening his eyes she saw that they were wild. He was no longer in touch with reality. She had him right where she wanted him.

"Michael, Michael," she mocked. "You're a failure, Michael. Nobody will ever love you, because you are a failure," she yelled at him.

Wild eyes flying madly around the room, desperately searching for a way to escape, his shaking hands reached into his pockets. Pushing him further, "That's why mother left, because she hated you, hated you because you are a failure."

Michael pulled a gun from his pocket, and Tessa had to keep herself from sighing in relief. She had been almost positive that he would have it on him. As a backup. Ever since the night he pushed his mother in front of a freight train and had been surprised by the homeless man he had carried it everywhere with him. It was his emergency protection.

Despite what her friends had thought she had no intention of spending the rest of her life as Michael Morley's wife, sex slave, bearer of his children, or whatever perverse way he thought of her.

This was exactly how Tessa had envisioned things turning out. If she pushed Michael far enough she was sure that she could push him back into madness. His past and all that had happened between them would overwhelm him. At worst, it would drive him to kill them both in a murder suicide, at best, he'd just kill himself in a straight suicide.

Leaving her to start a new life from scratch.

No matter how much she might want to, she would never go back to her old life. Everything, everyone, she touched was destroyed. She was poison. She would not ruin her friend's lives further. And she would not do anything to wreck Parker's life. She would bury her feelings for him and spend the rest of her life alone, where she would be unable to bring another person down with her.

Holding the gun on her, his hands trembling violently, she could see fear and indecision battling inside him. And she realized that in spite of everything that he had done to her, somewhere deep down inside him he had actual real feelings for her. Michael Mitchell Morley loved her as much as he was capable of loving anyone.

Indecision battling inside herself for a brief moment, as she thought of turning him in and trying to get him help. But then pure evil sprung up in his eyes as he lunged towards her. "If I can't have you then no one will," he screeched.

Crashing into her, the gun between them, they struggled for what seemed like an eternity but in reality could not have been more than a second or two. When a crack sliced through the stillness for a moment Tessa wasn't sure whether it was her or Michael who had been shot.

* * * * *

4:04 A.M.

"There it is," Parker pointed to the small white car parked under a tree just ahead of them. The lane that they had started down after he saw the tyre marks had quickly ended leaving them to weave their way through the thick woods. Their going made even slower by the snow that was now swirling around, and quickly covering the tracks they were trying to follow.

"You sure?" Wyatt asked.

Checking the plate number he'd jotted down earlier with the one on the car. "Yep, it's the right car."

Stopping, they both sprung out into the night, flashlights flicking on. Parker ran quickly to check Tessa's rental car in the vain hope that she might still be inside.

She wasn't.

Taking his scarf from his partner's outstretched hand, he wound it tightly around his neck, then pulled a pair of leather gloves from his pant's pockets and slipped them on, more from habit than need, he was too wired to really feel the cold. "She's been here a while, car's covered in snow."

"There's no way we're gonna be able to track her, the snow'll have wiped out any footprints she left behind."

Spinning around Parker searched for any sign that might point them in the direction Tessa had taken. Off to their left the trees looked like they thinned out a little, if they were looking for a house then it would make sense for it to be in a clearing. "This way," he gestured and started off at a brisk jog.

Wyatt followed without a word, and for several minutes they jogged through the snow in silence. Tall oaks and fir trees towered above them, the underbrush was thick and heaped with piles of soft, slushy snow, making it slippery. With the muted moonlight casting a thin, silvery light over the forest it would have been picturesque were it not for the reason of their presence.

After travelling what he guessed to be close to a mile without stumbling on anything Parker was about to give up and head back to try the other direction when suddenly they broke out of the woods and found themselves in a large clearing. Ahead of them sat an imposing Tudor style mansion. It was surrounded by acres of long, wild grass. The place looked like it hadn't been lived in for years. There was not a doubt in his mind that this was the right place.

Glancing at Wyatt he saw that his partner agreed.

Without a word exchanged between them, they both unclipped their guns and slowly moved towards the house. The windows were dark and there was not a glimmer of movement from anywhere within the dilapidated old building.

Crossing the overgrown lawn, they circled slowly around the outside of the house, checking carefully for any signs of life. It took every ounce of his resolve not to go wildly running inside to find Tessa. If she was still here then her life was in danger. And if he was going to get her out of here alive then he had no choice but to remain calm.

As they turned a corner, Parker felt his heart jump into his throat.

A body lay just ahead of them, covered in a light blanket of snow.

Throwing caution to the wind, he sprinted to the body and dropped down beside it. One hand desperately brushing away snow to uncover the face, the other felt vainly for a pulse. The snow around the body was stained a reddish pink.

Clearing enough snow, he saw empty eyes staring sightlessly at the sky. Letting out a shaky breath as he saw that the face was not Tessa's. It was Janice Peters.

Wyatt sighed behind him as he looked down at Janice's dead body then up at the window above them. Following his gaze Parker saw the jagged glass shards that remained stuck in the wooden window frame.

Scooping away some of the snow around Janice he saw shattered glass pieces scattered around her, sparkling like glass snowflakes in the thin torchlight. Reaching out a hand he gently closed Janice's eyelids.

"We were too late," he said softly more to himself than Wyatt, who was calling for backup. His hand lingering on Janice's thin, white face, he hoped that they weren't too late to save Tessa. "She hasn't been dead too long," he whispered to Wyatt, who raised his eyebrows in a silent question. "There's not that much snow on her, if she'd been dead for a while she'd be completely covered."

Reluctantly leaving Janice Peters alone in the cold, there was nothing more he could do for her, Parker followed his partner who was already making his way towards the open backdoor. Heading slowly inside, covering one another in case Dylan Riley was waiting for them somewhere in the dark recesses of the house.

From the outside the place looked slightly rundown on the inside it was a complete mess. Furniture was up ended, some of it broken into pieces, there were several holes in the walls and most of the doors, and almost every windows was shattered.

"This place looks like it was hit by a tornado," he muttered to Wyatt after they'd cleared the downstairs.

With no sign of either Tessa or Dylan, they slowly made their way up the stairs. Freezing as he reached the top, his eyes riveted to a small pool of blood. Wyatt knelt and touched a finger to it. "It's fresh," he said softly, eyes apologetic as though he were somehow responsible.

Refraining from letting despair take over he started down the long hall checking each room as he went. Most of the rooms up here were empty, no furniture and nowhere for anybody to hide. Unlike the rooms downstairs they still had their windows intact.

Reaching the end of the hallway Parker stopped to stare distractedly through the broken window and thought of Janice's final moments of terror. Looking down at her she was partially obscured by the snow that continued to swirl wildly in the night.

Opening the second last door he stood and stared. Unlike the other rooms this one was not empty. It was decorated as though for a little girl. The walls and carpet were pink, pictures of baby animals hung from the walls, a bookshelf full of children's books against the wall opposite the door, and an armchair full of stuffed animals was by the window.

In the middle of the room sat a four-poster bed, ropes lay on the pale pink blanket that covered the bed. "This was where he kept her," he called out to Wyatt who was checking out the final room.

"This is his room," Wyatt called back.

Leaving Janice Peters' prison, he crossed the hall and entered the last room on the floor. It was sparsely furnished with only a bed in its centre, stripped of sheets, and a dresser by the window. Wyatt had yanked opened the dresser's drawer's but they were all empty.

"We're too late," his voice sounding distant to his own ears. "She's gone. He's got her." Until this moment Parker hadn't let himself believe that Tessa was really gone. He had kept himself going by having faith that he would find her, but now . . .

A crack suddenly split through the silent night.

Exchanging glances, he knew from the look in his friend's eyes that he had jumped to the same conclusion.

It was a gunshot.

Before Parker even knew what he was doing, he was running.

Out of the room, down the stairs, through the first floor, and out the back door, running in the direction of the gunshot.

Wyatt was yelling at him. He couldn't make out the words but he could hear them in his head anyway. They weren't wearing vests. They didn't know where the shots had come from. They didn't know who had been shot. Back up hadn't arrived yet. Parker didn't care about any of these things. All he knew was that

Tessa could be lying somewhere bleeding to death.

As he started down the small hill atop which the house sat, there was a small building in the distance. Light spilling from its windows out into the dark night.

Sprinting down the hill, picking up speed as he went, he rushed madly towards the light as though it were a lighthouse guiding him to his destination.

Slowing only momentarily as he reached the building, barely registering that it was an abandoned stable, gun drawn he barreled through the door.

Stopping short as he surveyed the scene before him.

Dylan Riley, or whoever the man really was, lay on the floor at the other end of the building, in an ever-growing pool of blood. One arm bent underneath him, his neck twisted at an unnatural angle, legs straight out in front. A ragged hole in his chest, empty eyes staring in death, an almost surprised look on his face.

Tessa stood above the body. Her deathly white face a mask of shock, cheeks flushed red, eyes glazed and blank as she stared unblinkingly at the body that lay at her feet. She was breathing too quickly, struggling to suck in one shallow breath after another. Even from across the room Parker could see her pulse fluttering in the hollow of her neck, around which blue and purple bruises were already forming, in them he could just make out the shape of hands. Dylan had tried to strangle her.

In the middle of the stables sat a chair, ropes lay on the floor next to it, their ends shorn. Glancing at Tessa's wrists, he saw that they were rubbed raw, her fingertips and hands were bloody. Shaking hands that clutched the gun, which was still pointed at Dylan's bloody body, as though it were the only thing keeping her on her feet.

Tessa did not register his appearance.

Sucking in a deep breath to slow his own ragged breathing, from exertion, from fear, from relief, from all three. Parker had to keep repeating to himself that Tessa was really okay. Maybe not okay he admitted taking another look at her, but at least she was alive.

Putting away his own gun, he started slowly towards her. Hands out in front of himself in a non-threatening gesture, the last thing he wanted to do was startle her.

"Tessa," he began calmly, with an effort keeping his voice as soft and gentle as he could manage given his pounding heart. "Tessa, everything's okay now. I'm here."

She didn't move, standing so still she looked like she was made of stone.

"Tessa, it's Parker. Can you hear me?"

Reaching her he waved a hand in front of her wide eyes, she did not so much as twitch. Carefully placing his hand over hers, they were dwarfed by the enormous gun she clutched tightly. Her hands were tiny, childlike, and brought to his mind a memory of his recurring nightmare where another pair of tiny hands had desperately clutched a gun.

Gently pressing on her hands to lower them, so the gun no longer pointed at Dylan Riley. "It's okay, honey, its okay, you're safe now," he whispered soothingly, as he gently extricated the gun from her hand, slipping it into his waistband.

Despite his touch, his voice, his presence, Tessa continued to show no signs that she was even aware that he was there. She remained frozen in place as though she were a painted picture instead of a real person.

"Parker?" he heard Wyatt call from nearby.

"In here," he yelled back.

"Ambulance is on its way," Wyatt announced from the door as he assessed the scene before him. "She okay?" he asked nodding at Tessa.

"She's in shock," Parker answered absently, attention focused solely on Tessa, maneuvering himself so that he was now in between her and Dylan Riley. Her eyes seemed to stare straight through him, as if he were made of glass, to the bloody body behind him.

Taking her shoulders in his hands he gave her a firm shake. "Tessa," he barked. "Come on, snap out of it."

Still no response.

Forcibly turning her around so that her back was now to the body, hooking a finger under her chin he tilted her head up to look at him. Bending over so their faces were close, locking his eyes onto hers, giving her chin a gentle shake. "Tessa, come on, look at me."

Slowly her eyes blinked and cleared a little, finally registering his presence. "He's dead," she whispered so softly he could hardly hear her.

"Shh, I know, sweetheart, I know," he whispered back, trying to pull her into his arms.

But she pushed him away. "I didn't mean to," her eyes wild now, turbulent, begging him to believe her. "He . . . he jumped at me and . . . it just . . . just went off."

"It's okay," he soothed, once again trying to pull her into an embrace.

Shaking her head vigorously. "No, I killed him." Trying to turn back to look at the body but unable to because of his tight hold on her. "I killed him," she repeated in a tiny, frightened whisper.

"It was an accident," Parker tried to reassure her. "He tried to kill you," his fingers gently tracing the bruises on her neck.

Nearing hysteria, hands balled into fists she beat them against his chest, sobbing. "I killed him, I killed him, I killed him." Repeating it over and over, her mind frozen, unable to move on to anything else.

Pulling her against himself, she struggled frantically but he was too strong. "It's alright, it's okay," he soothed. Refusing to let her go he kept a tight hold of her, rubbing a hand up and down her back comfortingly, pressing her against his chest. Noticing the bright red blood that stained the back of her head, standing out in contrast to her matted blonde curls. He hoped Dylan Riley had not given her a concussion.

Eventually she stopped resisting him, her hands curling into fists as she clutched at his sweater as though she were drowning and he was her only lifeline. Holding her tightly while she sobbed, his cheek resting on the top of her head, as though they were the only people left on the face of the planet.

Finally, her sobs turned to sniffles and then to nothing. Hands still clinging to his sweater, she sagged against him as though all her remaining strength was gone. Tightening his hold around her waist to keep her upright, unable, no unwilling, to move, to let her go.

Letting his own fear and anxiety slowly ebb away, trying to convince his queasy stomach that things were finally over. Dylan Riley was dead. Tessa was safe, as were Tanner, Chelsea, Michelle, Melanie, Lauren and Carrie. Dylan Riley would never kill again.

Icy air swirled through the door as Wyatt returned to the stables, Parker hadn't even noticed his partner's absence. "ETA on the ambulance is ten minutes," Wyatt said crossing over to where he and Tessa were standing.

Keeping Tessa held tightly against him he spoke softly to Wyatt, "I want to get her out of here," nodding in the direction of the body. "We can wait for the paramedics at the house."

"It's freezing out there," Wyatt reminded him.

Unwrapping his scarf with one hand, the other continued to stroke Tessa's hair. "At least there's no . . . you know." Gently pulling back so he could wrap the scarf around her neck, covering the bruises that were progressively growing darker.

"Here," Wyatt shrugged out of his coat and handed it over.

Nodding his thanks. Tessa had resumed her near catatonic state, her eyes were unfocused and staring blankly into space, her face eerily empty. Dressing her as though she were a child, she didn't move to help him at all, as he slipped her arms into Wyatt's jacket and zipped it up. Her thin frame was almost swallowed whole by the enormous coat.

"Come on," he tugged lightly on Tessa's arms and started to guide her towards the door. Compliantly she came, her head turning dazedly in the direction of the body. Quickly reaching to turn her face away. "Don't look at that," he murmured, keeping his own body in between hers and Dylan's.

Following obediently where he led her, leaning heavily on him, but nothing seemed to register to her. Maneuvering her around the pool of blood, her eyes flickered briefly to the chair, he felt her stiffen in his arms, and for a moment Parker was worried that she was going to become hysterical again. But then her eyes flicked away and she relaxed.

Joining Wyatt at the door, they stepped out into the snowy night. They were passing around the side of the stable, heading towards the house, when Tessa suddenly stopped in her tracks. Eyes riveted to a spot on the ground. Following her gaze, Parker frowned in confusion when he saw nothing but snow.

Turning her to face him, her body moved but her eyes didn't. "Tessa, what is it?"

She said nothing. Eyes locked unblinkingly on the one spot.

Shaking her gently. "Tessa?" Exchanging a glance with Wyatt, "Tess, come on."

"What's she looking at?" Wyatt asked his eyes bouncing from Tessa to the ground and back again.

"I don't know," he shrugged, tugging on her arm. "Come on, Tessa, let's go."

Attempting to pull her towards the house, but she yanked herself free of his grip and dropped to her knees in the snow. She was shaking all over, from shock not the cold he surmised.

Both he and Wyatt squatted beside her, his partner running a gloved hand through the snow at the spot where Tessa's gaze was glued. "There's nothing here," Wyatt told him, even though they had both known there wouldn't be.

Taking Tessa's arm Parker tried to pull her to her feet, but she pulled it back and refused to move. "Tessa, it's okay, Dylan's dead now, he can't hurt you anymore. Come on, you're in shock, we gotta get you inside, out of the cold."

Wyatt stood and wrapped an arm around Tessa's waist, attempting to forcibly move her. Parker took her arm again. "Come on, honey, what is it?"

Managing to get her to her feet, she was wiggling and squirming wildly like a worm when you pulled it from the dark, moist dirt. "Tessa, stop it," he admonished, as they struggled to keep hold of her, she was as slippery as a fish.

They'd dragged her no more than a couple of feet when she twisted free from their grip and launched herself back to the spot where she'd been. She was murmuring something under her breath, over and over again. Frowning as he knelt back down at her side, ignoring the snow that froze his knees.

Leaning in close he could just make out the word she was repeating. "Ellie, Ellie, Ellie," she was whimpering as she rocked backwards and forwards, eyes locked on a scene from another time.

Everything clicking into place, this was the place where her friend had been killed. A wave of anger rolled over him at the cruelty of Dylan Riley, if the man weren't already dead he would have been tempted to finish him off himself. Painfully.

Sirens sounded in the distance. "I'll go," Wyatt called over his shoulder as he took of in the direction of the wailing.

His attention reverting back to Tessa, "This is where Ellie . . . Eleanor, was killed?" Parker confirmed softly.

Eyes slowly rising to meet his own, tears streaming unnoticed down her cheeks, she nodded.

"It's going to be okay, Tessa, I promise." Her blue eyes stared into his own as though she could look right into his brain to evaluate the reliability of his words.

Subdued now she nodded slowly and allowed him to pull her to her feet. As she reached up to wipe the tears from her face Parker realized too late what was about to happen. So far, Tessa had been distracted and had not seemed to notice the cuts that marred her hands, and the blood that still lingered there. Making a grab for her hand before she could see it, he was too slow.

For a second she froze, and Parker thought that she was too tired to really see the blood, but then her eyes sprung wide in horror, her face creasing in terror.

Jerking herself free she dropped to the ground. "Get it off," she shrieked, desperately grabbing handfuls of snow and trying to use them to wipe off the blood.

Dropping down beside her Parker grabbed her hands, forcing them to be still.

"Don't," she screeched. "I have to get it off," trying to wrench her hands from his iron grip.

"Tessa, it's okay, I'll clean them." She didn't hear his words, breathing quick and shallow, she was starting to hyperventilate. "Tessa, honey, you have to calm down, okay?" She was thrashing wildly, like a trapped animal. In her desperation to get the blood off her hands, she didn't seem to notice that she was struggling to breathe.

Worried that she was going to hurt herself. "Tessa, stop it. Stop," he repeated more forcefully than he'd intended.

At the sound of his stern voice she froze, eyes darting around in an almost manic manner as though she expected a monster to appear at any second. Given what she'd witnessed here, both tonight and as a child, he couldn't blame her.

Her eyes settling on him she blinked in fear and backed away. "Tessa?" he asked, confused.

Scrambling to her feet, she staggered and tried to run from him. Chasing after her as voices sounded nearby, help was almost here. Catching her Parker turned her to face him, hands firmly gripping her shoulders. "It's okay," he soothed, trying to make eye contact with her, grateful help was here, Parker didn't know how to ease Tessa's shock addled brain back to reality.

She shook her head. "No, he's coming. Let me go, please, he'll kill me," hands curling into fists holding tightly to his sweater.

"No," he stroked her cheek, trying to calm her. "No one's going to hurt you. You're safe now."

"Parker!" He turned as Wyatt and two paramedics approached. "EMT's are here but no one else yet," his partner explained.

"What've we got?" one of the paramedics asked.

"She's in shock, she's got a head injury and cuts on . . ."

"Please, I have to go, he's coming," Tessa interrupted, her eyes bored into his own, silently begging him to help.

"And I think she's having flashbacks to a murder she witnessed as a child," he added.

"Let's take a look," the older of the EMT's took a step towards them.

Seeing him approach, Tessa squirmed, petrified. "No, don't let him hurt me, he's going to kill me."

"Shh," Parker soothed, almost losing hold of her.

"I think we're going to have to sedate her," the younger paramedic announced, pulling a syringe and a small vial from his bag.

"No, no drugs. No, don't," wiggling desperately. "Don't let him drug me, please," she begged.

"Hold her still," the other medic warned.

Wyatt wrapped an arm around her chest, pinning her arms to her side, while Parker kept hold of her face, forcing Tessa to look at him. "Tessa, look at me, hey, look at me. Everything is going to be okay. I am not going to let anyone hurt you, alright?"

Her desperate eyes pleaded with him, her hands still twisted up in his sweater. "No drugs, please. Parker, don't let them drug me."

Realization dawning as he remembered that her mother had drugged her before trying to drown her in the bathtub. "Guys, just back up for a moment, let me talk to her."

"Parker, she needs . . ." Wyatt began.

"I know what she needs," he shot his partner a look telling him to just trust him. Reluctantly Wyatt released his hold on Tessa and took a couple of steps away, the paramedics shot him doubtful glances but also complied.

Once they were alone he returned his attention to Tessa. "It's okay, it's just you and me now." Thumb gently stroking her cheekbone, "Take some deep breaths for me." Breathing slowly in and out with her, when it had slowed somewhat he continued. "No one is going to hurt you, you can trust me."

Doubt lingered in the aqua eyes that stared up at him. Trust was not something that Tessa was used to. Her already deathly white pallor seemed to have drained even further, now a worrying shade of grey.

"I mean it, Tessa, you can trust me. Really. I would never let anyone hurt you." Looking down at her he realized how desperate he was for her to believe him.

Finally her eyes cleared and for the first time she looked as though she were really seeing him. Voice a tiny, childlike whisper, as she murmured her consent, "Okay."

Impulsively he leaned in and pressed his mouth against hers. One hand continued to cup her face, the other cradled her head, his fingers tangling in her hair. Tessa remained completely still at first, then she leaned into him and kissed him back. It was the softest, sweetest kiss he had ever experienced.

Unwillingly he pulled back, and Tessa sagged against him, pressing her ear to his chest, physically and emotionally empty. Absently twisting one of her ringlets around his finger. "The paramedics are going to come over now, okay? They're going to give you a sedative and we're going to take you to the hospital. I'm going to stay with you the whole time. Everything is going to be fine. I won't leave you, Tessa," he insisted before she could object.

When Tessa said nothing he took it as a sign of assent, and nodded at the paramedics, who crossed back over to them. Tessa didn't raise her head as the EMT took her arm, checking her pulse, and her blood pressure, then rolling up her sleeve to give her the shot. As the sedative took effect her fingers uncurled and her knees buckled.

"Let's go," one of the paramedics said. "We had to leave the bus in the woods, couldn't get it all the way through."

Swinging Tessa's limp body into his arms, Parker followed the others up the snowy hill and away, not just from this place, which he hoped to never set foot in ever again, but from everything it symbolized.

They'd take Tessa to the hospital. She'd get better, he would help her. And then they'd start their lives together.

Whatever it took.

He'd almost lost her once and Parker vowed that he would never let it happen again.

* * * * *

8:42 P.M.

A knock sounded on the door of her hospital room.

She ignored it.

Lying in the dark, Tessa had insisted earlier that the nurse keep the lights off and the blinds drawn. Laying on her side, back to the door, the hospital's scratchy blanket pulled up to her chin, she stared blankly at the wall. The only light in the room came from the machines around the bed that radiated a soft glow.

She was tired. Exhausted really. Completely drained.

Doctors had been in and out, checking on her regularly, but she hardly remembered a word they had said. Tessa didn't really care anyway. She didn't care if she had a concussion from the blow to her head. She didn't care if they wanted her to talk to a psychiatrist. She didn't care if the police were going to charge her with Michael's murder or rule it self-defense.

Tessa didn't want to see anyone either. She'd told the doctor to make sure that she had no visitors. She couldn't deal with other people's emotions right now. Couldn't even deal with her own.

Her friends had come by to check on her earlier, luckily while a nurse had been in checking her vitals, and Tessa had sent her out to send her friends away.

Most of what had happened after the gun had gone off was nothing more than a vague and fuzzy memory.

Bits and pieces had started to come back to her. Parker had been there, and she was pretty sure that she'd told him more than she should have about the night Ellie had been murdered. She wasn't sure exactly what she'd said, but she remembered blood on her hands, and she knew how she got when she saw blood.

It made her uncomfortable to know that she may have revealed more than she should have about her past. Not to mention that once again Parker had seen her while she was vulnerable, not in complete control of her emotions. In fact he'd seen her while she was in a blind, hysterical panic. It made her feel weak, defenseless, helpless, to know that someone had seen her lose control, it was something that she never allowed to happen, and knowing that it had happened left her feeling exposed, naked.

The only other thing she was positive of was that Parker Bell had kissed her.

And she had kissed him back.

It had been a mistake. Tessa did not intend to pursue anything with him, no matter how much she wanted too. Her life was in a downward spiral and there was no way she was going to bring him down with her.

Parker had been true to his word though. She remembered him telling her that he would not leave her, and he hadn't. Although she had been unconscious long before they reached the ambulance, and throughout the journey to the hospital and being treated in the ER, she had somehow been aware of his presence. It was like he had hovered on the edge of her dreams.

Reluctantly remembering how good, how safe, it had felt in his arms. Resting against his strong chest, his heart beating comfortingly beneath her, for a moment it had felt so wonderful to have someone to lean on. For a second she had allowed herself to believe that she was not all alone in the world. But she was.

When she had finally awakened, hours after arriving at the hospital, Parker had still been there, sitting patiently beside her bed, holding her hand in his. Tessa didn't want to hurt him but she couldn't allow herself to become emotionally attached to him and she didn't want him to become emotionally attached to her, at least not any more than he already was. So she had not alerted him to the fact that she was awake and had waited until he had left the room to go to the bathroom to call for a doctor.

Dr. Haddrell had a nice, calming face, and he'd been gentle and soothing, taking care not to upset her. Looking down at her hands she saw that they had been cleaned, the cuts on her fingertips had not been deep enough to require stitches. Her wrists, rubbed raw from the ropes Michael had used to bind her, had been wrapped in clean white bandages. Trying to remember whether the doctor had said she had a concussion but she was unable to recall the memory.

It hardly mattered anyway. It wouldn't change anything. It wouldn't change how she felt inside.

Part of her had died with Ellie that night.

That night had been the first time that she had ever felt truly scared and alone. The first time that she had realized that the world was not a friendly place. Right up until that night she had still believed, as only a child can, that her father was coming home, that her mother would get better and they would all be one big happy family.

Everything that she had seen that weekend had changed her.

Before Ellie's death, she had been so naïve. Despite her high IQ she was emotionally and socially a child. She had always rejected her intelligence, as had her family, and had refused to work hard or apply herself at school.

After her best friend's murder, that spark inside her had

extinguished. She had learnt the hard way that the world was a cruel and dark place, where no one could be trusted and even those who said they cared about you would betray you at the drop of a hat.

For years she had tried to fight her way through the darkness that had always been hovering just beneath the surface and threatening to engulf her. She had thrown herself into her studies, and then into her writing, she had gone to any length to protect her friends and all it had led to was more pain and suffering for everyone involved.

Tessa had always been so afraid of being alone. So terrified as one by one the people she trusted left. First her dad, then Ellie, and her mom, her brother, even the police officer who had found her had been killed by a drug dealer high on cocaine. She had fought tooth and nail to keep control of her life, to try and keep people around her. Now she was tired. Tired of always pretending to be confident and self-assured, of keeping up the illusion that she was calm and in control.

No more.

She was giving in to the darkness.

She was giving up.

Tired of fighting, of going on each day as though life was bearable. It was too much, too hard, and she simply wasn't doing it anymore.

Sensing rather than hearing the door open behind her. She didn't have to turn to know who was there.

Parker stood without moving, trying to assess whether she was asleep or awake. Not able to deal with him now Tessa closed her eyes, and pulled the blanket tighter around her chin. Deciding that she was indeed awake, he switched on the light.

"Turn it off," she murmured reluctantly.

Compliantly, he switched the light back off and crossed over to stand beside the bed, watching her. Eventually reaching out a tentative hand to touch her. "Tessa," he began.

Unhappily opening her eyes she pulled away from him. "Don't."

"I just want . . ."

Cutting him off, "What about what I want?"

He said nothing just stared at her with his serious caramel eyes, the long lashes fanning out around them gave him a sweet, innocent, little boy look.

"Please just go," she whispered, she was too tired to deal with this now.

Reaching for her hand, she yanked it back before he could touch it. Defeated he held up his hands in surrender. "Okay. I just want to talk," voice pleading. He ran a hand through his thick black hair standing it on end, and making him look even more endearing.

"I can't do this now," she whispered softly, closing her eyes to put an end to the conversation.

"Tessa, please," he pressed, she could feel his golden eyes studying her carefully, as though he expected her to break at any second.

Refusing to answer she kept her eyes firmly closed and her head turned away.

"Tessa," he tried again, "We're not charging you with Dylan Riley, or whatever his real name is, with his murder. It was clearly self-defense."

Saying nothing but relief washed over, at least that was one less thing to worry about. Not that it really mattered what happened to her anymore.

"Tessa?" When she didn't answer he waited a moment longer, then she heard him sigh and cross reluctantly over to the door. She thought he was gone when he spoke, "This is not the end. I am not giving up on you and I am not walking out on you. No matter what you say, no matter what you do, I am not going anywhere. Sweet dreams, Tessa."

With that, he left the room, the door swinging closed behind him.

When she heard it click shut she slowly opened her eyes and looked at the door through which Parker had just departed. Tessa was sure that he thought he meant what he'd just said, but in her experience people changed their mind almost as frequently as their clothes.

When a splash of water dripped down onto her gown, she raised a hand to her cheeks and was surprised to find them wet with tears. She never cried, at least she never usually cried, in the last week she had cried more than she had in the previous ten years combined.

Rolling over onto her stomach, she buried her head in the pillow and started to sob. Crying for Ellie, and for Janice, Tiffany, Bianca, Dorothy and Gina. And for herself. For everything that she had never had and for everything that she would never get to have.

Tessa was so busy crying that she didn't notice Parker's face at the door, watching her.

DECEMBER 2ND

7:26 A.M.

Driving down the now familiar driveway of Tessa's family's estate. For once, Parker was in his own car, he spent so much time being driven around by his partner that it felt strange to be in the drivers seat.

Parking in front of the main house, he climbed from the car and found himself staring at the huge stone structure that loomed in front of him. Looking at the place in a new light as he thought of a young Tessa asleep in one of it's rooms, awakened by her mother, drugged and nearly drowned. He knew that no matter how badly her cottage had been damaged in the fire there was no way that Tessa was going to spend a single night inside those walls.

Dragging his eyes from the cold, empty windows that seemed to stare back at him as though they were the house's eyes, he made his way slowly around the mansion and across the lawns.

Thoughts straying to the previous night. Tessa had not been happy to see him. Her eyes, usually kept blank with such careful control, had simply been blank with exhaustion. The only flicker of life he'd seen was the relief that had flashed across her face when he told her she would not be charged with Dylan Riley's murder.

After he had left the room, he'd stayed just outside, and had seen her sobbing brokenheartedly into her pillow. It was something he was sure she had spent many nights as a child doing. Crying alone in her room so nobody would hear her. So that nobody would come. It had taken every ounce of self-restraint he possessed to keep from barging into the room and taking her into his arms, but he knew she needed the time to be alone. To begin coming to grips with everything that had happened to her.

Parker had meant every word he'd said. They had come too far for him to let this go. No matter how hard she wanted to try there was nothing that she could do or say to push him away.

Arriving at the hospital early this morning to check up on her he'd discovered that she had waited until he'd left for the night before discharging herself at the crack of dawn, against medical advice.

Reaching the small clearing, he stopped short at the sight of the badly burned cottage. He hadn't seen it since the fire fighters had extinguished the flames, having travelled to the hospital in the ambulance with Tessa.

The stone walls had been broken down in several place leaving huge, gaping holes in the sides of the house. The grass in the clearing was blackened, as were several of the trees ringing the edge of the woods.

Through the broken walls he could make out Tessa standing alone inside the ruins. Her back was to him and she was too preoccupied with whatever she held in her hands to notice his presence.

Entering through the empty doorway, he surveyed the damaged room. Part of the floor of the second storey had collapsed, rubble had been partially cleared away but wooden beams and debris still lay in piles around the room. Furniture had been crushed, the huge wooden table had been split in half when a beam had fallen across it. The paintings that had hung on the walls were either burnt, waterlogged from the fire extinguishers, or utterly destroyed when the walls had fallen.

Trying not to startle her, "Tessa," he called softly.

Jumping she turned to face him, dropping whatever she had been holding, and for the first time since he had met her, her eyes were unguarded. Fear and loss and emptiness swirling together in the bluey-green mist. Not an emptiness like the one that been there before, the deliberate covering of her true emotions, now it was an emptiness that came from the deep depths of utter despair.

Too weary to bother covering her feelings she simply frowned. "Why are you here?"

"I told you I'd be back," he reminded her calmly, ready for an argument.

Apparently she was more exhausted than he had anticipated, she simply shrugged and bent to retrieve the item she had dropped. It was a book of some sort, badly burnt by the fire, but she held it tenderly in her hands.

"You were supposed to stay in the hospital for a couple of days, you have a concussion, and your lungs still haven't healed from the fire," he remarked. Her skin almost as pale as it had been out in the snow, dark circles under her eyes, however the bruise on her temple from the night of the fire had faded slightly.

Shrugging again, she answered with what seemed to be her standard response, "I'm fine."

Crossing to one of the kitchen benches, the only one that was free of debris, she placed the book on the counter and stood staring at it. As though she expected it to suddenly and magically repair itself.

"Chelsea's gone," he said finally, breaking the silence.

At first she didn't answer and he thought she was too lost in thought to hear him, but then she nodded. "I know."

"You knew she'd come."

"Yes."

Awkwardly, "She told us about your past, your family," he knew Tessa wouldn't be happy to have so much about her private life revealed.

"I know," she said again, voice laden with weariness.

"Tessa, I'm sorry."

Finally she turned to look up at him. "Why are you sorry? You weren't there. It wasn't your fault."

"I uh . . ." he fumbled for an answer.

Saving him from answering she continued, more to herself than to him, "I was never close to my parents. They never knew how to deal with me, they were scared of my intelligence."

"But what they did to you . . ." trailing off, anger welling up inside him as he thought of how lonely her childhood must have been. Torn between wanting to track down her parents to give them a piece of his mind, and worry about what he would do to them if indeed he ever did find them.

Tessa turned away again and crossed to the back window, her feet crunching over broken glass, she stood staring aimlessly out at the woods. When she spoke her voice wavered, "They never really loved me," turning to look at him, her face bloomed with all the vulnerability of a child. Eyes brimming with silvery tears. "I was always all alone," voice quivering brokenly.

Changing the topic to give her a break. "How did you meet Dylan?"

"Michael," she corrected, managing to regain some control over her emotions. "His name is . . . was, Michael Mitchell Morley."

"You knew him before he started at the school?"

Nodding, "He wasn't really a teacher, he faked his resume to get the job. When I met him he was posing as a counselor at the hospital where the psychiatrist my grandparents sent me to was working. He was . . ." she broke eye contact and stared steadfastly at a spot on the wall behind his back. "He was using the hospital to find vulnerable teenagers to . . . take advantage of."

"How do you know that?"

"A leopard doesn't change its spots. I found them, tried to help them, but . . ." her voice trailed off, it was clear she blamed herself, once again, for events over which she'd had no control.

"Tessa, why did Dylan only . . ." breaking off as he saw her shudder. "Why did he leave the others alone?" At first she wouldn't meet his gaze, and when she finally lifted her eyes to meet his he read the answer in them. "You made a deal. You for them."

Unshed tears once again glistening in the blue mist of her eyes, lifting a slim shoulder. "It was what he wanted anyway."

Watching her closely. "What did he do to you when you were alone together? Those classes where it was just the two of you?"

For a full minute, she said nothing and he thought that she wasn't going to answer but then she spoke, "He taught me."

"Taught you what?"

Swallowing audibly, "How to read people, body language, non-verbal communication, how to hide my feelings."

"Did he hurt you, when he had you alone?" Parker wasn't sure he wanted to hear her confirm what he was almost positive was true. Saying nothing, she just turned and resumed her aimless stare out the window that was as broken as her soul, and he had his answer.

Crossing to stand behind her, reaching out a hand to touch her, comfort her, he hesitated, not sure she would welcome the breach of her defenses. Deciding he didn't care whether it made her angry or not, he rested his hands on her shoulders and turned her around to face him, he was about to speak but she got in first.

Voice faraway, as though she wasn't really aware that she was speaking aloud, "I used him, took advantage of him. Michael was crazy and I used it against him."

"He tried to kill you," he reminded her softly.

Hand straying to the bruises encircling her neck, she winced slightly as she touched the black and blue line, but made no move to stop. Gently grasping her hand Parker pulled it away, unwinding his scarf from around his neck he took it and wrapped it around hers.

Fingering the scarf for a moment, then looking up at him she gave a weak smile. "This is the scarf you were wearing the day I met you. It's cute," her eyes falling again, she tried to pull away.

Keeping hold of her, he took her chin in his hand and forced her to look at him. "His death is not your fault," voice coming out more vehemently than he had intended, but he hated seeing Tessa blame herself for the actions of others.

Not breaking eye contact, her voice all the more powerful by its quiet and carefully composed air, "I went there to push him to the brink of insanity. That's why I had the razor with me, to get free, to scare him, to prove to him he could never beat me. I used him, I'm no better than he is," letting her eyes drop.

"No, that's not true," barely resisting the urge to shake some sense into her. "*He* used *you*, Tessa, Dylan . . . Michael. And he tried to kill you, not just that night but right here, he tried to burn you to death in your own home. He did this . . ." gesturing at the partially demolished house.

Raising her eyes slowly back up to meet his own, she blinked back tears and shook her head. "The fire, it wasn't him."

"Wh . . . what?" he stuttered, confused, tightening his grip on her arms to keep her upright as her knees buckled.

"Michael didn't tie me up and set fire to my house," she repeated, eyes distant, for a moment he thought she was going to pass out.

Shaking her. "I don't understand." Unable, unwilling, to comprehend the ramifications of what she was saying. If Michael Mitchell Morley hadn't tried to kill her then someone else had. Someone who was still out there. Someone who was free to try again. "Do you know who did it?" Realizing it was a stupid question even as he was asking it. Of course she knew. Tessa always knew what was going on, and there was no way she was going to tell him.

"Yes, I know who it was." Pulling away she leaned tiredly against the blackened wall, completely drained.

"Why did you tell us it was Dylan?"

"I didn't, remember," she snapped, then drew in a deep breath, deliberately calming herself. "I'm sorry, but I never said that

Michael tried to kill me, you just assumed."

Realizing his mistake. "And you just went along with us because it was easier."

Raising a shoulder half-heartedly she refused to meet his gaze, he assumed this was a strategy she employed on a regular basis. "Sorry," she repeated.

Understanding dawning, "Does it have something to do with Ellie, Eleanor's, murder?"

A darkness so deep it seemed to actually change the color of her eyes from blue to black passed across her face, and she answered his question with one of her own. "What did I say to you? After you found me?"

Knowing that if he wasn't honest from the beginning then any relationship they might have would have no chance of working out. "You said that someone was following you, that he was going to kill you. Is that who set the fire? The man who killed Eleanor?" Once again she said nothing, and when he reached out to her she took a step away. "Tessa, what happened that weekend?" he asked softly.

Her voice was so quiet he could hardly hear her, "I never told anyone what happened there. And I promised myself, and Ellie, that no one would ever know. I wish I could take it back, everything that happened that weekend, but I can't and I have to live with that for the rest of my life."

Swaying unsteadily, teetering on the edge of a complete emotional breakdown. Eyes were twin pools of guilt, she no longer bothered to shutter them, whether because she was starting to trust him or because she was just beyond caring Parker wasn't sure. Not that it mattered either way, he wanted to help her but he didn't know how, still he tried nonetheless, "Tessa, what happened wasn't your fault."

"Ellie didn't want to go," she continued as though he hadn't spoken. Hands gripping the window frame to keep herself upright, she didn't seem to notice the glass shards from the broken window cutting into her hands. "I told her that she shouldn't worry so much, that everything would be fine."

Reaching for her hands, Parker wiped them gently with his handkerchief. The gash wasn't deep but he was worried that the blood might set her off again. "There you go," he murmured softly.

The wounds on her hands not registering, her mind stuck firmly in the past. "I told Ellie that everything would be okay," she whispered again, haunted eyes looking up at him.

"Tessa . . ." he began.

Speaking over him, voice becoming louder, boarding on hysterical, "If I had listened to Ellie then she would still be alive. And if I had told everyone who Michael really was then none of this would have happened. Chelsea wouldn't have had to leave her life, Tiffany, Bianca, Dorothy and Gina would still be alive, and Janice . . ." she stopped short as a thought suddenly occurred to her. Turquoise eyes brimming with unshed tears, "Janice, Michael killed her didn't he?"

Reluctantly, "I'm sorry, honey."

"How? No, don't tell me, a fall. He pushed her out a window or off the roof or something?"

Raising a questioning eyebrow, "How do you . . .?"

Anticipating his question she continued, "Janice's little brother fell out of a tree. She was ten he was four, she was babysitting him, they were racing to see who could climb the highest the quickest. He lost his footing and slipped. He broke his neck, was killed instantly."

"I'm sorry," he repeated, feeling inadequate, wanting to say the right thing but not knowing what it was, or if it even existed.

Teetering once again on the narrow ledge between sanity and utter despondency. "I thought I could get her out before he knew I was there," ignoring the tears trickling down her cheeks. Another thing to add to the ever-growing list of things she blamed herself for.

"Why *didn't* you tell your friends? About what happened to Eleanor, about Michael, about what you were planning on doing? Didn't you trust them?" he pushed gently.

"I don't trust anybody," she sniffed, once again struggling to compose herself.

Trying not to take it personally, Parker desperately wanted her to believe in him, to lean on him, but he knew that trust was something that had to be earned. "Is that why you didn't tell anyone what Michael was doing to you?"

"He said he'd kill one of us if we told."

"And you believed him?"

"I knew what he'd done in the past. To his parents. I knew he was capable of anything. He wanted me to run away with him, but I was scared, I didn't want to be alone. I should have gone, saved my friends. I was a coward."

"You are the bravest person I have ever met," he told her fiercely, hooking a finger under her chin and nudging until she met his eye. "What happened with Eleanor, and with Michael, it wasn't your fault. I don't know how to make you believe that but I'm going to keep saying it until it sinks in. Tessa, you can trust me. I am not going to hurt you," he heard the imploring quality in his own voice, and realized how desperate he was for her to believe him.

Studying him in silence for several moments. "You say that I can trust you, but that night at the police station, when you told me about your sister, you were going to tell me that you had feelings for me, but you didn't. You pulled away at the last moment."

Guilty, he didn't know what to say. He'd know from the minute he pulled back that it was a mistake. He should have told her right then and there how he felt about her. "I'm sorry. I was scared, but it doesn't change how I felt." Reaching out to her, she let him cup her face in his hands, and he brushed his thumb across her lips. "It doesn't change how I feel."

Gently extricating herself from his grasp. "I'm sure that you mean what you say now. But things will change, you'll realize I'm not what you want, and then you'll leave."

'Just like everyone else' being the unsaid implication, she fully believed that to be true. Every person that she had ever counted on had left her and she had no expectations that he would be any different. He didn't know how to convince her otherwise, but he wasn't giving up, "the way I feel about you, I've never felt that way before."

Sighing deeply, from the very centre of her being. "I don't know how to be what you want. What you need. I never had a normal family. I don't know how to be part of one," he could see regret dancing in her eyes.

"What I want is you. Just you."

Taking a pointed step away from him. "I'm like poison, I ruin everything that I touch."

"You said that before," remembering the night at the station. "Do you really believe that?" She said nothing but the self-doubt and recrimination in her eyes told him that she did. "You are not poison, Tessa, it was the people around you that were. You are the sweetest, most dedicated, caring, self-sacrificing, and most beautiful woman I have ever met."

She blushed at the compliment and shook her head, "I'm not beautiful," she whispered softly, refusing to make eye contact.

"Yes, you are," he told her, tracing his fingertips gently across her lips then taking her face in his hands and tipping it up.

Deliberately moving the focus of conversation from herself to him, "The day I met you, I called you and Detective Wyatt the soap opera police, you were hurt by that, self-conscious. Why?"

Now it was his turn to blush and turn away, dropping his hands to his side, as painful memories from his childhood flashed through his mind.

"I think it's only fair you share something with me about your past, since you now know so much about mine," Tessa offered him a watery smile.

Smiling back, he reluctantly began, "I told you that my sister and I grew up in foster care." She nodded. "The last home we lived in was the worst. My foster parent's son, Malcolm, he used to hurt us, all the kids. He used to call me the 'little prince'. I was his favorite, he used to say I was striking. It's silly," feeling the familiar sense of insecurity course through him. "At school girls used to you know . . ." embarrassed, "I guess they used to have crushes on me, but I never dated anyone. I guess I never felt worthy of a relationship because of my past, and I was afraid to try in case I failed."

Indignation flashing through her eyes. "That's not fair, you'd make a great husband. You're thoughtful and caring and sweet and," looking up at him shyly, "You risked your life to save me."

Unable to help smiling at her double standards. "Yeah I guess just because I had a rough childhood I shouldn't have to spend the rest of my life alone."

Smiling back at him, but she wouldn't admit that she deserved a happy ending. Then her face clouded over, "That boy, Malcolm, was he was the one who . . . hurt your sister?" Tessa asked, still unable to say the word that had caused her so much personal pain.

"No. It was our foster father. But we were lucky. We got out and we had a great life with our adoptive family," he wished that Tessa had been as lucky. That she had had someone to rescue her, to take her away and give her the life every child deserved.

"I wasn't always sad, Parker," she was studying him seriously. "Before that weekend with Ellie I was happy, I was a normal little girl. I wished Emilie would be a real mother, and I wished Patrick hadn't left us, I was lonely, but I had Ellie, and I was doing okay," a hint of desperation in her voice, as though she needed him to believe her.

"Okay, honey," he nodded, telling her what she obviously needed to hear but remaining unconvinced.

"Do you know where she is, your sister?"

"No. She took off as soon as we graduated. I haven't heard from her in years," feeling the familiar twinge of guilt he always felt when he thought of his twin sister. "What about your brother, you heard from him since he left?"

"He sends me a card on my birthday," was all she said.

"I know what it's like to feel abandoned," he told her.

Studying him again through eyes that no longer attempted to hide what they were thinking. "I can't be your sister's replacement. Or Gina, the girl who tried to kill her baby, I don't need you to save me."

"You're not a replacement," he insisted.

Skeptical, "I understand that you feel like you let your sister down, believe me I know the feeling, but I don't want you to try to save me because you couldn't save her. I don't need anyone to save me. I'll be fine on my own."

"But you're not on your own anymore," he told her. "I promise you, you are not a replacement for Mattie. Or for Gina. What I tried to do with her, it was a mistake, I let my personal feelings get in the way of my job and I didn't see her for who she really was. I don't intend to make that mistake again. I like you for you, for who you are, and nothing that you can say is going to make me stay away."

Peering into his eyes, she nodded slowly, "Okay then, as long as we're clear."

"We are," chest tightening as his heart leapt with anticipation. "Does that mean that you want to . . .?"

"It means," she cut in, as they stared at one another, as awkward as a couple of adolescents, she was wavering, indecision battling in her eyes. Tessa had spent her life filing away her feelings, her emotions, hiding them away from the world because she thought that no one cared. Continuing slowly, "That I'm prepared to give us a go. But . . ." she warned, "I don't want you to get your hopes up. I don't know how to trust people and I don't know how to be in a successful relationship. I don't want to let you down . . ."

"You won't," he assured her. "And I'm no relationship expert myself. We'll take things slow and we'll learn together."

She nodded, and for the first time since he had met her he saw a spark of life in her eyes. Not quite of joy, he wasn't sure happiness was an emotion that she had a lot of experience with, but a sense of peace. Not wanting to upset her but needing to know the answer, Parker hoped he wasn't going to regret what he was about to ask, "Why did you go to him?"

Eyes clouding over again, he thought she was going to yell at him or withdraw inside herself and refuse to answer but then she shrugged, defeated, "I guess I went to end things once and for all."

"Did you go there to push him into killing you?" Not sure he wanted to know.

"I . . . I don't know," she answered finally, eyes turbulent. "Maybe."

"Why?"

"I was tired. Tired of living like this. Of always being afraid. I wanted things to finally be over. Same reason as Gina went walking out of the police station even though I told her Michael was waiting for her. I guess I felt like I had nothing to live for and nothing to lose."

"Do you still feel that way? That you have nothing to live for?"

Tessa said nothing for what seemed like an eternity then she smiled, a real smile that reached all the way to her eyes. "No. I don't feel that way anymore. I don't want to die." She seemed shocked by her own words, as though she herself had not been aware that she could ever feel this way.

Letting out a breath he hadn't known he was holding he smiled back at her.

Sheepishly she continued, "I have a confession to make."

Panic coursing through him. "What?"

"I knew about the GPS. The one you put in my jacket at the hospital after the fire. I knew that you were going to follow me and find the others."

Confused, he felt himself relax. "I thought that you didn't want us to find them, you wouldn't give us their names."

"I wanted them safe, I didn't want anyone else to die for my mistakes," eyes blackening slightly she deliberately pushed it away. "I just didn't want them to know I did it on purpose."

"That was a little risky, they could've confessed everything."

"I knew they wouldn't say anything until Chelsea got there. I just hoped . . ." voice faltering, "I had hoped that Gina might stay there."

"So are you really a genius?" he asked abruptly, he didn't want her beating herself up any longer.

The question caught her by surprise. "Yes."

"What's 3498 plus 5489?"

"8987," she replied without hesitation.

Impressed, "9274 minus 6471?"

"2803."

"7269 times 3518?"

"26,838,822."

Amazed, "That is so cool. How do you do that?"

Cheeks heating with embarrassment, lending some color to her pale face, and making her look even more beautiful. "I don't know."

"Do you like work it out in your head or do you just know the answer?"

"I just know the answer," she was still uncomfortable, but his distraction had allowed her to regain control of her emotions. Uttering a weary sigh, "I hate my intelligence. If I had just been a normal kid I would have been in class the day that Ellie and I were taken. And I never would have met Michael and none of this would ever have happened," chewing on her lip.

Giving her shoulders a comforting squeeze then crossing to

the bag he'd set by the doorless doorway, he pulled out a wrapped present. "Here, I got you something."

Surprised, she took the gift from his hands and pulled off the ribbon and colored paper, freezing when she saw what it was. Looking up at him, shock and gratitude battling in her face. "Where did you get this?"

Looking at the photo Tabitha McKreeney, the principal at Harlwood Academy had given them. "From your old school, it was the one I showed you at the hospital after the fire." He'd kept the photo and had it framed, guessing that part of keeping their secret had involved keeping as little physical links between them as possible, and therefore Tessa had few photos, few mementoes of the only people she had ever cared about.

Her eyes straying from the photo in her hands to the book on the kitchen counter, crossing over to it she picked it up, flipping through the pages. Following her, he saw that the book was in fact a photo album, the pages of which were badly burnt.

"This is all I had," her voice wavering. "The only photos of all of us together. They were ruined in the fire." Turning to face him, her eyes bright with unshed tears, bottom lip wobbling. "This is the nicest, sweetest, most thoughtful thing that anyone has ever given me."

Reaching for her he hesitated then stroked her hair, a single tear sliding slowly down her cheek leaving a glittery trail all the way down to her chin. Choking back a sob, she tried to turn away but he grabbed her and pulled her into his arms, pressing her firmly against his chest. Stiffening for a moment then she relaxed and, tears flowing freely now, held onto him tightly as she cried.

Eventually she pulled back so that she could see him, her eyes filled with a naked, desperate earnestness, "Parker?"

"Yeah?"

"Promise me something?" Looking at him with all the innocence and vulnerability of a child.

"Anything," he whispered, keeping her wrapped in his arms.

"Promise you'll never hurt me," her eyes pleading, tears still sliding down her cheeks.

Taking her face in his hands, he dropped a soft kiss to her forehead. Tipping her face up towards him she closed her eyes, leaning in he pressed his lips against hers, kissing her softly then deeply and passionately.

"What happened to the baby?" she asked suddenly.

"What baby?" he asked confused, his mind still on the kiss.

"Gina, the girl you . . ."

"After we cleared her boyfriend he took custody of the baby, moved back in with his parents, went back to school, took a job, he wants to make a life for himself and his daughter. Why do you ask?'

Embarrassed she looked away, "It's stupid."

"You can tell me," twisting one of her curls around his finger. "You can tell me anything."

Bashful, she smiled up at him. "It's just I thought that if the baby had a happy ending then maybe it might mean that we could . . ."

"Have a happy ending too?"

Tessa nodded, embarrassed.

Growing serious, "I am never going to leave you and I am never going to hurt you. I promise." Taking her face in his hands, his thumbs gently tracing her cheekbones, he pressed a kiss to her forehead. "I'm in love with you, Tessa. I don't care that we've only known each other a couple of days, that's how I feel."

Anxious aqua eyes examining him carefully, then relaxing, shock mixed with a glimmer of hope lighting her eyes. Reaching up she placed her thin hands on top of his. "I . . . I think I love you too," she stammered, as though she had genuinely surprised herself, never thinking that such a thing could be possible.

Smiling she nestled her head against him, wrapping her arms around his waist. Holding her firmly, resting his cheek against the top of her curly head. Enjoying the way the hairs tickled his nose, the way her breath warmed his chest. Marveling at how perfect it felt to be holding her in his arms, how well they fitted together, like two pieces of a jigsaw puzzle, it was as if they were made for one another.

Before this moment he would never really believed in a 'happy ever after' but the way he felt right now maybe it was possible.

Jane has loved reading and writing since she can remember. She writes dark and disturbing crime/mystery/suspense with some romance thrown in because, well, who doesn't love romance?! She has several series including the complete Detective Parker Bell series, the Count to Ten series, the Christmas Mysteries series, and the Flashes of Fate series of novelettes.

When she's not writing Jane loves to read, bake, go to the beach, ski, horse ride, and watch Disney movies. She has a black belt in Taekwondo, a 200+ collection of teddy bears, and her favorite color is pink. She has the world's two most sweet and pretty Dalmatians, Ivory and Pearl. Oh, and she also enjoys spending time with family and friends!

For more information please visit any of the following –

Amazon – http://www.amazon.com/author/janeblythe
BookBub – https://www.bookbub.com/authors/jane-blythe
Email – mailto:janeblytheauthor@gmail.com
Facebook – http://www.facebook.com/janeblytheauthor
Goodreads – http://www.goodreads.com/author/show/6574160.Jane_Blythe
Reader Group – http://www.facebook.com/groups/janeskillersweethearts
Twitter – http://www.twitter.com/jblytheauthor
Website – http://www.janeblythe.com.au

sic enim dilexit Deus mundum ut Filium suum unigenitum daret ut omnis qui credit in eum habeat vitam aeternam